A Dangerous Harbor

Happy Reading!

By RP Dahlke

RP Dahlke

A Dangerous Harbor vs 1.24.15

Published in the USA by Dead Bear Publishing

***

Credits

Edited by Christine LePorte christineleporte.com

Cover art by EDH Graphics
http://edhgraphics.blogspot.com/

Formatted by Debora Lewis arenapublishing.org

***

ISBN-10: 1470169886
ISBN-13: 978-1470169886

"Twenty years from now you will be more disappointed by the things you didn't do... sail away from a safe harbor, catch the trade winds in your sail.
Explore.
Dream.
Discover."

~Mark Twain

"No matter where you go, there you are."

~Yogi Berra

Dedication

Sharon Heitman: robin blue eyes twinkling, frequently followed by husky laughter, a generous and thoughtful friend of thirty-eight years: 1949-2011

***

Katrina Taylor Hunter, beloved godmother and dearest friend who always dreamed of sailing the deep blue ocean: 1910-2001

***

As always, my dear son John Shanahan 1964-2005

***

And to my darling granddaughters, Simone and Hanna Shanahan

***

And, last but not least, to my daughter, Dettre Schmidt-Galvan, and my husband, Lutz Dahlke, whose love, encouragement and patience never fails.

***

Many thanks to the authors and readers:

Authors: Lesley Diehl, whose sense of humor keeps any story fun and M. Louisa Locke, whose kindness, patience and thoughtful suggestions are an inspiration to this author.

Cousin Beth Englehart, who is the best of the Phillips writers, she's just too stubborn to admit it.

Foreword

This book was the result of several years aboard our cutter rigged Hylas 47 sailboat spent sailing in Mexico, and as most California sailors know, first port of call into Baja, Mexico after San Diego is Ensenada. Most of the town is clustered around the harbor where working marinas like Baja Naval still service American boaters.

I found this sleepy little town to be fascinating, full of endless stories, with a culture that was, and still is, struggling to gain a foothold in the twenty-first century. The irony is that I started this book ten years ago, based on a local news story, which at the time was staggering in its brutality. This story is no longer unique as the Mexican cartels daily murder with impunity. But, just as the cartels are not all that is Mexico, this story isn't all about them, it's about what happens when you try to run away from your problems, or as Yogi Berra would say, "No matter where you go, there you are."

It's about Americans, the ones passing through and the ones stuck in A Dangerous Harbor.

Chapter One

Except for the mermaid on a weedy patch of sea grass ghosting in her wake, Katrina Hunter's solo sail into Mexican waters had been monotonous and uneventful. And now her thirty-two-foot Westsail was on a leisurely stroll with only the current and the thrum of the auxiliary engine for companionship—except, that is, for the mermaid.

Katrina rubbed at gritty eyes, the result of too little sleep and too many hours at *Pilgrim's* helm. "Sure it is. Last night it was Mickey Mouse reciting Robert Frost on top of a following wave, so why not mermaids?"

Shivery, bleary-eyed and slow, she blew at cold, stiff hands, then reached over and tapped at her handheld GPS. Arrival to her destination at the port of Ensenada in forty-five minutes, it said.

She peered through the early morning light at the sun-fuzzed tan cliffs of Baja. The bare corduroy hills folding onto themselves, then breaking apart, humped up again into another cluster of barren monotony. Bored with the dull scenery, she cupped a hand over her brow and glanced back at the patch of weed again.

Like all solo sailors, Katrina talked to herself. And in this case, it was more to ease her worried mind than for the sheer entertainment of hearing her own voice.

"Definitely not Mickey Mouse. It's a busted white fender stuck on some seaweed, that's all it is."

Rubbing at her tired eyes again, she peered at the seaweed wallowing in her wake. The white plastic fender was now a pale arm swimming in slow, lazy strokes, moving to some genetic Latin rhythm.

There was also a head with long dark hair and a body to go along with the arm.

"Yeah, and gold watches are this year's accessory for every boat fender. Shit!"

Katy swatted at the clanging alarm going off in her head—that litany of cautionary instruction drilled into her by her superiors when they heard about her solo sail to Mexico. Never mind that she'd been sailing since she could stand, or that she was frequent crew for any racing regatta on the San Francisco Bay. She was one of their own, or would be if her paid leave of absence played out as intended.

There would be no calling the American Coast Guard now; she was already too far away from San Diego and the American border. She stoppered her ears against getting involved with even the slightest whiff of trouble while she was in Mexico and stabbed at the Man Overboard button on her GPS, marking her exact location.

Yanking at the furling line of her jib until it curled obediently onto itself and crabwalking forward, she uncleated the main and let it drop into the lazyjacks, worked her way back to secure the boom into its cradle, dropped down into the cockpit and shoved the tiller hard until the bow was aimed at the patch of weed, then tied off the tiller, idled the throttle, and with boat hook in hand, waited for the patch of weedy sea grass to slide across her waterline.

Katy leaned over and deftly nudged the weedy raft around so that its reluctant passenger was facing her, and then ever so gently pushed back the wet strands of black hair. Dark winged brows stood out in stark relief on pale olive skin. It was a girl, maybe all of sixteen, she guessed.

"Where'd you come from?"

As if to answer at least part of her question, the ocean swelled, lifting up the maiden's bier until Katy was looking into slightly open eyes. There were no petechiae, the telltale red dots freckling the cornea and typical of strangulation.

"Not strangled, but still...."

A frothy red bubble clinging to a nostril and a few more at her mouth said drowned, but not in the water very long as the limbs were still pliant and the skin wasn't bloated or damaged by fish or sea birds.

Katy noted the time as seven a.m. for the investigation that was clearly going to happen, and gave her guess at a couple of hours earlier, which would put the death about three or four a.m.

"Did you fall off a party boat, my little mermaid?" She lifted her head to scan the horizon for any sign of a disappearing yacht or cruise ship.

The empty horizon made her sad and then angry, but not at the dead girl. Detective Katrina Taylor Hunter, recently of the San Francisco Police Department, would never be angry at a victim and certainly not one so young. "All right, let's get this over with," and she went below to twist the dial on her marine radio to 2.182 MHz and did as she was trained to do when finding dead bodies in Mexican waters—called the Mexican Navy.

Chapter Two

Held in solitary confinement since she was met at the public dock by a chubby Mexican police officer, she had every reason to agree with veteran travelers who made it their policy never to stick around after an accident in Mexico. He had her write it all down on a pad with a stub of an old pencil and then read it back to him as he slowly pecked out the letters on a manual typewriter. Then he had her sign it and, leaving her a copy, bowed out the door of the interview room.

Every hour or so he would pop in with a cold soda or offer to escort her to the ladies' room, which was depressingly dingy, and without any windows to tempt her with escape, she naturally followed him back to the room.

"The chief inspector specifically asked for your patience, please," he said, smiling and backing out again.

A dead girl had been found floating in the ocean. What was so hard to understand about that? Katy's passport said she was an American citizen, her driver's license said she was a resident of San Francisco and her police ID said she was a detective with the San Francisco police department. The ID photo sucked but so did her attitude about now.

Just when she was beginning to think she might be here permanently, her jailer whisked open the door for a broad-chested suit, a thick file under his arm. The uniform stood guard while his superior squeezed his big shoulders around his sergeant, loosened his tie, thumped the file down on the table, and with a heavy sigh, lowered himself into the chair across from Katy.

"I am Chief Inspector Raul Vignaroli and this is Sergeant Moreno," he said, as if she hadn't already become best friends with the sergeant. The Chief's basso profundo was clearly upper-class Mexican, but it was also intertwined with something akin to a Louisiana patois. Odd, and maybe she would find it interesting in some other situation, but this wasn't a social call and there was no offer of a handshake as one does when encountering another police officer, especially since that police officer has gone out of her way to willingly report a suspicious death.

The slight momentarily bothered her, but what she really wanted right now was to unstick her butt from the worn plastic chair she'd been occupying for most of her first day in port and leave for the marina and her boat *Pilgrim*. She had plans to get some deck work done while she was here then haul the boat back to the States, and with a little luck, she'd have a job to go back to. Today, however, was not going well at all. Six hours here, and now she was getting the snub by the chief inspector? What the hell was going on?

She knew better than to initiate small talk; it only compounds the problem for suspects. Suspect? She sat up in her chair, about to ask if she needed an attorney, then reminded herself that she was in a foreign country. Maybe things were done differently here and, resisting the temptation to fold her arms in a defensive posture across her chest, instead calmly folded her hands onto her lap, and did a quick assessment of the chief inspector.

The man in question pointedly ignored her and continued to study the folder in front of him.

Maybe forty, she figured, lifting first one cheek and then the other off the sweaty seat of her chair. Black wavy hair dipped over a high forehead patterned with a load of worry that wasn't any of her business. His skin was olive and the cleft in his square jaw said some Italian had splashed across his gene pool not long ago. *Not so bad looking if you like the dark Latin type.* Her eyes wandered up to the clock again. *Jeez. Over six hours. Now, if it was just the sergeant, I could give him a quick hip shove, make it out the door and down the hall, through those swinging double doors faster than a jackrabbit...*

Then she noticed the inspector idly appraising her from under long, dark lashes. *Is that amusement on his face? The bastard!*

He snapped the folder shut and stared at her as if suspecting her of having bunny feet.

"You alerted the Mexican Navy at seven a.m. this morning, is that correct?"

"Correct," she answered, and straightening her spine, looked him in the eyes, hoping she sounded like the conservative, upstanding citizen her mother always wanted her to be. "If I'd been in the States, I'd have alerted the Coast Guard. But I understand that mariners here are to call your Navy. So, do I need a lawyer, Chief Inspector?"

"That won't be necessary, Miss Hunter." Then, as if he couldn't help himself, he gave her a quick dazzling smile, causing long dimples to bracket the wide mouth. Wrap it all together and the man was not just incredibly masculine, he was downright attractive. "We're not such a third-world country that we arrest tourists who report finding a dead body. At least," he added dryly, "not without cause."

"Of course. And, as an American police officer," she said, pointing out once again what he already knew, "I'm glad I was able to help. So, are we done here?"

A twitch, or was it a smirk, tugged at the corner of his wide mouth. But instead of answering, he went back to studying the pages in the thick folder while the clock on the wall slugged out another five minutes.

She clenched her hands together and stared at the clock, then rubbed her tongue over her teeth, trying for some moisture.

"Have you been offered anything cold to drink?"

She jumped at the sound of his voice. Was he *trying* to make her look guilty?

Ignoring the crumpled paper cups littering the table, he snapped fingers at his sergeant. "A couple of cold sodas, *por favor*?"

Turning back to Katy, he added, "Regular Coke okay with you? We don't have diet."

Katy sighed. Standard police tactics. "What do you want from me, Inspector? I've told your sergeant everything I know. But now that I've been here for six—oops, make that six hours and fifteen minutes, I'm sure by now you know more than I do. So, did she fall off some party boat or what?"

He gave her a noncommittal stare. His eyes, she noticed, were the color of burnt sugar and there was some kind of golden ring around the edge. Wolfish eyes combined with that low, threatening voice and she would've considered him a very sexy package—except for the wedding band on his left hand. She did like her bad boys, just not *married* bad boys.

"Sure, a cold Coke would be nice, thank you."

Peering at her over imaginary reading glasses he said, "You have a husband, a friend, anyone who can account for your whereabouts?"

She knuckled her tired eyes. "Inspector, if that fat file says anything about me, you already know that I'm on sabbatical from the San Francisco PD, I'm single, I live in a studio apartment on Columbus Street. There are ten, maybe twelve people who know where I was this morning at seven a.m. because I checked in with them after I called your Navy." Then she added with a tilt of a smile, "But, whatever you do, please don't call my mother."

He answered her smile with a deep chuckle, and this time his demeanor relaxed a bit. "As a dutiful son with a constantly worried mother, I can assure you we will not call your mother."

Sergeant Moreno backed into the room with two cold cans in his hand. He set the cans down on the table, and giving her a timid glance, bent to whisper in his boss's ear.

The chief inspector blinked. Then suddenly purposeful, he scraped back his chair and stood. "Señorita Hunter, we will detain you no longer. In the course of your brief stay here in Ensenada, I hope you will not hold this unfortunate incidence against us. Please enjoy the rest of your vacation and thank you for your cooperation." He nodded once to his sergeant and turned to leave. When he saw that Katy wasn't standing, the black brows went up a notch.

"So, nothing to share, Inspector? Like, was she murdered?" Katy asked in a voice that quavered from the pent-up emotion of the last six and a half hours.

He looked down his long Roman nose at her as if he'd just encountered something smelly. And she probably was, too. Her last shower being now almost twenty hours ago.

"I can only give you the standard reply; I am not at liberty to divulge anything at this time. And, as they say in Mexico, *Que le vaya bien.* It means—"

"I know what it means, Chief Inspector. As for having a good trip, I think that boat already sailed."

She waved a floppy hand to indicate she had no intention of explaining American slang to him and, with as much dignity as she could muster, marched past him out the door and down the hall, trailing the sergeant behind her. At the lobby, she turned to the sergeant. "Will you call me a cab, please?"

"Oh, that is not necessary, señorita. I will personally drive you to the marina."

Baja Naval was expecting her. It was a good working marina and she had been looking forward to the respite. Scrub the boat, get the teak work done and leave Mexico and its troublesome problems behind—wait. Wasn't that why she sailed to Mexico—to leave her own troubles behind?

Shrugging off the sense of dejá-vu, she nodded thankfully to the sergeant. She could almost taste the late afternoon sun, the fragrance of tacos frying in local stalls. Oh, and there was the fish market. Maybe she could persuade the sergeant to stop long enough for her to pick up some fresh fish, or better yet, some fish tacos. Her stomach rumbled at the thought.

She was still thinking about fried fish tacos when the double doors of the police station slammed open with such force that the ceiling fan stuttered in its lazy rotation. Two policemen marched in, dragging a listless prisoner between them.

A thick, sun-bleached blond head of hair flopped over half-closed eyes, the buttonholes missing their mark on a faded Hawaiian shirt.

Katy judged him another drunk American giving Mexicans cause to believe everything they've heard about privileged Yanks with their big wallets and bad manners.

He was a good foot taller than the two Mexican officers, but with his hands manacled behind his back, it was obvious that he wasn't going to give them any trouble. But before Katy could dodge around him for the exit, he raised his head and a startling pair of aquamarine eyes met hers.

He straightened his back, wincing at the angle of his cuffed wrists. "What the... Whisper?"

Suddenly, the sound of the ceiling fan was terribly loud. Blood pounded in her ears, her mouth went dry, her palms were damp and her feet were nailed to the floor. In a knee-jerk reaction, she hissed, "Don't call me that!"

Realizing her mistake, she backed up to scoot around him—and bumped into Inspector Vignaroli. She gasped, and then blurted, "Is he being arrested for the murder?"

The chief inspector's eyes narrowed briefly, then with a nod to his sergeant, indicated there would be a detour in the prisoner's march for the holding cells, and to Katy's freedom.

Chapter Three

Chief Inspector Raul Vignaroli herded them down the hall and into the same windowless interrogation room where Katy again flopped into the nearest plastic chair. The blond American stood awkwardly next to her.

The inspector looked from Katy, who preferred to stare at the clock rather than meet his eye, to the prisoner. Noting the alcohol-blurred expression, the fresh cut above his left eye and the fading bruise on his jaw, Raul Vignaroli wondered how the lovely American police woman knew this man—who was obviously a vagrant. There was a connection here, he could see it in the shift of her body as she crossed her legs and tried to distance herself from the other man. In any other circumstance the man would be pushing back his floppy blond hair, re-buttoning his shirt, shoring up his image, if not for the chief inspector, then certainly for this attractive young woman. Instead, his hands hung by his side, his eyes begging for an exit.

They were about the same age, and there was an air about the two of them, something almost tangible in its familiarity. Ah yes, that was it—money. The man may have had it at one time, but obviously had lost it. A refugee from the States—had he been in some kind of trouble there? Ensenada was rife with Americans in one kind of trouble or another. The attractive police woman—vacation, she'd said.

Under other circumstances… well, it was better not to go there.

"Excuse me a minute?" The chief inspector quietly left the two people alone.

When he left, Katy looked over at the blond man and sighed. "There's no two-way mirror in here, but they could have a microphone somewhere. Oh, what the hell, this day is already screwed. So, Gabe, what happened to Canada?"

"Too cold. What happened to San Francisco?"

"I think it's safe to say we both picked the wrong border. And to think, only moments ago I was thinking about bunny feet and here I am again with the biggest bunny of them all."

"It was no picnic, I can tell you that much. I hitched so many hay and animal trucks just to get this far I can still smell goat."

"Oh my God! Don't tell me you're thinking of sneaking back across the border?" Katy reached over and punched him on the shoulder. "All you had to do was keep two promises and now you're reneging on both? You dumb shit—you're going to ruin my life, yet!" She began to pummel him in earnest.

They were interrupted by the shark-like grin of the chief inspector as he and his sergeant stepped back into the room. The sergeant left, but the inspector stood where he was. With a flickering light now dancing in his eyes he said, "Now, who wants to go first?"

Chapter Four

They gave the chief inspector an abbreviated version of their childhood friendship, omitting that awkward and embarrassing episode during her second year of college. The inspector looked from one to the other, and though he kept his own council, Katy noticed that little bit of amusement remained on his handsome mug.

She would have to sort out this incredible coincidence somewhere out of earshot of the inspector. Gabriel Alexander here in Mexico. What was he thinking? Was he going to go home, do his time, clear his name and ruin her life? Her life before Gabe was all innocence—finish college, become a lawyer, follow in her daddy's footsteps and become a judge. Then there was life after Gabe where her plans seemed to be cast in an ever-shifting line of sand.

Only a week ago her only thought was to do her time in purgatory and then go back to work.

"Don't worry about a thing," her chief had said. "The hearing is mandatory, and you can think of the leave of absence as a vacation, and the department's attorney has your sister's deposition that the stalker was taking aim when you wrestled him for that gun. Now get out of here. I'll see you in two weeks."

She had a life. A job she loved. Unless Gabe destroyed it all by turning himself in to the feds.

Finally they were released and politely instructed not to leave the country. Not likely, since the inspector had, with a knowing smile, slipped her passport into his folder and tucked it under his arm.

Gabe mumbled something about not having his passport with him but if the inspector would allow, he'd come by with it the next day.

Outside, she stood on the sidewalk waiting for her ride.

Gabe sidled up to her, and sticking his hands in his pockets said, "Well, that was close, but I guess it turned out okay."

She glanced at his profile. That was it, of course. The shock of seeing him again after all this time and in this place. What was it—ten, fifteen years? She felt a bubble of hysterical laughter threatening what was left of her composure.

She held her chin up like a boxer about to take a hit, but the effort proved to be too much, and when she started to teeter off the edge of the pavement and into oncoming traffic, Gabe reached out and pulled her back onto terra firma.

She righted herself and jerked out of his grasp.

Oblivious to the insult, he said, "What do you say we get a bite to eat. You'll feel better."

She decided she'd been wrong about Mexico and certainly this stupid idea that she could outrun her problems if she left them seven hundred miles behind her in San Francisco. It was a truism her dearly departed dad had vainly attempted to pound into her head: *"You take your problems with you, Katrina."* Her dad, Judge Roy Hunter, spent a goodly amount of time and money to make sure her secret wouldn't become known by anyone except himself and a few trusted aides.

Never mind the warm sun, the perpetual blue skies, the friendly people, the cheap rum and those fish tacos her mouth was watering for; the emotional roller coaster she'd endured over the last hours made the hardship of her week-long solo sail look like a cakewalk. As for reporting any more dead bodies to foreign police, she would forget about her pledge to "Do your duty" and give it a wide berth. Let somebody else take the heat.

Gabe, keeping his distance, probably in case she decided to smack him again, asked, "So—which way?"

Sergeant Moreno pulled up to the sidewalk in his patrol car. He opened the back door and waited for a sign she had decided against his offer for a ride to Baja Naval.

Katy marched over to the squad car and, silently declining the sergeant's offer of a potentially urine- or vomit-stained back-seat ride, slid into the passenger seat. She adjusted her belt, rolled down the window, and curled a finger at Gabe.

Pretending he wasn't uncomfortable with his proximity to a police car, he stepped over to the car window, and with his hands on his knees, bent down to eye level. "I'll pass. Thanks anyway."

She grabbed him by his Hawaiian shirt and growled through her teeth, "It wasn't an invitation, Gabe. You broke every promise you ever made to me, so I don't know why I should expect you to keep this one, but I'm asking you, begging you, stay away from me." And then because her mother taught her to be polite, added, "Please."

Gabe jerked back as if he'd been slapped.

The sergeant, carefully ignoring anything that might keep him from his appointed task, plopped a size-too-large policeman's cap on his small head, scuttled around to the driver's side, got in, put the car in gear and pulled out into the thick afternoon traffic.

Katrina glanced back at Gabe, taking in his sun-bleached hair flopping over the aristocratic forehead, and sighed. The man actually had the audacity to look hurt.

She turned around and stared out the window. The sergeant's driving was typical for Mexico—tapping his brakes lightly at every stop sign, then speeding through, all the while keeping up a running dialogue.

"You like the movies?" he asked cheerfully. The side of his police car did have the words 'Tourist Officer' printed on the side. "Yes? Did you see *Titanic*? Excellent. They made the ship for the movie outside Rosarito." He snapped the wheel to the right, missing a couple of jaywalkers. "It was only half a ship, not the whole thing, but I was a—how you call it—extra? Yes, that is the word, no? I was behind the fence with a baby in my arms. Not a real baby, of course, only a bundle of rags. They told me to yell some words, didn't matter that it was in Spanish. You aren't from L.A., are you? I have cousins in L.A., none of them legal—stupid cousins. They get homesick and come home every year and then I have to pay some coyote to smuggle them across again."

His driving was amazingly capable, even if he wasn't watching the road. "My friends tell me I look like John Travolta. I think it's the chin. What do you think?" Thrusting out his chin for her approval, Katy gasped. It was a big one alright, and so was the Tecate truck bearing down on them. The sergeant swerved back into his lane and avoided clipping the truck with only a grunt to acknowledge the near miss.

"They did *Zorro* here too, with Antonio Banderas. Did you like that movie? Yes? Excellent. It was my very good fortune to have been an extra in that movie, too. I was an officer for the governor." He took his eyes off the road again to ogle a couple of American girls in shorts and halter tops, then punched the accelerator, and without missing a beat, continued. "I take the governor's cape and then give him a message. They cut my lines, but you can see me in the background, holding his cape."

Relieved to see the marina building ahead, Katy envisioned walking through the gate, and settling in with a nice cup of tea and some peace and quiet. The sergeant slowed, taking the roundabout to the marina, he parked and nodded to the guard who returned his nod with a quick salute. "I have enjoyed our talk, Señorita Hunter. I am also available for tours of the city should you wish and I am very cheap." When she didn't answer, he shrugged. "The guard is my cousin, Manuel. If you need anything, he's the man to ask."

Katy ignored the suggestion that she should hire either of them, and seeing the top of her mast peeking through the forest of sailboats in the marina, she was now more than ever ready to get out of the patrol car and be done with the local police.

The sergeant tried one more time. "Groceries, a nice map for all the best places to visit?"

Her hand went for the door handle. *Pilgrim* was there waiting. Iced tea ... something herbal would do the trick, chamomile to soothe her jittery nerves. Then a shower and she'd walk the mile or so to the fish market, get some of those hot, crispy tacos she'd been craving.

"Nightlife? Whatever you want."

But the memory of the girl in the water ground her hopeful ruminations to a halt. She turned back to the sergeant and he popped his head came out of the window. "Sí, señorita?"

"There is one thing…"

"Sí?" he asked hopefully.

"The dead girl I found in the water, was she from Ensenada?"

He swept the big police hat off his head and fidgeted with the brim. Stealing a glance at his cousin, he said, "You shouldn't think about it anymore, señorita. Nightlife, maybe a few beers at a nice place like Carlos Murphy's, and then you go home, no?"

"I'm not much for bars, Sergeant. And as you well know, Chief Inspector Vignaroli has kept my passport. Did he tell you when I might be getting it back?"

The sergeant licked the edge of his mustache, his expression showing his indecision. Her expression said she wasn't going to budge, so he switched to a rapid Sonoran Spanish. "What a shame. She was one of the *putas* working at Antonio's. Only sixteen years old. I myself have three young daughters close to that age." He crossed himself, ending with a kiss on his thumbnail. *"Pobrecita."*

She surprised him when she responded in Spanish. "You're right. It is a shame." She was sad to hear the policeman confirm what she'd suspected; the girl was indeed only sixteen and already a prostitute at a local bar. "I have seen a lot of bodies in my work," she said in Spanish, "sometimes young women, drug overdoses, even murder. It is the same in the States as it is here." Then she switched to English, hoping to draw him in. "I saw no signs that she was strangled, however, that doesn't mean she wasn't murdered."

The black mustache quivered uncomfortably as he answered in Spanish. "That place is known for its wild parties where men buy whatever they desire. It is not on the list for tourists and certainly not for young ladies of good family. No, a beautiful young woman such as yourself... no, you do not want to go there."

"Where is this place you're talking about?"

"I have said too much already, señorita. The *jefe* would not want me to speak so much about his investigation."

Then why did he send me off with this chatterbox who obviously can't keep a secret under his big hat? Something's afoot here, I just don't see it yet.

She reached out and lightly patted his arm. "I wouldn't want you to get in trouble. I guess I'm just at a loss as to why he would keep me at the police station for so long."

Relief washed across his face. "Oh, that much I am glad to tell you. He didn't want the *conejo* to run." Then he rolled his eyes. "*Entiende*?"

He didn't want the rabbit to run? There it was again—bunny feet. The expression and its meaning were the same in either language. She did a mental head smack. Putting herself in the inspector's shoes, she ticked off the list of suspicious behavior—woman sailor reports finding a floater, then encounters Gabe, shackled and stumbling into the police station between two officers. And because she was quite frankly sleep deprived, she'd blurted out the one thing that gave the chief inspector reason to suspect Gabe. "*Is he being arrested for the murder?*"

Never in her ten-year career as a police officer had Katy Hunter been so careless, and certainly not when someone's life depended on it. Gabe Alexander might be a lot of things, but he wasn't a killer. He'd been drinking, fighting too from the looks of him. But now she'd given the inspector reason to think he was a murder suspect. She was going to have to talk to Gabe again after all, clear up this misunderstanding with the inspector, get her passport back, get the boat hauled onto a truck, and get the hell out of Mexico—before anything else happened.

Katy made a show of cheerfully thanking the sergeant for the ride and even waved as he left. She brightly smiled at the clutch of sidewalk spectators, then took the stairs for the offices of Marina Baja Naval where she would start the process of checking in and, even if it was wishful thinking, a quick haul-out and trailer home to northern California.

With the paperwork and bathroom visit done, and marina keys in her pocket, she walked through the boatyard for the gate and her boat. She gave the guard her name, boat name, the marina paperwork and tramped down the ramp to where a cluster of American boaters were gathered around her boat.

When she saw why they were staring at her thirty-two-foot Westsail, she angrily flushed and cursed. The chief inspector had someone chain her boat to the dock *The bastard!*

Ignoring the puzzled questions and offers of assistance, she turned on her heel and stomped back into the office where she asked a secretary to make the call. The secretary, a round-faced young woman who looked to be more Indian than Mexican, gave her a sympathetic smile, calmly punched in the number and listened to excuses. A few expletives went with her demand that the inspector return her call. She hung up, giving Katy a rueful grin. They both knew that it could be any time between now and next Christmas. After all, this was mañana land.

Katy spent the next two hours taking out her frustrations on her boat, washing the salt water off the brightwork and stainless stanchions, vigorously scrubbing the topsides with a stiff brush and, in honor of Chief Inspector Vignaroli, practicing her hangman's knots while she secured her boom to its cradle. She also gave the curious boaters on the dock a truthful, if condensed, version of her encounter with the floater.

"I expect to have this chain off tomorrow, latest."

Clucking sympathetically, the crowd finally thinned out, probably because the story was now being transferred via the ham net, aka the "Coconut Telegraph." Guilt or innocence to be decided along with tomorrow's weather report.

Her cabin fan had been on the fritz since San Diego, and since there was still no return call from the inspector, she decided that a trip to replace it would be just the ticket to get away from the intense curiosity of her dock mates. Gathering her purse, she swept out the gate and took a taxi to a downtown marina store she thought might have one. Surely, replacement boat fans would be a popular item in any marine store. She also expected it would be a high-ticket item.

The inside of the store was cool from a hardworking, if somewhat noisy, air conditioner. It also had the friendly and familiar smell of rope and teak of marine stores everywhere. No one was at the sales counter so she snagged a small, rusted, wobbly-wheeled grocery cart and walked up and down the aisles while she thought.

If she was free to go, then why did he chain her boat to the dock? And not available when a fellow police officer wished to speak to him? Obviously his cell number wasn't available to the likes of her. Probably home having a siesta. What was the man up to and what could she do about it? She could take it up with his superior, if he had one. He had the look of the top man, and unless her eyes fooled her, she also knew a handmade Italian suit when she saw it. The man was an egotist to think he could pull this kind of stunt. *Well, we'll see about that, Inspector Vignaroli.*

While she was cogitating on the inspector and whereabouts of Gabe Alexander, she passed up the display for electrical wall fans. Backing up and going down the aisle again, she slowed and looked more carefully, knowing that Mexicans didn't always stock shelves as Americans would. Teak decking could just as easily show up next to toilet paper, and her fan jmight have taken up residence next to marine toilets.

Giving up, she found a ship's bell anchored to the counter, and in her frustration she gave the short monkey's knot a hard pull. The clanging bell brought a short, thin Mexican from the back of the store. He signaled for her to wait, then wiping his face with a napkin he scurried down the aisle to take his place behind the counter. Giving her a toothy, gold-filled smile, he wiped his hands on his shirt and asked in broken English if he could help.

"Yes, please," she said, handing him the fan. "I'm looking for one of these. You had them last year when I came in, but I don't see them on the shelves now."

He turned it over, examined it carefully, tugged at the wires hanging out of the back and then handed it back. "Yes, we used to carry these, but no more."

"Really? You can't get them?"

He shrugged. "*No hay.*"

"Yeah, yeah, I got that. You don't have any now, but when will you get them again?"

"*Lo siento. I don't have one.*"

"I'm sorry too, but look," she said, pointing to his collection of marine parts on the wall behind the counter, "there's one on your wall."

He turned to admire the fan on the wall. "We used to have them, but they sell out. We buy again, but too quickly they sell. They do not stay in the store, so we no buy them anymore."

She started to giggle then stopped herself. The man was serious. This reminded her of the time she and her friends flew into San Carlos. With reservations in one of the top favorite beach hotels, they were shocked to see the place mostly empty. When she asked why no one else was there, they were told that business had been bad lately. Katy then waved a price sheet in front of the desk clerk. "Then why're your prices now twice what we paid?"

The desk clerk answered in a small voice, "Business is bad?"

Incredulous, Katy was unable to throttle back her astonishment. "So the cure is to raise your prices?"

The desk clerk ducked his head between his ears and quailed at this American woman. "Sí?"

Grabbing her broken fan out of the store clerk's hand, she stomped outside and finding a passing ice cream vendor, bought herself a Mexican fruit ice and sat down on a nearby bench. Pulling the paper off the crushed and frozen treat, she bit into the solid and deliciously ripe strawberries and laughed. "Well, some things are still as they should be."

Chapter Five

High above the town of Ensenada, Chief Inspector Raul Vignaroli pushes open the heavy door of his hill-top home to the hush of the air conditioner and the faint sound of children laughing. At the drop of his keys onto the entry table, a woman cheerfully calls, "*Cena, querido!*"

"Yes, my love, dinner. I'll be right there." But instead of following her call, he detours away from the light where children laugh and his wife's voice echoes in his head. Raul stumbles for his bathroom and a shower, chastising himself for his weakness. Every night the same, and every night, if only for a few bright moments, his life is what it once was.

After the shower, towel wrapped around his waist, he rubs the steam off the mirror and faces the dour face and shadowed eyes. His thick black hair curls wetly around his ears, indicating a much-needed haircut. He rubs a hand over the stubble on his chin, then fingers the shaving cream, considering… and he hears her voice calling again, "Dinner, my love!"

He curses loudly and explodes, tossing the can across the room. Ashamed at his outburst, he dips down to pick up the can, replacing it back in line with his toiletries on the sink. The turns the labels to the front as if they were tin soldiers in the fight against unruly beards and sweaty armpits and a life that extends no farther than the walls of this house.

The ongoing argument with his sister was finally beginning to wear on five years of denial. She'd told him it was madness to remain in this crazy house, and crazier still to keep a grieving, featherless parrot.

"*Cena querido!*"

But then, how else would he ever hear their voices again?

After cobbling together a late dinner of tinned food from her dwindling food locker, Katy sat in her cockpit and gazed across the night-time marina.

What a mess, she thought. *I suppose it would be too much to expect Gabe to read my mind and show up here tonight. And didn't I tell him to stay away from me? Now I gotta take it all back. Gabe may be on the lam, but if anyone can find him, it'll be me.*

She'd ferret him out of his latest hidey-hole, see what he knew about the girl and her murder. She was sure of it now, it was a murder, and if she wasn't a suspect she certainly was of some interest to the chief inspector, if only because of her association with Gabe. Why oh why couldn't she have kept her mouth shut? She could only hope that the chief inspector didn't have the resources to dig up the history between her and Gabe.

Surely she was being paranoid. It was simply a coincidence and the shock of seeing Gabe again that had stuck her feet to the floor and subsequently given the Mexican chief a possible suspect.

Time changes people. *Look at me. I've changed. Not the same naïve little sweet-on-Gabe Alexander I was in college, that's for sure.* And Gabe. God knows he'd changed, what with living on his wits all these years, surviving on God-knows-what to live on. Okay, so he'd had it rough, but if anyone deserved a time in purgatory, it was Gabe—after what he did to her.

She would find him, talk him into leaving town immediately—but not back to the States. Then they would both be safe.

Tomorrow, she would make inquiries as to where she might find him. She'd start with the sergeant's cousin, the gate guard. Granted, he'd immediately tell the sergeant and then the chief inspector, but what choice did she have? She had to start somewhere.

And that comment by the sergeant—that Tthe bar was a dangerous place where men could acquire anything they wanted. She wondered if it was the sort of place Gabe frequented. Maybe she should look there. Then again, she didn't have her badge or backup should there be trouble she couldn't handle.

She knew some of what the sergeant hinted at about Ensenada. Just as Thailand was a Mecca for pedophiles, there were hot spots running the length of Mexico where men could buy girls of all ages—Mexican, South American, and girls from as far away as the Ukraine have been lured with the promise of work as au-pairs. Beaten, drugged, raped and reduced to abject slavery, they would lose their will to resist or escape. With a shudder, she saw his point; that if she went to this place, she might disappear into that dreadful maw of human slavery. Even with her police training in hand-to-hand combat, could she fight off a kidnapping attempt? Fight until she either escaped or died trying?

Reluctant to use the dwindling space in her holding tank, Katy took a walk to the marina bathroom where she showered, washed her hair and smoothed Lily of the Nile lotion over her legs and arms.

Feeling rejuvenated from the shower, she swung her bag over her shoulder as she walked through the dry dock to the marina gates. Seeing the overhead phosphorescent lights had left broad pools to splash through, she smiled and leaped from one to the next. But she found her enthusiasm cooling at the sight of a man leaning on a lamppost near the gate. The guard? No, the stance was different and he was smoking. Gabe? The square, blocky shape was all wrong for Gabe's lanky build.

Giving the hulking figure a wide berth, she picked up her pace and opened the gate with her key.

The man stubbed out the cigarette he'd been smoking with the heel of his shoe, pushed off the gate and called her name.

She turned. There was no mistaking the solid frame beneath the weak light. "It's about damn time, Chief Inspector Vignaroli."

"*Buenas noches* to you too, Señorita Hunter." The voice was still pitched at that low rumble, but it held none of the authoritarian behavior from earlier. "I had to work late. I just came from my mother's home. She lives not far from here." He patted the rock-hard abdomen of his white shirt with a thickly muscled forearm. "She is a wonderful cook."

All the frustration and anger at her good deed gone wrong came out in a growl. "Why in God's name did you chain my boat to the dock? You can't possibly think I'm a suspect."

Raul paused, reappraising this angry young woman—the wet curls of her long honey-colored hair held back in a still damp ponytail, the baggy sweats, the swell of her breasts under a thin white tee-shirt and then down to the flip-flops on her narrow feet, noticing with an odd pang to his heart that her toenails were painted a bright pink. *No,* he thought, *whatever Katy Hunter is, she's not dangerous, at least not tonight.*

He took her arm and gently led her through the gate and toward her boat. "I do not think you're a suspect, but perhaps we can take this conversation somewhere more private?"

"It's late, Inspector," she said, jerking out of his grasp. "Unless, of course, you've come with bolt cutters?"

Her voice was pitched for war and it also was attracting an audience. He said, "Perhaps you'd like to show me the inside of your boat?"

She turned on him, hands on her hips. "If you didn't come with bolt cutters, then why *are* you here?"

"I am not your enemy, Miss Hunter," he said, softly. "I can understand your anger, but I can assure you that if you will allow me to explain—"

"You can start here and now."

"Don't you want to know *how* the girl died?" She was furious and beautiful, even now with her full mouth pulled into a tight line. With a certainty born of his self-imposed year of celibacy, he knew he wanted her.

"Why so forthcoming now, Inspector?"

He lifted a hand at the gathering crowd of curious boaters. "Are you sure you don't want to show me your sailboat?"

One man stepped forward. "This guy bothering you, miss, you just say the word and we'll chuck him over the side."

"Er, no thanks, he's uh… a friend."

"Well, if you say so, miss. G'night then." The guy nodded and herded his dock-mates to their own boats.

"Follow me, Inspector," she said, and briskly led him to her boat slip.

Raul followed her down the ladder, now unsure of himself as he stood in her own private space, filling up her small cabin with his bulk.

When she pointed him to a settee behind a small teak table, he gratefully slid onto the cushions.

Tapping a finger on the table, he said,"I am here unofficially, Miss Hunter."

She stood where she was, arms over her chest, showing him she was not going to allow him an unnecessary minute.

Raul's lip twitched in a half smile. *In another minute she'll be tapping that cute little pink-toed foot. Get on with it, Raul. Your motives may be pure but your hormones are not, and once again, your timing sucks.*

"The medical examiner has completed his examination of the body and his report says that though she had water in her lungs, which was the final cause of death, she was also shot."

He was only slightly surprised that she seemed to already know this.

"Caliber?"

"Nine millimeter and though we have the bullet we don't have a weapon." Seeing her confused look, he waved a hand across his face. "A match, if we had the weapon, could take months since our government is up to its armpits with the cartels. I was thinking that you might be interested in this case, since the suspect is an American."

Her eyes narrowed and she went on the offensive. "This is why you humiliated me in front of my countrymen, chaining my boat to the dock, so you could bully me into helping you with a homicide case? Not me, Inspector. Mexico is way out of my jurisdiction. Besides, I have exactly two weeks left on my sabbatical, and I don't have any interest spending that time working a murder case in a foreign country, much less helping the likes of you!"

Díos mio. He liked this woman. She had attitude and she used everything in her arsenal to throw him off track. Good. He would use that. He continued as if she wasn't red-faced and angry. "She was a dancer at a local strip club and it was well known that your Gabe Alexander spent time there."

"He's not mine, Inspector. I haven't seen Gabriel Alexander since I was in my second year of college and he came by to say he was leaving town." Which was true—her dad always told her that when lying, be sure to get as much truth into it as possible.

Then her demeanor changed and with a quick smile, she said, "You asked for a tour of my boat. Let's do that now, shall we?"

He nodded, now wary of her temper.

She began pointing out the items at her interior helm. "I have radar and GPS, depth sounder, single side-band and VHF radios are all here and wired for the cockpit helm outside." Then she turned to the narrow galley and showed him the fridge/freezer box and her storage for food and dishes.

"And you're standing on a bank of six deep cycle batteries under the floor boards. I also have two solar panels mounted on my stern."

Giving the interior of her floating home a nod of approval, he said, "It takes a crew of six to work my brother's fishing boat and he doesn't have sails to deal with. How do you work the lines by yourself?"

"On a sailboat they're called sheets and all kinds of people single-hand sailboats. There was a famous English yachtsman, Tristan Jones, and not even the loss of his second leg to diabetes stopped him from sailing alone. Karen Thorndike was fifty-six when she sailed her thirty-four-foot sloop solo around the world, and besides, I hear that she didn't have an autopilot or a nifty GPS."

"I know radar and GPS. My brother has a big unit on his console."

Turning the tables, she asked, "Is your brother a sport fisherman?"

"No, he does it for a living." The answer was simple and his way of keeping his personal life out of her hands.

Raul turned away and squeezed forward as far as her miniscule shower/head combination and then halted at the line of photos secured on the bulkhead.

She tapped a finger on the first one and couldn't keep the smile out of her voice. "My dad. He taught me and my sister to sail this boat on the San Francisco Bay. Said if we could conquer those wily waters, we could sail anywhere. He was right. Unfortunately, he's gone, but my mom," she said, pointing to the next one, "lives nearby and that's me and my sister and the guy… the guy in this photo is my fiancé, David Bennett."

Her stumble at the fiance's name caused Raul to lean in for another look. The man's bored expression and expensively barbered head told him all he wanted to know about the man—but not why Katy wasn't with him anymore, which secretly cheered him more than he thought possible.

Raul sat down at her settee and lightly tapped the table top to indicate she should join him. He enjoyed watching her trying to keep her composure as well as her distance.

But when he saw a rosy blush rise up her neck a fissure of lust ran up his spine. So the attraction was mutual.

"So," she said quietly, "have you arrested a suspect?"

Unable to resist a teasing tone, he said, "Did I say we arrested a suspect? You must have misunderstood me. Sometimes my English is not so good."

"You kept me in your police station for most of the day because you suspect Gabe Alexander and you were afraid I might warn him before you could pick him up, is that right?"

He toyed with the edge of her place mat, rolling the edges up and down. "Did you come here to meet Mr. Alexander?"

She choked out a laugh. "That, Inspector, would be stranger than you'll ever know. But then I stood in the lobby of your police station and practically begged you to arrest him for the girl's murder, didn't I?"

The Inspector slanted a glance at her. When her breath hitched up, he allowed himself a private smile. He had an effect on her as she did on him. "I am very grateful that you had the foresight to call the Mexican Navy and not use your VHF radio. If you had, the wrong person might have heard your message and our ability to take action would have been lost."

"And that person would be Gabe Alexander?"

He shook his head. "We have no interest in your friend, Gabe, and I have no interest in what he says you are to him, either."

She let out the breath she'd been holding and went on the offensive. "You still have a chain and lock on my boat, Inspector."

He preferred to ignore the lock and chain for the moment. "I know that your record as a police officer is, except for shooting your sister's stalker, exemplary. In Mexico, there would have been no forced leave of absence for one who goes to the aid of a woman in distress. He had a gun aimed at her head, no? End of story."

Raul stood, indicating that he was finished.

Katy stepped in front of him, her hand inches from his chest as if she could stop him from leaving.

Raul looked down at her face tilted up, the sweep of her full lips slightly open as he saw her mentally calculating her next move. She was a scant few inches away and certainly within reach, so close the scent of her freshly washed hair tingled his nose. Without a hint of makeup, she was definitely a beautiful young woman. She would be a stand-out amongst the cosmopolitan model types his friends trotted out like sleek polo ponies. She was also unfashionably curvy, with hips, thighs and breasts that made his insides heat up in a way that he'd thought long forgotten.

The clear tanned skin would be abhorred by the women, and the wonderful tiny laugh lines radiating from the corners of her very blue eyes would only elicit suggestions for a favorite clinic where they could be erased. His guess was that Katrina Hunter would laugh at such nonsense.

He wondered if she'd be here long enough for him to see those eyes sparkle with laughter. He certainly didn't have to be here—alone with her. He had resisted the temptation until it was almost too late and gave himself over to it only because he could convince himself that it was business. He was not one to break his own rules, but this time....

Katy broke the spell when she tilted her head to one side and asked, "Cat got your tongue, Inspector?"

Surely she had a sense of his inner struggle but was making light of it.

Resolving to bring his blood pressure back to normal would be no easy task, but he was sure that any discussion about this case would do the trick. "This will be a delicate case and one we are told to handle with kid gloves."

"A politician?"

"Worse," he said, watching her very nimble mind work up an interest.

"What do you mean, *worse*? You don't strike me as a man who is easily intimidated."

He almost laughed at her use of flattery to get answers. "You know it is illegal in Mexico for any foreigner to be found with drugs or weapons."

"It is no secret that your police force is out-gunned by the cartels who can force them to take twice their salary or be shot."

"Yes. There is that. There are some of us who can't be bought, as in my case."

"Politically ambitious, are you?"

He lifted a hand as if to brush away the lock of hair that touched her cheek, then thought better of it. "Not in the way you would think. He's an American who has political influence. To arrest him would mean that the police officers involved would soon be sweeping streets for a living instead of attempting to clean our streets of crime."

The relief on her face was almost comical. "That definitely leaves Gabe out of the equation."

He chuckled. "When I got word of a young woman's body found in the ocean, I left everything to Sergeant Moreno and did a background check on you. After your credentials were verified, I saw no reason to hold you."

"But you *thought* you might have had reason to hold me?"

Hold her? If only.... He bit back these unusual and bothersome emotions and continued. "Ah, but then your Gabe walked in and everything changed, didn't it?"

"What makes you think I care?"

He ignored her outburst. He had her. There was a history with Gabriel Alexander that she didn't want known and because of it, she would do what he asked. What was it, a rift between them that sawed against the grain of her powerful family back in San Francisco? Or was it something that could affect her standing as a police officer? He would eventually wrinkle out all the sordid little details, but for now he had all that he needed, at least enough for him to get the help he needed to solve a crime. Carefully—he would have to handle her very, very carefully.

He said, "In spite of this man's influence, we can get a conviction, I'm sure of it… that is, if you're willing to take just a little time from your vacation—to question a few of the witnesses. As a sailor and an American, they will gladly talk to you."

"Where?"

"In another marina close by."

"What're the chances they already know who I am and why I'm there?"

"I am guessing it is your natural tendency not to reveal secrets to strangers. That is why *no* one but my sergeant and I know what you do for a living. I apologize for keeping you in the station for so long, but I'm sure that if you were in my position you would do the same thing."

She squinted up at him, a dimple appearing at the side of her mouth where it tweaked up in a slight smile. "Yeah, I guess."

"We have a very limited amount of time before your position is compromised."

"And the suspect gets wind of why I'm there and kills me too, right?"

He gave her a pained look. "I have a man on the dock. You do not need to know his name, but he will be there to look out for you."

"Details?"

"The suspect is Spencer Bobbitt. We had an anonymous phone call saying that gunshots were heard coming from a certain yacht in the marina. We found him passed out in the bedroom of his yacht, blood on his bed, blood on his hands, on the walls and a trail of it across the floor from his bed to the door. Our government has some interest in Mr. Bobbitt, but our main concern now is to discover his guilt or innocence."

"I'm going to ask a stupid question—"

"He remembers nothing. Nada, zip, zilch, zero. Only that she was picked up and brought to him on the yacht. They shared a drink and after that he can't tell us what happened until we woke him."

"Did you test the drink glasses for roofies?"

"The date rape drug? That would be an irony for someone like Spencer Bobbitt. He prides himself on his ability to seduce young women, and as you know the drug quickly leaves the body. We did not test him for any kind of narcotics—we were too busy looking for a body."

"Ah. Was he still unconscious when you boarded the yacht?"

"Quite. The suspect's captain had the engines running, ready to leave while he tried to clean up the blood."

"Do you think the captain was your anonymous caller?"

"No. He actually appeared relieved to have the responsibility taken off his hands. But he was also, how do you say, cagey about his earlier whereabouts. Ironic, don't you think? If someone hadn't called the police we might not have any case at all. Even so, there is still the riddle: How does a girl who is shot in the stomach walk across the floor, jump into the ocean and die of drowning without leaving behind any hand or foot prints?"

"The captain?"

Raul Vignaroli was warming to Katy Hunter in more ways than one. She was a good police officer. She was perfect. Perfect for the job he had in mind; that is, if he could manage to keep his eyes from straying to her tender mouth and his hands off her luscious body. He smiled down at her then stepped on the first rung of the ladder. "I'll have my sergeant come tomorrow and remove the chain."

She grabbed his arm, his hard muscles bunching under her fingers. He looked down at her open mouth. So close he could reach out and take her lower lip between his teeth and… he swallowed hard, his immediate and unintentional response coming out as a growl. "What?"

She instantly removed her hand. "How… how do you want me to contact you?"

His plan was working, so why should he feel this worm of disappointment? "I'll be in touch."

Was she trying to guess how much the inspector knew about Gabe, his past, her involvement with him? "'Kay."

"Okay? You don't want to sleep on it? I could come back tomorrow and we could discuss this again."

She swallowed and shook her head. "I'm good."

He was teasing her again and her response delighted him.

She followed him out of the boat and onto the dock. She held out her hand as a way to seal the agreement and maybe her fate. He took the proffered hand, and in one swift gesture, lifted her knuckles to his lips and lightly kissed them.

He took a step back, breaking the connection, and taking a piece of paper from his pocket, handed it to her. "This is the complete list of witnesses at the marina. Your reservations at Marina Mar are confirmed with a slip on the same dock as the suspect's yacht."

"You're very sure of yourself!"

"Not at all," he said, his voice now confident that she would do what he asked.

Then he turned on his heel and strode off into the dark, whistling.

Chapter Six

As promised, the chain and its lock were removed at dawn, doing a lot to improve Katy's disposition. But then so did the bright sunshine and promise of an early morning sail. Accepting the stern line from one of the dock boys and the bow line from an American sailor, she returned their salute, gunned the engine and motored away from the dock.

Gliding for the breakwater, Katy tightened her tiller lock, went forward to pull up the main, cleated it off and let it flutter in the slack. Back in the cockpit she bore off a few points and the main filled. With one hand on the tiller she reached out and yanked on the jib line, freeing the triangular-shaped foresail from its roller furling, and slipped between the red and green harbor markers for the open ocean.

Katy put the boat on a close reach and *Pilgrim* lifted her skirts like the very good girl that she was and scooted across the bay. It was pure joy, taking the wind and the waves on her bow, and it did everything it was meant to do to soothe her jittery nerves for the half hour that it took to reach the new marina—the one that held a connected American suspect and hopefully witnesses.

Closing in on her destination, she got a lesson on entering a windward-facing estuary when a sport fishing trawler juked its big engines as it caught the crest of a powerful wave and barreled through the narrow chute of the estuary into the calm water of the marina.

The Potato Patch, that gnarly snag of white water outside the Golden Gate Bridge, had taught her a lot about riding waves. So in preparation she waited, counting rollers until she saw a break in their pattern, and grabbing the tail of the smallest, rode it safely through the entrance.

At the dock a couple of Americans motioned her to throw her docking lines. One line went to a beat-up rooster in a pair of disreputable shorts, the other to his goosey-looking friend. The men neatly cleated off her lines and stood back to allow her to step onto the dock.

She pulled off her damp sailing gloves and offered her hand to the rooster.

Make that bantam rooster, she thought, since his head barely came up to her chin. He also had a recent surgery scar running from sternum to belly button showing through his unbuttoned Hawaiian shirt.

"Appreciate the help, fellas. I'm Katrina Hunter, but my friends call me Katy."

"Well, Katy, I'm Tennessee Booth but *you* can call me Booth."

Goosey, on the other hand, stood with his hands in his pockets, his shirt buttoned to his big Adam's apple and his mouth zipped shut.

Booth ignored his silent companion and nodded at a Mexican boy in khaki. "Julio is one of our many fine employees here at Marina Mar. He'll tend to your lines if you need to leave your boat for the season or any time at all. We got some powerful tidal currents in here and you'll want to stock up on more o' them rubber-baby-bumpers, 'cause the damn things bust out twice as fast as anywhere else. You stayin' long?"

"A few days, then I'll have her trucked back to the States."

Booth gave her and the sailboat a quick once-over, and nodded his approval. "You sail by yourself?"

"Yup," she answered, matching his folksy patter with her own.

He shrugged and scratched at the scar. "California?"

"Uh-huh," she said, turning away to adjust the dock fenders.

"Well," he said, "garbage goes in the covered box at the end of your slip but Julio likes the empty soda cans in a plastic bag on your bow. Recycling here is very big."

She grinned at him over her shoulder. The Mexicans invented recycling, mainly for the extra income. She tipped an eyebrow at Booth's friend.

Booth tsked. "This here's Wally. Ah, come on, Wally, say howdy to the pretty lady."

Wally gave her a shy grin, but his hands remained in his pockets.

Booth pitched her another comment. "He don't say much. Wally prefers to watch, don'cha, ol' buddy?"

The salacious comment, she knew was meant to tease Wally and embarrass her. But Booth also didn't seem to be in any hurry to share other news, either. Like the recent police raid on the big white yacht taking up most of an end dock. The inspector's list had a Wallace Howard on it, but not Tennessee Booth, and she had to wonder—why not?

Booth caught her wary look and gave her a friendly smile. "As your official welcoming committee, I hereby invite you to a cocktail party tonight at Spencer and Myne's boat. That's spelled M-Y-N-E and you'll see why when you meet her." He winked at her, another teasing gesture. "See, Wally? She likes it here already."

That made three on the list—Wallace aka, Wally, and now Spencer and Myne. She should just take out her list and ask if the rest of them would be there, too.

Booth stuck a thumb over his shoulder. "Can't miss it. It's that big motor yacht on the end."

"I dunno, Booth," she said, not willing to sound too eager. "I'm really beat and I need a hot shower. Maybe some other time?"

"Showers are inside the hotel, but you make friends with Spencer and Myne and they'll let you have the run of the place. Hot showers, cold drinks, good food. Besides, you gotta eat, don'cha? Get'cher shower, come for the food, meet a few nice folks and then go home. You'll see we're a pretty tame bunch here."

"Alright," she said, smiling again. "What time?"

"Six-ish? When you've had your fill of food or us silly old farts, go home. Ain't that right, Wally?"

Wally nodded.

Tame crowd, good food, huh? We'll see about that. By the end of the night she intended to meet most of that list and have at least some of the answers to the chief inspector's questions.

It was late afternoon by the time she stepped through the airy, open lobby of the resort hotel. Intent on finding the showers, Katy slowed to admire the modern architecture and local art. The place was all high beamed ceilings, glass and chrome blended with sculptures of Aztec warriors that looked to have been quarried out of local stone. The club-wielding Aztecs, she noted, were strategically placed next to exits. *Nice touch,* she thought. *Too bad they can't follow me back to the boat and become my bodyguards.*

She passed a rock wall hugging a seascape the size of a picture window. The artist had perfectly captured that moment when a rapidly changing sky releases its light on an unsettled sea. Thunderous clouds chased the hopeful blue of better weather off the canvas while water appeared to be in danger of sloshing onto the stone hearth.

Turning left, she found a lineup of land-line phones next to the hotel bar and took out her calling card. Cell phones were great but digital meant nothing if the police used Mexican Telecom to eavesdrop. Plugging one ear against the roar of American football on the TV in the bar next door, she started to call her friend Bruce at the department and see if anyone in a Mexican police department had been asking about her, but at the last minute, changed her mind and punched in the number for her mother's apartment, hoping to leave a message.

"Hello?" The smoky voice answering the phone didn't match what she knew was her much younger looking mother.

"Mom. I'm glad I caught you at home."

"Katrina, darling! Of course I'm home. I saw David a few days ago, and he seems terribly glum—even for David. Darling, I made a joke. Aren't you listening?"

"I heard. Didn't he tell you?"

"Tell me what? Did you start another fight you can't win? If you wanted to argue with him, you should've gotten a law degree. Katy? That was another joke."

"Mom, David called off our vacation for the Delta and announced we should see other people." She didn't add that all this happened after she was put on leave of absence from the shooting.

"Good God!" The other end of the line hummed with the sound of her mother's mental arithmetic for what it would cost to cancel the big wedding. "Does his family know? God, I'm getting slow—of course they do. Everyone knows but me. Katrina, you know I love you, darling, but honestly, this is incredibly inconsiderate. The invitations are out, the hotel! The caterer!"

"Sorry, Mom. Really, I am. I thought surely David would've said something to you by now. I mailed him back his ring before I sailed for Mexico."

"Mexico! Are you sure?"

"Of course I'm sure. I got my passport all stamped and everything." She didn't add that it was still being held by the Mexican police, but that wasn't going to be a conversation she intended to have with her mother.

"Katrina Hunter, don't be obtuse! I can't believe you broke up with David, when the wedding is less than a month away!" There was a moment of silence and then her mother's voice softened. "Maybe it was a knee-jerk reaction to all the stress you two have been under; his job, that horrible incident with your sister's stalker. I know you took it hard when the department put you on sabbatical but I'm sure it hit him hard, too. You should never run away from problems with a spouse, Katrina. It only exacerbates the problem."

Katy snorted "Mom, David isn't my spouse and it doesn't look like he's ever going to be."

"Alright, alright, but you're coming home soon, aren't you? The department hearing is in two weeks and I'm sure you can resolve your problems with David with a little TLC."

Her mother's comment, that it should be her job to soothe David's hurt feelings, rankled to the bone. "It was his decision and I'm good with it and now I'm here where I should be," she said, leaving out the body she found in the water, Gabe, and that she was now obligated to help with a murder investigation in Mexico.

"And where *are* you in Mexico?" her mother asked. "At least tell me you're on dry land again."

"I made it to Ensenada day before yesterday," she said. "You'd love this marina. Very modern, lots of art and a high-end hotel and spa."

"Ensenada. Isn't that close to the border? You know those towns are rife with all those nasty cartels. It seems every night the newscasters have some grim new story about beheadings."

"Oh, Mom, don't worry. All those nasty cartel guys are out lounging by the pool."

"Katrina Taylor Hunter! Don't you make jokes about something like that!"

"Mom, I'm perfectly safe. This is a very well-run operation; they have guards and locked gates and everything." Katy was eyeing the bar, wishing she'd thought to fortify that boast with a big glass of wine or two before calling her mother.

"Well, I must admit the place sounds nice, not that I wouldn't go within a mile of anything north of Punta Mita. We were in Puerto Vallarta all last week and stayed in that wonderful Westin out on the point."

Here was the reason why her mother missed the gossip about her daughter's breakup with San Francisco's next district attorney. She had a new boyfriend.

"Anyone I know?" In the five years since Katy's dad died, her mom had stepped out with any number of gentleman friends, all of whom were only too willing to accompany the wealthy Judge Roy Hunter's widow anywhere she chose, as long as she paid their way.

But then her mother surprised her and said, "Believe it or not, your sister put her very busy life on hold so that we could have some mother-daughter pampering."

Katy grinned into the phone. "Our Leila? How'd you drag her away from L.A.? Didn't she get her contract renewed for that soap opera... what's it called?"

"*All My Tomorrows*. Now, if you will remember, I invited both of you since it might be the last time we had some girl time before the nuptials. Unlike you, your sister sees the merit keeping in touch with her mother."

Her beautiful sister had been throwing herself at Hollywood for almost twenty years. Even with the security of a full-time job on the soaps, she still auditioned for secondary characters in whatever indie or TV pilot appeared likely to give her faltering career a jolt. Katy cautioned her sister against random networking, vigorously arguing for some reasonable vetting of invitations, warning Leila that that's how beautiful women sometimes ended up dead. That stalker found it incredibly easy to find Leila's home address, and if Katy hadn't answered the door, well, she didn't want to think of it now.

"Katrina, I asked you a question. Are you, or are you not, going to talk to David? Oh, wait—I just got back today and there were no messages on my answering machine, maybe he hasn't yet told his family. Oh, that's it, don't you see? He *must* be having second thoughts. Katrina, there's still hope."

"Uh-huh. Look, I'm making arrangements to have the boat trucked home and I'll be back in San Francisco in a week or so, and then, well, we'll see."

"Another week? Good God. I don't suppose you've thought to call Roberto either, have you? One simply does not blow off wedding planners like Roberto Marquez, not if you expect him to ever do another one, you don't. And I'm not doing it for you either, young lady! Your father would be spinning in his grave if he knew you'd broken David's heart and sailed off for Mexico."

Her father would be cheering her on if he knew the details of why she'd sailed for Mexico.

Katy ground her teeth, took a deep breath and let it out. "Daddy left me that money to use as I wished, Mom. If I choose to blow it sailing around the world instead of marrying David Bennett, that's my choice."

She wished she hadn't brought up her father in this way, not now in a phone call when she was too far away to find the words that could placate her mother's steely silence.

Finally her mother said, "I think you're making a terrible mistake, Katrina, but since it's your money to do with it as you wish, blow it all on that stupid sailboat of your father's if you must, but make the appropriate calls to cancel the wedding plans or forfeit the deposits. And don't ask me to do it. I'm too disgusted with you."

Katy murmured something that might have been an acknowledgment of her sins but it was all said to dead air.

Her mother had every right to be angry at her. Katy had run away from home, leaving behind the responsibility of tangling with David's family, wedding planners, caterers, hotel accommodations, and it was reprehensible and irresponsible. She looked at her watch. She'd deal with the wedding planner tomorrow, but a call to Leila was overdue.

In a cheesy Spanish accent, Katy gushed, "Is theese the famosa Señorita Leila Standiford?"

"Katy!" the laughing voice of her sister responded. "You rascal! Where are you?"

"Ensenada, Mexico, *darling* girl."

"You talked to our *darling* mother before you called *me*? And why are you in Mexico? You and wha's his name were going to use some of that paid leave of absence for a trip up the Delta, weren't you?"

Katy said, "Remember when I said that David would be a welcome change from the bad boys I've been dating?"

"Right. So what's Mr. Stuffy-Butt done to ruin his chance at marrying Judge Roy Hunter's daughter?"

"He said a whole week cooped up in a small sailboat trolling the Delta wasn't interesting. Never mind that he'd gone along with the idea until we were packed and ready to leave. That started a fight that led to him saying he thought we should give each other some space because he was no longer sure we were right for each other."

Leila hooted. "Oh God. That's priceless! Who on earth is she?"

"My question, exactly. Remember Karen Wilke?"

"Eeuww. That old thing? She's ten years older than David, thinks of herself as prime Cougar, which she isn't. So, what's she want *him* for, anyway?"

"Probably because she can."

"She'll eat him for lunch. Two months with that bitch and he'll come running back... that is, if you still want him?"

"Mom thinks he may be having second thoughts 'cause she hasn't heard anything from his side of the family. I'm good with it but I'm seriously considering including a no-man clause to this trip south."

There was a pause on the line. Leila's voice came back tense with worry. "Oh, honey. Don't say that. You aren't really sorry about David, are you? You know I never liked him. He's an ambitious suck-up and I suppose you know he just dumped you 'cause your job's now on the line... the bastard! You just need your juices primed. Want me to come down there? I've got friends with a beautiful home in Acapulco. It has this amazing infinity pool. I can do a few days… oh, what the hell, let's make it a whole week. We can swim, get drunk, chase boys, what do you say?"

What a wonderful thought, but not with the chief inspector and the investigation she'd been roped into doing for him. "I would, but I've got a date with a truck driver."

She laughed. "Well then, why didn't you say so? Does he have a friend?"

"*Pilgrim*'s going to get all his attention and I still have things to do to get her ready."

"Okay, fine, but promise me you'll stop over her on your way home. I owe you, little sister," she said, her voice going soft with tears. "You know I do, so why fight it? Let me fix you up with some of those bad boys you used to love so much. We'll tear up the town… or better yet, take the show to Vegas."

Katy chuckled. "Bring it on then. But I'll pass on the bad boys."

"Why? Don't tell me you're going all squishy 'cause that dweeb dumped you? Come on, where's your grit? You got your cherry popped and your heart broke at high school graduation with Gabe Alexander and that never slowed you down, so don't tell me you're losing sleep over David Bennett."

Katy felt the guilty blush rise to her face. Good thing Leila couldn't see her right now, but then Leila always was able to zero in on the source of her troubles.

Interesting that Leila would bring up Gabe now. For all Leila knew, Katy had shed him with shoulder pads and high school graduation. But Gabe was Katy's very own unhappy secret. And if all went well, she should be able to keep it that way.

"Kat… you still there?"

"Yeah, honey. Someone wants to use the pay phone, so I'll talk to you later, okay?"

"But, Katy, don't you ever wonder what happened to that gorgeous ever-lovin' heart-breakin' lyin' bad-boy?"

"Nope."

Chapter Seven

At six o'clock, she sprayed herself with the light floral scent she kept on the boat, something feminine she'd bought for the vacation she'd planned with her now obsolete fiancé. After David's hasty retreat she'd FedExed his ring in its box to his office. Her boat would go home on a truck and she could use up the last of her sabbatical doing—what? Lolling around L.A.? She hated to think of the tap dance she'd have to do to get her career back on track if she was demoted to street cop status. The union had specified that her paid leave of absence was mandatory but she was assured of a position with SFPD. And what might that be—crowd control at the ball park? Pulling nickels out of downtown parking meters? Not what she signed up for with a degree in Criminal Justice, that's for sure. And, if she was demoted she'd be stuck in vice for another hundred years. Maybe she should start over somewhere else, like up Mendocino way. Wasn't there a posting for an officer in Ft. Bragg? A new start, a new home, away from San Francisco, could she, should she do that?

She pushed at the fabric clinging to her hips and wished the wrinkles out of her only sundress. She was proud of her sturdy little vessel but at thirty-two feet, *Pilgrim* had less than twenty-four feet of usable living space and her cabin allowed only a couple of cubbyholes and a few drawers.

She was grateful, however, that Chief Inspector Vignaroli was sensible enough to leave her to do her job with the list. He did not, thank God, try to tell her how to conduct an interview. If the information she found tonight was enough to report on, then he could finish what she'd started.

Katy yanked a brush through sun-streaked curls then added delicate earrings with dangling silver leaves. Twisting her head from side to side, she checked her appearance in the narrow mirror. The mirror on her tiny bedroom door said sparkling earrings would do nothing for the worry she was carrying around. Besides, the earrings tangled in her hair. She tried sweeping her hair back but the earrings only burrowed deeper into the thick locks. She glared at her image. Shit! Tangled hair, tangled up in this stupid scheme to get a bunch of wily American boaters to talk about a murder by one of their own. She pulled off the earrings, grabbed the bottle of her favorite Napa Valley chardonnay, squared her shoulders and set off for *All Myne*.

A tanned young man in sailor whites tipped her a two-fingered salute and pointed towards the stairs. "Everyone is topside, miss. Watch your step, please." If there was an American in Northern Baja *not* on this yacht, it would be a surprise to Katy. They spilled out of the salon, clogged the stairs and were so tightly packed together that some of them were actually perched on the rails.

This is the dumbest thing I've ever done... well, except for Gabe, that is. I'll be lucky if the witnesses here don't put roofies in my drink and toss me overboard.

She pushed through the crowd and into the salon where the AC was barely keeping pace with the crush of perfume, cigar smoke and sweat, then wiggled through a hole in the crowd, and in a victory slam dunk of a quarterback at the end zone, plunked her bottle of wine on the bar.

Booth grinned at her. "Congratulations. Not many folks have the wherewithal to navigate this crowd."

"What's the occasion?" she shouted over the megawatt music and raucous laughter.

Booth cupped a hand around his ear and cocked his head to indicate she should try again. When she shook her head in the negative, he reached into a tight circle of men and extracted a tiny blonde. Draping an arm over the girl's bare shoulder he moved her in front of Katy.

"This here's Myne," he yelled over the noise. "She's Spencer's significant other."

Katy tried not to stare at the oversized breasts spilling out of the expensive red cocktail dress. Myne was a fifteen-year-old's wet dream and an older man's prized possession. The five-foot kewpie doll held out her long red-tipped nails and in the dirt poor accent of East Texas, drawled, "Hi, I'm Myne."

Myne. On the list. Get her out of the noisy room. Talk to her. See what she knows. Yelling was hopeless, so Katy used hand gestures to indicate a move for the door. Myne dimpled a smile and winked, then grabbed two beers out of the ice-filled bucket, offering one to Katy as they slid out of the door to lean against a recently deserted spot on the aft rail.

Looking for an opener, Katy held up the beer. "People are always trying to hand me a glass of wine when all I want is a nice cold beer."

Myne giggled. "Me, too! All that 'doesn't this wine have a hint of apple to it?' don't get it for me. Gimme a nice Michelob or Coors. Though this Tecate ain't too shabby. So,

Katy, they do call you Katy, right? I been dyin' to ask, you sail that li'l ol' boat all the way from California to here?"

"All the way from San Francisco."

"On purpose?" Myne asked, squinting up at Katy. "You ain't one of them lesbians from Castro Street, are you?"

Katy took a pull of the beer to hide her laughter, then looked down at the pint-sized Mae West and smiled. "No, no, I'm definitely not one of those. Nice dress."

"You think so? It's a Wanger."

This time Katy let the smile out. It was Vera Wang and probably cost Spencer a cool two grand.

To grease the skids, Katy said, "I don't know a Wanger from a Wallabie, but my sister gets to wear some nice designer dresses to the Emmys every year."

The little blonde squealed. "Get out! Who's your sister? TV or movies?"

"She's got a long-standing gig on *All My Tomorrows*."

"Oh..." Myne put her hands over her heart in a near swoon. "I *love* that show. Which one is she, Tamar or Rachel? Don't tell me she's that scheming bitch, Suzanne."

"Bingo. But she's an actress, so to take the sting out of her bad girl image she's always looking to do different parts in movies. Did you see *Knives* with Bruce Willis? She was Bruce Willis' sympathetic psychiatrist."

Myne's red lips widened into a grin. "Then she's a *real* actress, not some naïve walk-on whose work ends up on the cutting floor along with her clothes 'cause that's all the producer thinks she's good for."

Well, thought Katy, *that explains where Myne was headed when Spencer Bobbitt found her.* But before she could move on to questions, a gray-haired, grim-faced woman angrily brushed past with Wally in tow. Still tight-lipped, he managed a brief, apologetic nod to Katy and Myne, as resigned to his fate as a hooked bass.

Myne, however, wasn't happy to see Wally leave, and in a voice that could project the length of a football field, bellowed, "Hey, y'all ain't leavin' the party! Come on back here, I got somebody y'all oughta meet."

Ignoring his wife's desperate attempt to drag him away, Wally did a U-turn, towing the angry wife back to Myne.

Myne ignored the older woman's sour expression and chirped her introductions. "This here's Wally and Ida Howard. They've got a sailboat too, *Consolation Prize*. Ain't that cute?"

Ida Howard, her mouth set in a thin line of disapproval, nodded curtly at Katy and went back to eyeing a path for the door. Wally, however, open-mouthed and glassy-eyed, appeared to be under some kind of spell.

Two more faces to match the inspector's list. "Wally was kind enough to help me tie up this afternoon."

Through gritted teeth, Ida muttered, "Of course he did."

Wally blushed, closed his mouth and stuttered, "G—g—glad to be of h—help." Five words appeared to be it for Wally, and continued his longing stare at Myne.

No wonder his wife was desperate to get him off Spencer's yacht. A few more minutes of this and Wally would disappear into a pulsing vortex of lust for another man's possession.

Seeing her chance to escape, Katy excused herself for the buffet table. She picked up a sausage with a miniature Mexican flag skewered through it, added some carrots and celery and a dollop of ranch dip.

As if on cue, Booth appeared. "So, how's it going, Katy?"

Katy was impressed at the engineering of his introduction to Myne and wondered what he had in mind.

"Did you try the bean and sour cream dip? It's my specialty."

Booth's dish of bean dip looked to have grown a few hairs.

"Um, no thanks on the bean dip, but I am having a good time."

He nodded, waiting.

"Myne seems nice."

"You liked her, huh? Then you should meet Spencer Bobbitt. There he is," he said, pointing at a tall man in a pale yellow silk shirt and matching linen slacks. In his fifties, she guessed. Big head of graying blond hair styled into a poufy comb-over, a predatory brow and a long stubborn jaw radiated a cool self-confidence that said he wasn't worried about any murder investigation with his name on it. He also had a cigarette holder jammed between a row of perfectly capped teeth and a pair of round tortoise-framed glasses perched on his nose. The FDR image could not have been accidental. The big head turned in their direction, and with a nod to Booth, Spencer motioned to the man next to him.

The guy's piercing whistle got the attention of the people nearest to Spencer, and the volume on the party settled down to murmur. In a warm and perfectly pitched baritone meant to be heard without benefit of a mic, he said, "Ladies and gentlemen, I'm pleased to introduce tonight's entertainment."

As whoops and jeers broke out he held up a cautionary finger. "Not that kind of entertainment. Not tonight, anyway. I give you Frederic the Magician and his beautiful assistant, Astrid Del Mar!"

The magician, in a flowing white peasant shirt and tight leather pants, bowed deeply enough to show a speckled, egg-shaped bald spot nesting in the frizz of his dyed black hair. He was the same man who had been leaning on the stern of a fifty-foot motor yacht smoking and watching as she struggled to bring her little boat safely into the estuary. Passing his boat, she'd momentarily locked eyes with him. But instead of a welcoming nod, he flicked his cigarette into the water and turned away.

Frederick and Astrid Del Mar were both on the witness list. Was his earlier boorish behavior because he was expecting her? He was all jokes and smiles now as he clumsily flipped cards for the boozy crowd. His colorful assistant was a slim whirl of red shimmering sequins on four-inch heels and reminded Katy of a wood sprite with her magenta pixie cut hair, mostly absent light brows and heavily lined big brown eyes. She did her job well, dazzling the drunks and deflecting attention away from the sloppy work of the magician. Most of the crowd was too drunk to notice when he palmed and layered a card so that it appeared on the top of the deck.

Her dad used to do card tricks in chambers to diffuse angry confrontations. *"Material witnesses popping up in the middle of a trial?"* he'd ask, clucking his tongue and leaning over the desk to draw a card from behind a lawyerly ear. *"Disclosure is the law. That way we can all see the tricks each of you has hiding behind your ears, right?"*

With a lurch of her heart, she could only wish her dad were here to critique the magician's work. Anyone who wasn't falling down drunk could tell this guy had just slipped that birdcage out from under the stand. Add boor to bad magician and she had enough reason to want him for murder. He was obviously guilty of something.

On his worst day, and towards the end of the cancer, her dad was way better than this guy. Despite a howling air conditioner, Katy yawned at the close warmth of too many bodies and too little sleep. Booth, Myne and the Howards, she noticed, had already disappeared so she might as well call it a night.

She stepped out of the overcrowded salon and into the sweet evening air. Feeling better, she headed for the stern exit, but at the last moment decided to do a little reconnaissance, walk off the liquor she never touched and skirt the perimeter for an unlocked door. With no one to say she couldn't, she took the steps to the lower level. This level would be the bedrooms. Maybe she could find where Chief Inspector Vignaroli and his police found Spencer Bobbitt stretched out and unconscious with blood on his hands.

Katy ambled along the deck, glancing into each dark window until a porthole illuminated the night like an attractive spotlight. Naturally she leaned forward to peer inside.

The room was mostly unfurnished, lit with overhead fluorescents; lockers sprouted along one wall and diving equipment hung off another. A semi-circle of men, most of them sleekly well-fed and middle-aged, lounged in arm chairs with drinks and cigars. The group had the look of pigeons about to be given the ubiquitous condo sales pitch as they puffed and drank and waited the plucking. A drumbeat pulsed against the glass of the porthole and a short blonde, her back to the window, slid into the room wearing white heels and a short pink gingham dress. The dress may have been childish, but there was no mistaking her curtsy. To their roar of delight the dress came off her shoulders in one pull and was kicked out of range and she turned around to wriggle her bare ass at the men. Without her red Vera Wang, Myne was a rounded, pink confection right out of a Donatello painting.

Seeing enough to know what came next, Katy backed away and bumped into something solid, and from the boozy breath on her neck, a drunk. Heavy hands landed on her shoulders and then a voice said, "You mush be the new girl."

Katy froze. She didn't recognize the voice but she wasn't looking forward to fighting off a drunk when she might have to face him in the next couple of days.

The hands slid around to grope her breasts as his mouth slobbered wet kisses on her neck. "Whad'ya shay we take it to my cabin?"

Without turning around she jammed her elbows down to break his hold. Then redistributing her weight, lifted a heel and came down hard on his instep. The drunk reeled back, grunting and swearing.

Damn, she thought, *too drunk to get the message, but let's see if he gets thi*s. She turned, and slammed her fist into his adam's apple. Satisfied he would be too busy trying to breath to bother with her again, she hurried along the passage only to bump into another male body. This one was shorter, sober, and put up his hands to keep her from colliding into him.

Booth.

He nodded at the lighted porthole behind her. "Enjoy the peep show?"

The question was obviously rhetorical, since she was getting the picture that Booth made it his business to keep tabs on her. But did he know she was a cop, one who was here to see if she could get the goods on his friend Spencer Bobbitt?

She sighed. *Might as well see what I can do to fix the damage.*

"Can we talk someplace else?"

"Sure. Foredeck should have cleared out some by now." He indicated they were to head back the way she came.

She stiffened, remembering the nuisance drunk she'd left behind. "I'd rather not go that way, if you don't mind."

Booth laughed. "I didn't take you for the prudish kind, but okay, top-deck is nice and quiet this time of night." Doing an about-face, he took a staircase to the next level up.

He pointed her to some deck chairs set out for daytime sunbathing. "Take a chair and I'll get us a coupla Cokes."

Katy enjoyed the few minutes of quiet to admire the inky darkness of the Mexican night and the brilliant stars in the Baja sky.

Booth came back and handed her a cold can. "Noticed you don't drink. Gets in the way, don't it? So, where were we? Oh yeah, guess you got an eyeful down there, huh?"

"The magician in the salon keeps the women entertained while the men go downstairs for a strip show. What're they signing up for...Nigerian blood diamonds, shares of nonexistent gold mines in Canada?"

"Want to know how Spencer got his start?"

She waited. He was going to tell her anyway.

"He had a secret formula for copying French couture and sold it to gullible housewives."

"This is a far cry from gullible housewives," she said, waving a hand at the expansive yacht.

"It's a fun story, if you wanna hear it."

He was too smart by half, in spite of his folksy speech pattern. What was Booth to Spencer? Sycophant? Surely not just a gofer. More like consigliere to Spencer Bobbitt's Don.

"As Spencer tells it to his friends," said Booth, "of which I count myself one, he'd roll into some Midwest burg, get himself on the local radio station, and with a heavy French accent, proclaim that he was sick of France, hated the French. Midwesterners hate the French, so they were ready to listen.He's stolen the secret of French couture, see, and if the fine women of Bum-fuck Missouri, or wherever he happened to be at the moment, wanted his secret, he'd meet them at such and such time at a local auditorium or high school gym, and reveal the secret that every French woman knew—how to make beautiful couture with only a simple pattern and a sewing machine."

"Did it work?"

"Boy, howdy, did it. He would fill up a high-school auditorium and then pretend to measure off his assistant, consult his secret book, cut a pattern and in minutes he'd have haute couture. But, like all good cons, one day he misjudged his audience, and climbing outta bathroom windows to escape the law taught him a lesson. See, women are not as proud as men when it comes to admitting they've been had. That's when he decided to switch his game to the weaker sex—primarily married, wealthy, retired men with a taste for very young flesh. Now, don't get me wrong, eventually men wise up to a con. Land or condo or whatever deal he has them hooked up to, it's all smoke and mirrors. Some try to cut their losses and back out of the deal, but the few who do get an envelope with some photos delivered to their homes. Then it becomes a write-off for a Lolita fantasy."

"Well, as my daddy used to say, 'A fool and his money are soon parted.'"

"Your daddy said that, huh? Then he was a wise man."

She thoughtfully rolled the can between her hands. "I saw some kind of message pass between you and Spencer tonight. What's he hoping to accomplish, Booth?"

Booth's jolly expression slipped into a complacent smile and he sat back in the chair, hands clasped over his belly.

"You were also conveniently there to help me tie up my boat. Very anxious that I come meet all these swell people; the Howards and Myne and pointing out what a generous fellow Spencer Bobbitt is, considering he might be guilty of murder."

He held up both hands in surrender. "Okay, okay. We thought you should meet him, see what a swell guy he is, though I guess that didn't go so well. You wanna talk to him, right?"

"How do you know who I want to talk to?"

"Oh," he said, squashing the aluminum can between his hands, "I know what's going on around here, who comes into the marina and why." He stood up. "Don't be sore, honey, it's my job. I'll set it up for tomorrow."

"What exactly is it that you do for Spencer Bobbitt?" she said, getting out of the deck chair.

"I didn't remove a dead girl's body if that's what yer thinkin'." Then with a quick nod, said, "Tomorrow afternoon I'll come get you for that interview with Spencer. G'night, Katrina."

He left her then, leaving her to wonder what was next and how safe she really was here in this dangerous harbor.

Chapter Eight

Tucking a pillow up against the coaming of her cockpit, Katy sat where the early morning sun could warm her as she studied the list from the inspector. Handwritten—was that because he didn't trust any of his staff to see what he was up to? A leak in the police department would explain how someone like Booth might know who she was and why she was there. But it didn't answer why his name wasn't on the list. So far, at least three people knew who she was and why she was here. Tapping her pencil on her lip, she pulled her notepad from under her thigh and started to make notes

Spencer Bobbitt: Swindler, con artist according to Booth. Rap sheet?

Myne: Young, impressionable, susceptible to Hollywood types. How attached was she to Spencer Bobbitt? Get her real name and/or rap sheet.

Booth: Was Booth the man the chief inspector put on the dock to watch her? Could that be Booth?

Wally and Ida: Find out how long here, why? What's Wally's relationship to Spencer, if any?

Fred McGee aka Frederic, the magician: If he also knew who she was did he see her as some kind of threat? Might he be a suspect?

Astrid Del Mar: Fake name,Star of the Sea, but good assistant to a lousy magician. Need more.

Boat Captain: Jeff Cook… didn't meet him last night so…

What the... ?

A beam of light smacked her in the eyes. She blinked, and thinking it a reflection off another boat, moved to the right. It hit again, this time flashing across her face, forcing her to close her eyes. "Ugh, that hurt!" she mumbled to no one in particular and closed her eyes to watch round black dots bounce around her retinas. She gave it a moment then opened them again.

Shaking it off, she went back to work on the list. She would call Bruce Sullivan, her partner in the SFPD, see if he could help with these names.

When the searing light did another pass across her face, she jerked out of her seat, banging her head on the metal ribs of her canvas bimini.

Now she was mad.

Rubbing at the sore spot on her skull, she stumbled off the boat and peered down the quiet length of dock. There it was again, smacking her in the face. If it was the reflection off one of the boat windows, then why did it follow her like this? Curious, she hurried up the ramp to the parking lot. Someone may be opening a door, or moving a car in the early morning light. But all the windows were still opaque from last night's wet marine air.

A sharp whistle and another flash of light blistered her corneas. When her vision cleared, she looked up to the cliff overlooking the marina. A figure held up a hand, waved, and motioned for her to come up. Who was this Boy Scout signaling her with a mirror?

Adrenaline propelled her through the quiet parking lot to where a path had been carved into the rock. She took it, scrambling up the rocky path, and in a few more minutes, she was on the top of the bluff. He stood his ground, she had to give him that much, calmly smoking.

"What the hell you think you're doing, Gabriel Alexander? You could put someone's eye out with that thing."

He waited until she finished the tirade, then stubbed out the cigarette with the heel of his huaraches. "You're in trouble 'cause of me, aren't you, Whisper?"

"I told you before, don't call me Whisper!" She hated this reminder of the schoolyard taunt, the result of an overpowering shyness that earned her the hated nickname. That is, until an older boy turned the tables on her tormentors, forever winning her trust and devotion. The rest, as they say, is history.

"Okay, *Katy*. Happy now?"

"I'm here, aren't I? And I'm not in any kind of trouble. I just moved from one marina to another, that's all."

"Sure you did. I came to check on you over at Baja Naval. Your dock mates said your boat got chained up, but the next day you and your boat are pulling away from the dock bright and early."

"Then how'd you know I'd be here?"

"I live in this RV park. Spend most my afternoons sitting out here watching the sport fishermen come into the marina, so when I saw this little sailboat get washed through the estuary, I figured it had to be you. I'd ask what you're doing here, but I guess that's a redundant question. So, *are* you doing this on account of me?"

That got her stubborn up. "Why do you think this is about you?"

Gabe shook his head and walked away. Katy started to follow and then thought better of it. This was Gabe she was dealing with here, and where she used to be like iron to magnet, she wasn't that person anymore.

She stood where she was and spoke his name. "Gabe."

He turned. "Did he tell you that my trailer is here? No, of course not. That would make it too easy. You're in dangerous water, sweetheart. You know that, don't you?"

His comment brought her back to the present. Now if she could only convince him that she had his best interests at heart. "You're the one who should leave. Why don't you take off for Costa Rica, or Brazil?"

"I'm tired of running, Katy. I thought I could live the rest of my life hiding, but I might as well have stayed and testified against the mob for all the good it's done me. I'm miserable living without a name or a home. I want to get a lawyer, take my chances in the States."

"Gabe, I'm on a forced sabbatical from my job with the San Francisco police department and if you go back now, the truth will come out and I could still be prosecuted for helping you jump bail. Is that how you want to thank me?"

"Let's get out of the open and talk about this, okay?" He turned and walked through a row of dilapidated trailers, all of them devoid of wheels and so abysmally rusted on their stands that it was obvious that they were never moving again.

Gabe opened the door on a twenty-four footer with a riot of bougainvillea permanently welded to its sides.

Katy took the step and entered through a pockmarked and rusted door. The interior was about the same space as her sailboat and just as tidy. Gabe motioned for her to take a seat at one of the two bench seats between a bolted-down dinette scrubbed clean of most of its original color.

"I rent it from a guy who's in the hospital up in the States," he said, lighting a burner on his small stove and setting a kettle on it. "Had a heart attack so he's probably not coming back any time soon."

Leaning against the sink, he said, "You look good. You've grown into all that wild-child hair you had when we were kids. "

"Hair products, flat iron—when I can find a place to plug one in. You know Mexico may be *mañana* land but that doesn't mean the inspector can't get your records, if he chooses."

"You don't have to worry about that, Katy. I can take care of myself."

"Oh, Gabe, don't be naïve. There's no statute of limitation on jumping bail and skipping out of the country so you can avoid federal prosecution."

He shook his head and gave her a lopsided grin. "Mathematical genius only works when you're savvy about how things roll and I've learned a thing or two about surviving on my own, but I'm sorry I didn't give you a lot of thought in this equation. When did you decide to become a cop instead of a lawyer?"

"Disbarred or dismissed, either way I'm out of a job, if not in jail, for what I did back then. I was over eighteen and you were a rat. If it weren't for my dad...."

"Roy still hate me?"

"He died last year, Gabe. He never said boo about you to anyone who wasn't part of his inner circle and I think it's safe to say none of them have any reason to talk about it. He promised me he could make it all go away and he did, swept up all the loose ends so it looked like I was never there. But I understand that your conscience says you need to stand up to a federal judge and tell him the truth. Good luck with that, but hey, you do what you gotta do."

"Sorry about your dad. I liked him. Wasn't mutual, but I know he cared about you and your family."

"Thanks."

"So… just one question?"

"Yeah?"

"If you're not staying because of me, then why are you in a marina with a murder suspect from hell instead of on your way home?"

"I… I…"

He looked at her with such poignant longing that she almost reached across the table to take his hand in hers, but stopped herself when she saw that his expression wasn't what she thought. It was disappointment. Gabe was disappointed in her. She almost laughed. Instead, she hid behind her cup of tea and let him talk.

"Katy, I messed up, but please believe me, I'm not a killer. I never touched that girl and I hate it that someone did kill her."

"Then the best thing you can do for the both of us is get on another freighter and head south."

He grimaced, as if swallowing a very bad pill, and said, "Let me think about that."

She sat at the table inside her boat and traced a finger along the eight names and thought about her conversation with Gabe and how her life had changed.

She was in her second year of college and Gabe was already working as a stockbroker. They were in love then, with plans to marry. Then he was arraigned on charges of money laundering for the mob. He explained it all—that that he'd been foolishly duped by his bosses. "I thought only of the quick buck. But I did it for us, Katy, so we could get married."

The feds offered him amnesty if he would testify against his bosses.

She'd encouraged him to take the deal, but Gabe was terrified. "They're all mobsters, Katy. They'll kill me if I testify, Katy."

And because she loved him, and didn't want him dead, she told him to run, go to Canada.

He held her to his chest and wept. "That wouldn't be right. How could I live with myself?"

And then there was the heartache of being apart and they were so young. Would they ever see each other again?

"Katy, I couldn't think of living in Canada without you. No, I'd rather take my chances, do the time in prison, that is—if you'll wait for me." They stood looking at each other, trying to imagine what the other would look like in ten or twenty years, if Gabe took a jail sentence instead of testifying against the mob.

They argued about it, her trying to get him to leave, him arguing that he didn't want to ruin her life either, that she shouldn't wait for him. She finally convinced him that they should both go to Canada.

"Yes," he said, hugging her again. "We'll get married there, change our names. Start over. It'll be great."

Katy withdrew all her savings, and taking her little Miata sports car, they ran for the Canadian border. They got as far as the Washington Bridge when a police car pulled up close enough to read the dirty California license plate, and as they exited the bridge, the cruiser lit up and a siren signaled them to pull over.

Gabe silently put on his right blinker, slowly took an off-ramp to a side street, then jammed the accelerator to the floor and careened around a corner into one-way traffic. He dodged honking traffic and bumped over curbs trying to dislodge the police car behind them. Hearing the sound of smashing metal, they turned and saw their tail collide with an unsuspecting motorist.

Gabe turned onto a two-way street, then slowed to see if they were being followed. Nothing. They both took a deep breath and let it out. Gabe leaned over, and taking her face in his hands, kissed her deeply. When he drew back he looked her in the eyes, his voice a sad note to their predicament.

"I'll always love you," he said. Then he unlatched her safety belt, opened the passenger door, and much to her amazement, pushed her out the door.

She fell onto her knees, the momentum rolling her once, and then sat up in the dirty rain-washed gutter and watched him speed away in her Miata, the one her daddy bought her for her twenty-first birthday. Gabe had taken her car, her purse with her cell phone and all the cash from her savings. Surely he didn't mean to leave her here, stranded? She waited twenty minutes, then limped into a nearby store and asked to use the phone, where she made a collect call and confessed her part in a humiliating episode to the one person she knew she *could* trust—her dad.

Katy put the page under the cushion, and dragging her garbage topside, slipped the bag into the container at the end of the dock, which just happened to be next to Spencer's mega yacht. Leaning against a light pole she noted the hailing port—Bahamas—no surprise as a Bahamian port of call allowed any yacht owner to avoid paying American taxes. The Bahamas also had discreet banking practices.

"Don't let the name fool you," said a voice coming from topside.

Katy looked up and saw a good-looking young man in sailing whites leaning on the stern rail.

He tilted a square chin at her. "You the one who crash landed through the estuary yesterday?"

"Yup, that would be me."

"Nice to know we didn't have to scrape you off the jetty. Can I buy you a beer to celebrate your death-defying feat?"

This could be interesting. "I'll take a cold soda."

"I'll open the stern gate."

His white, even teeth flashed a genuine welcome. He was shorter than she thought he would be, probably because his shoulders were so big, maybe all of five-eight. He was also fit in that way that said a workout was more than hefting a beer to his lips.

"I'm Jeff, by the way. Come inside, it's already hot enough to roast hamsters out here," he said, guiding her through the sliding glass doors into the big salon.

"Hope it's cool enough for you. The AC costs a son-of-a-bitch, so the boss decrees we keep the doors closed and the thermostat set to seventy-eight. If you're considering summering here, you'll become one of the mole people, only popping out at night when it's cooler." He pointed her to a long leather sofa and then went to the bar fridge and drew out a couple of cans. "Damn... out of everything 'cept Coke. But I have ice and a glass, if you like." He held up a clean tall glass.

Jeff cook was Spencer Bobbitt's captain. "The can is fine. I wouldn't want you to have to wash any more dishes on my account."

He settled into the luxurious deep cushions of the couch, handed her the Coke and pushed a bowl of last night's peanuts over to her side of the huge glass-topped coffee table.

"Babe, captains don't do dishes."

The "babe" moniker was annoying, but she smiled anyway. "I didn't see you here at Spencer's party last night."

"Night off," he said, popping a handful of peanuts into his mouth. "And the caterers cleared out the whole mess by the time I got back, thank God. I hate messes."

Yes, he would, she thought, since the police found him trying to clean up the blood in his boss's bedroom. "Have you worked for Spencer long?"

"The job as his captain is my first, and hopefully, last."

"You don't like being a captain on this yacht?" she asked, hoping the bland question might lead to Jeff revealing other tidbits on Spencer Bobbitt.

"Babe. I'm getting my twenty-ton license for commercial shipping. Way better than this crappy job."

"I never got a chance to really see the place last night, what with all the people stuffed in here," she said, examining the spacious and artfully decorated interior.

"So, you were one of the guests, huh? What'd you think of the floor show?"

Her head swiveled around to see Jeff's smirk. Was the smirk for the lousy magician, or because Myne stripped for a bunch of businessmen?

She gave him a neutral reply. "I guess some would say it was entertaining."

"Ha! Thought you might say that. He calls himself Frederic the magnificent, but mostly he's just another bum looking to mooch off ol' Spence. So, you like the interior, huh? Spencer's wife did the decorating."

While Jeff stood to point out some of Mrs. Bobbitt's designer pieces, Katy gingerly lifted his Coke can, and careful not to smudge his prints, switched it with hers."Yes, I met Myne last night."

A grin wide enough to allow her to see most of his back teeth split his face. "As much as Spence likes to trot out the bit of fluff as his, Myne is still not, nor will she ever be, Mrs. Bobbitt. I've met Mrs. Bobbitt, and let me tell you, if it were up to her, this ship would be in the Med right now, not hanging out in Ensenada. This is nowhere-ville for people like Linda Hinkle."

"The designer on TV?"

"Yeah, ain't that a hoot? She doesn't use his name or she wouldn't have any business, that's for sure. Can't you see the men with their hands over their nuts every time she walks in? And Spencer, this cracks me up, names the yacht after his mistress. The man sure has the *cojones.* Any time now, that other shoe's gonna drop."

"Divorce?"

"Spencer wasn't born yesterday. He's not one to give it all for love, married or mistress. She's never here anyway. She's doing some rag-head's house up in L.A."

Another reason to dislike this wise-ass. "So, where's Spencer today?"

"He's not staying here. Not after what happened."

"Why? What happened?"

Jeff tucked his chin to his neck and swallowed. "Girl was murdered on the yacht."

"When?"

"Other night. I got on board about the same time the police arrived. He didn't do it. Someone drugged him to make it look like he did it. Man's got a lot of enemies."

"Wow. Still, this is Mexico. I heard they arrest you and then ask questions."

"Not Spencer Bobbitt, they don't. He's got connections."

"So what's he do that makes him so connected?"

"Business deals down here, I guess. Say, do you like the waves?"

"Surfing? Never learned." It was a clever switch of subject. But it wasn't going to keep her from asking the questions she needed to have answered.

"You look athletic," he said, letting the sandy lashes lower as his eyes swept the outline of breasts under her tee-shirt. "I could have you snarking up the back of tubes in no time."

Him on top of her on a board? Not a chance in Hell. "I'll keep it in mind. When are you off?"

That brightened him a bit. "I'm bored silly waiting for us to move this tug, though I'm told it won't be anytime soon. So can I ask a question?"

Thinking he wanted to talk sailboats, she nodded, holding the smile.

His very blue eyes had a mean glitter in them. "What kind of a cop are you? I mean, street cop or detective or what?"

Not a very good one since the list of people who didn't know why she was here was shrinking fast. "I'm on sabbatical from the San Francisco Police Department. I had a struggle with a stalker for his gun."

"Ouch. Remind me not to get on your bad side. Well, offer still stands for the surfing lessons. Knock on the hull, call me on the VHF, anytime, babe. You finished with the Coke, I'll put it in the trash."

"I'll finish it up on the walk home, if you don't mind."

"Sure. Anytime," he said, walking her to the door, and with a whoosh, opened and closed the sliding door on her and any more questions.

She was halfway down the metal steps when a young woman, head down, barged into her.

"Oof." Katy put out a hand to keep the two of them from going over the side. When they were balanced again, she let go. "That was close."

"Yeah," the girl said, giving her a perplexed stare. Same elfin face with just a trace of eyebrow, the same slim body, but this time the hair was a blond pixie cut and the big brown eyes were forest green. "What're you doing here?"

The question was rude enough to give Katy the impression of trespassing. Jeff and Astrid, huh? This should be interesting. "Just talking to Jeff. That okay with you?"

Without answering, Astrid put her head down and pushed past Katy and disappeared into the salon.

She mentally noted the facts. One: Jeff knew who she was and why she was there. Two: Though he wasn't planning on confessing his role in the cover-up, he did appear less like a killer than a young man who simply wanted to keep his winter job until he passed his exams. But she'd met plenty of people who would kill and then cover it with lies to keep what they had, so why not Jeff? Three: Astrid Del Mar had a blistering case of jealousy.

At her boat, there was an envelope with her name on it stuck between the slats of her hatch board. She opened it and found a penciled note on the back of his card. *"Tonight, 9 p.m. at the street outside the marina."* This was Chief Inspector Vignaroli's request that she report in on what she had learned so far. In less than twenty-four hours? Not nearly enough time.

Katy was inside her boat when she heard someone loudly singing. She popped her head out of the cabin to see who it was. She hopped off the boat and caught up with Booth as he lurched along the dock. Katy hooked her arm through his to keep him from falling into the water. "Hey, Booth, where's the party?"

"Hey, Katy, girl—af'ernoon toddy."

Afternoon toddy? Katy hadn't heard the word *toddy* since her grandmother died. "Who were you drinking with?"

"Uh-uh," he said, shaking a finger at her face. "Shecret…me to know an' … you later."

"Okay. This your boat?" she asked as they passed sailboats and sport fishing boats. "No? This one? No? How 'bout this one?"

Last night she saw him with one soda in his hand, and wasn't he the one who said alcohol only *gets in the way*? So why was he drunk now? Secrets, huh?

When he blundered toward the steps of a thirty-five-foot trawler, she followed, keeping an eye on his equilibrium. Inside, Booth folded onto his settee and began to snore.

Katy shook his skinny arm. "Hey! Booth! Wake up!" She thought about how she ought to let him sleep it off, but there was that nine o'clock meeting with the chief inspector looming in front of her, too.

"Don' shout," he mumbled. "Tol' you it waz af'ernoon toddy with m'friends."

"Oh yeah? What was in that toddy? TNT?" In the closed space his breath alone could fumigate the boat.

"Importan' meetin'. Me'n friends. Need to save ol' Spence… not guilty." Then his eyes closed and he snored some more.

She lifted his bony legs up onto the seat, nudged the AC a bit cooler and quietly closed the slider after her. Looking around, she was glad the dock was empty of curious boaters. Of course, anyone could be watching her from their porthole, wondering why a young woman would be steering a very drunk Booth onto his boat.

As she hurried back to the relative safety of her own boat she could almost hear that coconut telegraph tearing a rip in the ozone.

Chapter Nine

With a cup of strong tea, Katy took the list out again and went over it. Most of these people revolved like weak planets around the strong gravitational pull of Spencer Bobbitt's sun. Fred performed his magic act at Spencer's party, Myne stripped for his business associates, Booth hustled drinks and girls for him, and Jeff—why would Jeff endanger a potential career as a commercial ship captain to cover for Spencer Bobbitt? And then there were Wally and Ida. Something was keeping this couple stuck here in Spencer's orbit, so what was it?

She grabbed her shower kit as a prop and went to look for Ida Howard. On the way, she saw Astrid glumly stacking bottles into the recycle bin.

Deciding a detour was in order she smiled at the girl. "Hello. Can I talk to you for a minute?"

The green eyes squinted a warning.

"If you're thinking I'm horning in on Jeff, I want to assure you I'm not. And I think you're a terrific magician's assistant."

Astrid momentarily brightened, nodded and followed Katy to her boat

Inside, Katy offered Astrid a cold soda.

"Anything without aspartame, please. I'm a vegan."

Katy turned away so the girl wouldn't see her smile at the aspartame/vegan comment. She sifted through her fridge until she found a can of regular cola. She brought it up, carefully wiped it dry and handed it to Astrid.

The girl downed half of it, and wiped her mouth with the arm of her sleeve. "Nice boat. Is it yours?"

"It belongs to me and my sister. We learned to sail on the San Francisco Bay with our dad, and when he passed away last year, he left it to us."

"I have a sailboat, too. You know Bandido's?" When Katy responded with a questioning lift of her brows, Astrid said, "It's next to Baja Naval, but without all those nice things like electrical and water and security gates. I'm not anyone's kewpie doll, so that's what I can afford. I get a paycheck and sleep peaceful knowing I don't have to whore for some old rich guy."

"You mean Myne?"

The green eyes slitted. "Yeah, her, the conniving little bitch."

"In what way?"

"She'll steal anything that isn't nailed down."

Katy leaned forward and put her hand on Astrid's. "Did she try to steal Jeff from you?"

"Last week he was going to drive me up to LA for an audition with *American Idol*, but then Myne has an *e-mergency,* so I had to take a bus."

"Really? You sing, or what?"

"Sing, dance. I worked hard on that routine and she probably broke a nail or something and I missed my big chance."

"So, then Astrid Del Mar is a stage name?"

Instead of answering, Astrid got up and wandered over to look at the bulkhead where Katy's family was lined up and framed in non-breakable plastic. Dad, Mom, Leila and Katy… David.

After hungrily devouring Katy's life in pictures and said, "My parents were hippies and I was born on a catamaran, so I guess Astrid Del Mar's better than Rainbow."

"You said *were*. Are they still alive?"

"Lost at sea," she quipped, dragging her eyes away from the photos. "I was sixteen and fed up with their crackpot ideas of what constituted 'paradise.' Their response was to dump me and my duffel bag on the dock at PV and sail away. Never heard from them again. So, yeah, I guess I am an orphan, aren't I?"

"I'm sorry to hear that."

"Oh, please. They were a sorry excuse for parents. Not like yours, I bet. Nice-looking family you got. I sure could've been happy in a family like that. But I guess you hear a lot of sad orphan stories, being a cop and all. San Francisco, wasn't it? When are you going home?"

"Soon." Katy sighed. *One more person who knows why I'm here.* "So, where were you the night the girl was murdered?"

"On my boat, asleep."

"Alone?"

She shot Katy a thoughtful look, then said, "I'll take the fifth on that one… at least, for now. So, we done?"

"For now."

When Astrid was gone, Katy took out the list and made some notes: One: Astrid was a pathological liar. Her attraction to Katy's family photos only whetted her appetite for an embellished version of her parentage. And, if that weren't enough, the girl had lifted Katy's favorite hair scrunchie. Astrid calling Myne a thief was a stretch when the girl obviously had an uncontrollable desire to steal. Katy added klepto beside Astrid's name and wondered what had provoked the girl this time… the mention of family? A touchy subject for a lot of people.

If Astrid had a thing for Jeff, had she offered him an alibi? Did she have anything to do with the murder, or Jeff's attempted cover-up?

Katy carefully stuck her forefinger in the opening of the soda can Astrid used, put it in a plastic baggie, and before zipping it shut, laid it on the floor of her cabin and added enough foot pressure to squeeze the sides flat.

Another ID for Bruce Sullivan, and the results should be very interesting.

She was on her way to the marina office where she planned to FedEx the package with the two cans and a note to Bruce, when she almost stumbled over Ida Howard. The older woman was kneeling over a plow anchor, her chin-length gray bob swinging in time to her energetic polishing of a stainless anchor. Katy looked from the anchor up to the shabby sailboat. When attached to the boat, the anchor would hang like a shiny Christmas star on a moth-eaten fir tree.

"Good afternoon, Mrs. Howard," said Katy. "That's a, uh, nice big anchor."

The older woman got up off her knees and dead-lifted the heavy anchor up in her arms. "*This* is the only thing on this boat that isn't worm-eaten." Ida dropped the forty-five-pound Danforth anchor on the dock and spit on it.

This was one angry woman and she could see why; worn and rotting teak decks, splitting teak rails and peeling paint on the main mast, and green algae doing a hula with the water line. The boat was a wreck.

"How'd you come to buy it, then?"

"*Buy* it?" Ida squeaked. "You're a sailing woman, tell me the truth, would you buy this piece of shit?" she asked, giving a grand sweep of her arm at the floating wreck. "And just for fun, he had *Consolation Prize* painted on the stern. Now do you understand why that silly little bitch, Myne, was laughing?"

"I see."

"Do you? Really?" Ida leaned forward to look Katy square in the face."The boat was supposed to be Wally's farewell gift for thirty years of loyal service as Spencer's CPA. He brought us the brochures, produced an equipment list that included new sails, a fully functioning engine, newly painted bottom, redone teak decks. It had everything we needed to sail to Tahiti, at least it did on paper. We sold our home on his *promise.* Packed up and moved down here with every expectation of stepping on board a brand new fifty-foot sailboat, provisioning, and then leaving for our lifetime dream of cruising the Pacific."

Obviously, Spencer didn't think so highly of a thirty-year employee. If Spencer could climb out a bathroom window to elude an angry mob of American housewives, he would have no problem bilking a loyal employee.

"This must've been a disappointment."

Tears welled up in the older woman's eyes and she angrily swiped at them. "You have no idea. This is the sort of thing he does because he can get away with it. And why should it be any different with us? But my silly husband convinced me that Spencer would come through. I'd kill him with my bare hands, given the chance…" She reddened and tried to back-pedal. "Not that I would you know, but it galls to think he's going to wriggle out of a murder charge, too."

Katy looked from Mrs. Howard to the boat and back again. "I've been here for less than twenty-four hours and I already heard about the police finding a dead girl on his yacht. But is Spencer in trouble for something else/"

"I... I just meant that the bastard always has a loophole."

"So you think he did this to punish you and Wally?"

"The only thing I did wrong was to believe the man. Wallace got out with his life. It could've been worse. Spencer's up to his wrinkled neck in illegal business schemes."

"If Wally wants to cooperate with the authorities, I'm sure he could get immunity from any prosecution against Spencer."

"It's too *late*." The older woman's face crumbled and she sobbed into her hands.

Katy reached out to comfort the woman. "Why is it too late, Ida? Tell me what's happened and maybe I can help."

Ida wiped her face with her sleeve, sniffled once, and then looked around. "Oh God. Look at me, crying my eyes out here in the open where everyone can see me. I can't talk about this anymore." She turned and staggered up the boat steps and disappeared below.

Well, thought Katy, here's an interesting development for the inspector. If Wally Howard was Spencer's CPA, he would know all the man's dirty secrets. There was no doubt about it—the derelict sailboat was a gift and a message. Now she would have to find out the message.

There was no capital punishment in Mexico, but it wouldn't be hard to imagine someone wanting to see Spencer Bobbitt suffer a long and slow death in a Mexican jail. Could these two people have committed the murder as revenge for the derelict sailboat? And why did Ida Howard say it was too late?

Checking her watch, she saw she would have to hurry if she didn't want to keep the inspector waiting. Still hot and humid at eight p.m. she took her kit bag to the marina showers, changed into her only sundress, pulled her hair up into a knot at the top of her head, spritzed herself lightly with fragrance and added a little lip-gloss, then exited a side door that led around to the front of the hotel. She was walking to the main street when she saw a familiar figure leaning against a late model black Mercedes under the hotel's portico. Chief Inspector Vignaroli was waiting for her.

Only when she was practically in front of him did he break the concentrated stare he had on the hotel entry. Startled out of his private reverie, he dropped and then crushed the cigarette he'd been smoking and gave her a small formal bow. "Good evening, Señorita Hunter."

"Hello," she said, now feeling awkward. He was dressed in a black suit, crisp white shirt and black tie. "You look… uh, nice."

"I am supposed to look like a chauffeur. Please," he said, and opening the back door of the luxurious sedan for her, he waved her into the back seat.

When he was satisfied that she was settled and buckled in, he walked around to the driver's side and got in.

She asked, "Do you really think anyone is going to believe this?"

He looked at her in the rearview mirror and started the engine. "Why not? It makes more sense than having the watchers see you get into a police car."

"Are there watchers?"

"Of course," he said, pulling out into traffic. "And why is my disguise not perfect?"

"You don't hurry enough to be a chauffeur." And he looked at her too much.

He chuckled, the deep rumble leaving a warm spot somewhere in Katy's middle.

A block away from the hotel, he turned onto a highway leading out of town. Then he pulled over, got out, opened her door and beckoned her out.

"Here?" she asked. "Don't you want to talk inside the car?"

He smiled. "I am off duty and hungry. So if you will join me for dinner, I would very much appreciate it. We can talk there, *sí*?"

He walked her around to the passenger side and opened her door. She hesitated. "Wouldn't you rather be home with your wife and family tonight, Inspector?"

"This is business, Señorita Hunter. And we will be in a public restaurant owned by a family member, so I will expect by tomorrow my entire family will have questions, if not opinions, on the subject."

She nodded, got in, fastened her seatbelt.

"So, where did you borrow this nice car, Inspector Vignaroli?"

"It's mine," he said, with just enough humor in his voice to let her know he was enjoying himself. She wasn't going to ask, as well he knew, how a Mexican policeman could afford a luxury German car like this one.

He hit a button on the dash and immediately the air conditioner quietly lowered the temperature to a comfortable seventy-two. "Let me know if you're cold."

Another button and classical music washed through the interior.

"Chopin okay with you?" The car was headed north, and soon they were climbing higher into a dark, mountainous region.

Katy was beginning to wonder what she had gotten herself into. She was in a foreign country in a married police officer's very expensive private auto heading for God only knew where in the dead of night.

He looked at her. "I see that this is making you uncomfortable. Please rest assured that I am after only two things; one of which is to get us both away from the center of Ensenada so that we can talk in private, and the other is so that we can both enjoy a very good meal."

With each turn of the wheel the headlights twisted away from the road to throw a spotlight into the moonlit sky. She stole a glance at his shadowed face in profile. The high clear forehead, that prominent brow with those perfectly carved black brows and impossibly long eyelashes. In any other circumstance, she would be pleased to be going out to dinner with a darkly handsome man who made her insides go all fluttery.

He caught her looking and nodded. "Are you perhaps just a little hungry? I can promise you will love the food here."

"So, where is this place, Kansas?"

"You'll see." Rounding a corner, he pulled off the road and swung the wheel around until he rolled up next to an adobe building with wide steps leading up to cathedral-size double doors.

Two valets scurried down the steps to open their doors and Raul handed one boy his keys while the other opened Katy's door to offer her his assistance.

The chief came around the car and offered his arm.

They stepped through the entry and were greeted by a beautiful young woman whose dark liquid eyes smiled warmly at the chief and widened when she saw Katy. Even so, she graciously indicated that their table was ready and that they should follow her.

The foyer opened into a garden setting with huge old trees, their thick limbs forming a high, leafy green canopy. Hanging from the limbs were lighted round woven baskets in a variety of sizes. Tables were scattered throughout the garden between plantings of flowers and hedges, giving the atmosphere of privacy.

"Do you approve?" he asked.

"It's incredible." As they were led to a table set apart from the rest she added, "This is a beautiful setting. And from the cars outside, I'd say very popular. Not that I've ever heard about it."

"The marina hotel offers it to their guests. Otherwise, it's word of mouth, and every night all the reservations are filled."

A waiter rushed up and pulled out her chair, set her white linen napkin on her lap, laid two menus on the table and asked if they would like a cocktail.

Raul leaned towards her and whispered conspiratorially, "It is my one vice, once a week, one margarita. Say you will have one, too. I can promise you they are very good."

She smiled and nodded. One drink. And some food because everything smelled so good, she thought as another waiter passed by with something colorful and tasty looking.

When the waiter left with their drink order, she took it all in, the lush, yet quiet setting, the sigh of the breeze gently nudging the lighted baskets into motion. "This is an unexpected treasure. Do you come here often?"

"Not nearly enough."

Remembering the surprised look on the hostess's face she guessed that his presence here with a woman other than his wife was unusual. Now, why would a married man come here alone? She leaned back in her chair, and then because she was also a cop, said, "We could have brought your wife with us tonight, you know. It might have pleased her to be with her husband, even if you are here on business."

His earlier good humor was gone in a flash. He looked around the lighted patio garden, as if seeing it for the first time. "My wife," he said quietly, "would forgive me for coming without her."

Something he said, or the way he said it, touched her. She knew she was prying, but she couldn't seem to help herself. Just as she opened her mouth to apologize, a small man with a white starched chef's coat spread across his round middle rushed up to them. He stood beaming with arms extended wide, crooking his fingers in a proprietary signal, no dispute allowed.

Raul sighed, scraped back his chair and gave the little man a hug. In Italian, the two conversed amiably, then the chief turned to Katy and said, "This is my uncle, Blake."

Katy flashed the short round man a wide smile and held out her hand. Who wouldn't love this amiable Chef-Boyardee character named after an English poet?

Saying something in Italian, the little man grabbed her hand and gave it a feather-light kiss. Then with a wink and a waggle of his forefinger at his nephew, he said, "Forgive me, señorita, but I am so very pleased to see my nephew has honored us with your presence tonight."

When he left, Raul sat down again, put his napkin back onto his lap and smiled, his good mood now reinstated.

Katy, unable to wait another minute, said, "Blake? Not too many Blakes in Italy, I'll bet."

The light was back in his deep gold eyes. "You think that's funny? My father's name is Byron and my aunt is Emily Bronte Vignaroli. She never married, poor thing, and she still blames our grandmother for that mistake. Of course it didn't help that my aunt looks like a horse."

Katy giggled. That got her funny bone, as he must've known it would.

He toyed with his spoon and continued, "My grandmother thought emulating the upper-class English would bring some sort of civilized deportment to our squabbling dinner table. Then my grandfather moved the entire family to Ensenada to start the cannery and my grandmother's dreams were dashed."

"Your family sounds good to me. All of you are educated, gainfully employed, successful. I hear a bit of southern American in your accent. Where'd you get that?"

"I went to law school in Louisiana. Fell in love with the south there and almost stayed."

She sipped a taste of her margarita, wondering if he also had stayed in the States long enough to meet and marry and move back to Ensenada. They probably had five kids. She gave up the useless mental beating and took a sip of her margarita.

"You're right about the margarita, though I think putting this fine tequila into a cocktail is a waste. What is the brand?"

"It's my Uncle Blake's. Named after his daughter, who fortunately has a very nice Spanish name… Angelita."

"It's also very strong. Perhaps we should order some food to dilute it."

"May I make a suggestion?"

When she nodded he ordered the food: veal saltimbocca and spaghetti with meatballs.

Katy noticed a guitarist had taken up a spot on a stool, close enough for the music to drift their way.

Raul considered the musician. "Shall I ask him to leave?"

"No, please. I think it's nice," she said, reaching for a breadstick.

"I'm sorry," Raul said, watching her take the breadstick out of the basket and bring it to her lips.

"Why? I'm not bored. We'll eat then discuss the case."

He traced a forefinger over the checkered pattern of the tablecloth. "You are anxious to get back to your life in San Francisco, are you not?"

"If you're asking whether I still have a job in the SFPD, the answer is yes. I'm expected to report for duty in two weeks and I still have to have my boat trucked back to California."

"I wish I didn't have to involve you, but I have many cases on my desk with all of them crying out for my attention."

"What could be more important than the death of one of your own citizens?"

"That is exactly why I am so grateful for your help in this matter. Your record with the SFPD is exemplary."

"You mean it was until I shot my sister's stalker."

He shook his head sadly. "If it had happened in Mexico, there would have been no paid leave of absence for one who comes to the defense of a potential victim."

"Well, that may be so in Mexico, but not the States."

"My sources tell me that you have the makings of a good homicide detective but you work in vice."

Her job and that promotion from vice to homicide hung in a decision of her department's internal investigation. She pushed the margarita glass away. "Let's concentrate on this job, shall we?"

He pursed his lips as if trying to keep something inside but nodded to indicate she should start.

"Your ruse to fool the American boaters lasted less than the time it took me to sail from one marina to the next. Word is out on who I am and why I'm there. You're surprised? Along with the weather report, rumor is spread throughout the entire American fleet over a cruiser's radio net. I can tell you right now that every boater from here to Acapulco knows about the floater, that my boat was chained to the dock by the police, and after a late night visit from the investigating detective, I'm motoring for Marina Mar, where the main suspect is docked." At his deep frown, she added, "Look, it's not all bad. For now, your witnesses are more interested in covering their own butts than to care about any connection I have with you."

"I'm sorry."

"Please don't apologize again. If you're really sorry you can release me from this job."

When he didn't jump to that idea she continued, "It wasn't a coincidence that I was invited to Spencer's party the first night I got there. I was, however, impressed at the number of Americans who showed up. I think it was his way to thumb his nose at your investigation and to size me up. So, I guess my question is who spilled the beans?"

"Beans?"

"You know what I'm talking about. Spencer knew I was coming."

He started to say something, but a young waiter shuffled over with two hot plates, thrust them onto the table, sighed loudly and shuffled away.

Katy couldn't help but smile. "New waiter?"

"That is my nephew, Alphonso, who is supposed to be in college in the States, but because he was caught drinking on campus, he's doing penance here at his father's restaurant. He hates manual labor, so we expect to see the back of him soon. I can only hope his good behavior lasts until he graduates.

"Please, *mangia, mangia*. Enjoy your meal and we'll talk on the ride back."

She was only too happy to dig into the savory saltimbocca; veal layered with prosciutto and cheese in a wine sauce over polenta. When she was finished, she wiped up the last of the sauce with her bread. "That was beyond yummy."

Raul said, "Saltimbocca means *jumps in the mouth* and it's one of my uncle's best dishes." Then he stood and lifted her shawl off the back of her chair, and in an intimate gesture that caused her breath to stop, lightly lifted her hair away from her neck to gently lay the shawl across her shoulders.

For a moment, the music from the guitar player, conversation of nearby diners, waiters delivering and retrieving plates of food… it all faded into the background and she was standing there alone with him. Their eyes locked and only with great difficulty was she able to break the connection.

At the door, Katy looked back and gave one last look at the garden with its hanging lighted baskets. "It's like a secret garden. From the outside the walls are simple and plain. One would never know all of this is inside."

He was standing close to her, his voice warm in her ear. "I'm glad you liked it. Shall we go?"

Replete from the very good food and charmed by this magical night, she got into the car, belted up, and sat back to enjoy the moonlit night. At her contented sigh, Raul broke in on her quiet thoughts.

"I think Spencer Bobbitt will attempt to bribe you. You're a beautiful young American, a skillful sailor and you will be a sympathetic ear to many of the people on the list. He will want to have you on his side to make sure your investigation clears his name."

"Now it's my investigation?" The spell was broken. "Booth said he was going to get me an audience with the great man today, but either Spencer has changed his mind, or he's avoiding me. Which only looks bad for Spencer. Now, I have a question for you. Why isn't Booth on the list?"

When Raul didn't say anything, she said, "Booth is too smart, too cagey, to be anything less than Spencer's consigliere. Is he also perhaps working for you?"

Instead of answering her question, he asked, "What do you think of Spencer Bobbitt as a suspect?"

She rolled her lips under as she wondered why he wasn't willing to answer and decided to leave it, for now. "He's a ruthless and cunning barbarian who has lived by his wits for so long I doubt he'd know human kindness if it hit him in the face. Slimy business practices aside, I can't say yet. He checked me out at his party, and I suppose he'll be offering me that bribe soon. I'll let you know. But as for murdering the girl, I don't have enough information yet."

"No one has spoken to you about the dead girl, or Spencer's interrogation at the police station?"

"Spoken? They're all waiting for me to ask the questions. Astrid, Booth, Spencer and Jeff all know I'm a cop. That leaves Fred McGee, Ida and Wally and Myne, but that's only because I haven't cornered them yet." She wasn't ready to mention her conversation with Ida. She'd talk to Bruce first then see what he could dig up on Wally.

Then he surprised her by asking, "Why did you sail to Mexico alone?"

"You mean why didn't I come with my fiancé?" She momentarily thought about telling the chief inspector about David's grand schemes and political aspirations, but remembered she needed to keep as much of her life private as possible. Besides, he was a married man, no, make that a Mexican-Italian married man, and might think her susceptible to an affair should she appear in the least bit vulnerable.

"Well," she said, "just because I obviously had some time on my hands didn't mean my fiancé would be able to get away from his job."

His hands did a tap dance on the steering wheel. "What does he do that is so important he can't take a vacation with the woman he is about to marry?"

"He's with the district attorney's office."

The car slid into the entrance of her marina hotel. Her mixed feelings about an evening spent with a married policeman were interrupted by the sight of several policemen clustered at the entrance to the hotel. Raul said, "Wait here, please. I will see what this is all about."

Chapter Ten

Raul got out of his car and Katy watched as he shook off his relaxed demeanor from earlier in the evening, squared his shoulders and marched for the knot of police next to the entrance. At his approach the men gratefully broke rank to include him. Minutes passed, he listened, nodded, then held up a hand and directed first one and then another officer to different points.

He hurried back, got in and started the engine. "I turned off my cell phone, which I should never do, even if I am off duty. I will drop you off on the other side of the hotel away from the curious."

"What's happened?"

He curved the big Mercedes around to a darkened corner of the hotel, parked, and keeping the car idling said, "Please, go now."

It was police business, she knew the drill; still, she felt an almost visceral feeling of despair, even abandonment at this sudden rush to get her out of his car. She gritted her teeth and did as he asked, pulled open the door and got out.

Ducking behind the building, she could hear him put the car in gear and drive away.

Disoriented in the dark alley, she hugged the wall and proceeded to follow it all the way to the marina security fence. The marina, she noticed, was strangely silent under the pale yellow sodium lights. Not one single sailor en route to a late shower, no guards to greet her as they pedaled past on bikes, their radios banging against their knees as they checked dock lines and fenders for damage against the errant tide.

Something was very wrong.

Using her marina key card, she walked through her gate. On the dock, boaters gestured, voices rising and falling in agitation as they clustered around a dock slip.

She pushed through the crowd to where a man stood offering redundant advice to a frustrated policeman poking at an object in the water with a boat hook.

She turned to the person next to her and asked, "What's going on?"

"Floater," he said, staring at the dark shape in the water.

One of the dock guards tried to grab at the clothing with a boat hook, but the body rolled away as if dodging capture.

An American pointed at the water and, in exaggerated English, said, "*Drag* him with the hook over *here*. No! Here, *aquí*. To the *dock* ... damn Mexicans can't understand English... no, no, not *that* way, you imbecile."

Seeing Ida and Wally huddled together, she tapped the woman's shoulder. "Do you know who it is?" Ida acknowledged her with a stiff nod then shook her head, unable to say any more.

Wally pointed to a beam of light running over the water. "P—p—police are here."

Fred, the magician, stood at the edge of the crowd, a bicycle at his hip and a helmet under his arm. Though he appeared to be interested in the doings, he didn't try to help, Katy noticed, and his eyes kept swinging from one side of the group to another. Katy followed his stare and saw Myne clinging to Jeff Cook, Spencer's captain.

"No, turn your pole the other way," another boater said. "Use it to snag the damn shirt."

Edging closer gave Katy a better visual on Fred. In another moment, his pebbled bicycle shoes clacked across the wooden dock as he ran to intercept Astrid, her claws extended and aiming for Myne's back.

Fred, missing his chance, scrambled out of the way as the two girls rolled around the wooden dock.

Astrid got the upper hand and, grabbing a handful of Myne's long curls, viciously slammed her head onto the planks. Momentarily stunned, Myne appeared to collapse, then as Astrid loosened her grip to stand, she wriggled out from under her attacker and kicked at the other girl's head. The kick sliced open Astrid's cheek. Furious, Astrid reached out and shoved, giving Myne another taste of the splintered wood. With a fierce howl of pain, Myne grabbed Astrid's shirt and yanked hard, and using the momentum, tucked her knees into Astrid's midsection and tossed her over her head to land on the boards. Astrid lay moaning on the dock while Myne bounced up, knees bent, talons clenched and ready.

Jeff tried to reach for her, but when she snarled at him, he backed off. Astrid turned over and instead of getting up, kicked out at Myne with a spike-heeled boot. Quick as a mongoose, Myne caught Astrid's boot and twisted, causing the girl to roll painfully onto her stomach. Now, with booted foot in hand, Myne braced and yanked backwards.

This time, Astrid's forehead hit the dock hard enough that Katy could hear the crack as Astrid's head hit the wood. Astrid rolled over clutching her head, then struggled to her feet, fists clenched.

Katy stepped between the two girls to stop the fight. "Enough!" But Astrid had already let fly the roundhouse meant for Myne and the fist slammed into Katy's left cheek, snapping her head back. In an automatic motion, she ducked, swung and clipped Astrid under her chin and regretfully watched as the girl collapsed into a heap on the dock.

A few people applauded until they were shushed with a quick reminder of why they were here. Katy then took the initiative to push the stunned Jeff at Myne. He nodded and dragged her away, murmuring softly in her ear.

Fred moved in to peer down at Astrid spread-eagled and out cold on the dock. When he reached down to shake her, she opened her eyes and groaned. Katy was surprised to see him gently pull her to her feet and, holding her protectively to his side, move away towards his boat.

With the show over, Katy and the rest of the boaters went back to watching the guard try to snag the floater. Someone muttered an oath and voices rose and fell in disgust.

Then Katy felt Raul Vignaroli next to her. "I have my men at the gate. No one is to leave," he whispered, then moved off to where the guard was now being helped by two uniformed policemen.

She saw that the body was now up against the side of the slip. Stepping up to the front of the crowd she said, "Excuse me, Inspector Vignaroli, I'm sure you know it's going to be impossible to bring the body out of the water without a hoist. If you'll allow me?" When he nodded, she pointed to a sailboat in the adjoining slip. "Is the owner here?"

The guy next to her said, "He won't be back till next summer, miss."

"We'll use his rigging. I'll get my sling and we'll move this boom out over the water, pay out enough line, attach his main halyard to the sling and winch the body up onto the dock."

Without waiting for a reply, Katy ran to her boat and by the time she got back, one sailor had the main halyard around a self-tailing winch and another had uncovered the main mast, released the boom from its cradle and moved it over the deck for the line to cleat onto the sling.

With the sling in her hand, she said, "Someone's going to have to get into the water, work the sling under him."

A few of the Mexican policemen shuffled their feet, but it was Wally who removed his shoes and shirt and slipped into the water. With the body wedged up against the dock he worked the sling underneath, then clipped the snap-shackle onto the main halyard and twirling a finger, indicated that someone could start winching.

Scattered applause went up at the sight of the limp, dripping body being hoisted up onto the dock. The crowd murmured, speculating as to whom the floater might be, but they all went silent when they saw the wet strands of gray hair covering the face, the Hawaiian shirt gaped open to show the long belly scar.

Wally stumbled over his words finally getting it out. "B—B—Booth."

A deep and heartfelt moan went up. It was one of their own.

Raul stepped forward and bending down, tilted the man's head from one side to the other then lifted an eyelid. Katy knew he was looking for signs of strangulation. He stood up and indicated with a roll of his hand that his policemen were expected to go do something and quickly. To a man, they all took off running for the gate.

Katy heard someone next to her say, "You're gonna have a hell of a shiner tomorrow, kiddo."

"Gabe!" she hissed, turning to him before she could think about the wisdom of doing so. "What're you doing here?"

He shushed her, and with his hand still at his side, pressed something small, plastic and rectangular into hers.

"What…?"

"Not now. Come to my trailer later, when *he's* gone."

She watched him fade into the background and slowly move up the dock for the gate.

By the time Raul turned around again, Gabe had disappeared behind the cars in the parking lot.

Raul, now all business, swept them all into a line-up with Katy on the far left. As if it were the most natural thing in the world, he asked the obvious. She mumbled something about a dinner out and he dismissed her with a curt nod and went on to the next person.

She opened her boat and went below, heatedly tossing her fringed shawl on the bed. Damn. It was his investigation, but if he would only leave it to her, she might have gotten more out of the stunned boaters. That was why she was here, wasn't it? To get the witnesses to talk about their own? She saw the shock on their faces. None of them expected it to be Booth. But then, not all of them were there, were they? Spencer was conspicuously absent. Myne, Astrid, Jeff and Fred left at her prodding, didn't they? She hoped Inspector Vignaroli got what he wanted out of the crowd, because tomorrow, by God, they would all become clams again.

Booth. Did he walk off the end of the dock because he was drunk? Or did someone push him? And what was it that Gabe put into her hand? She was still tightly clutching it when she got back into her boat.

She unclenched her fist and a little black tape cassette tumbled onto her bed.

Chapter Eleven

Gabe waited for her in his trailer. He cleaned a spider web out of a corner, then watered the hanging plant in his window. When he heard a knock, he wiped his hands on his faded jeans and opened the door.

"Nobody follow you?" he asked, suspiciously eyeing the dark behind her.

"I didn't hear anyone."

Satisfied that no one was lurking in the dark, he pulled her inside his tin can and motioned her to the small banquette.

"Want some tea?"

She waggled the tape cassette she held in her hand."I'd rather you tell me what this is and why it's important."

"Did you play it?"

"Who has a tape deck anymore?"

"I do. They're dirt cheap here." He took it out of her hand, slipped it into a player, sat opposite her and pressed the play button.

At the distinct rumble of Inspector Vignaroli's voice, she sputtered, "That's…"

He shushed her. "Wait. Damn it—missed what he said. Let me run it again." There was Raul's voice, his tone preoccupied as he answered what she could only assume was a question. *Yes, it is possible, Booth, let me know as soon as you find out.*

Katy pointed at the player. "He's responding to a question that's not on the tape. Is there no other voice on it but Raul's? Where'd you get this?"

"Your *Raul* is the only one on the tape. As for where I found it, I was outside my trailer getting a smoke. It was getting dark, I guess about eight, and I heard angry voices coming from the marina and I worried you were in trouble so I came down to see what all the fuss was about. By the time I got here, it was quiet again. That's when I see this little cassette next to the gate. So where were you tonight?"

She couldn't look him in the eye.

"Good God, you were on a date with Inspector Vinegar!"

Katy scrubbed her hands in her hair. "It wasn't a date. If you will remember, *I'm* helping his investigation, so we can both get out of here."

"You can't trust him, you know."

"Why? Because he's a cop? You keep forgetting I'm one of those, too."

"You should've turned me in when you had the chance."

"Too late for that. Gabe, a tape like this is used for blackmail. Do you swear that you found this next to the gate?"

"Of course I did. What're you saying?"

"You know these people, don't you? Booth, Spencer, right?"

"I didn't have anything to do with Booth's death, if that's what you're suggesting, and I've never seen this tape before tonight."

"It looks suspicious."

"No, it doesn't," he snarled, disgusted that she couldn't, wouldn't let go of her hurt feelings at what he'd done all those years ago. "It looks bad for your chief inspector."

"Maybe you're right. But he's got the local police department on his side, and you're just another gringo hanging out in Mexico because you've got nowhere else to go."

"You should worry more about Inspector Vinegar, maybe he dropped it after he killed Booth."

She shook her head. "Timing doesn't fit. He picked me up at eight. What was Booth asking?"

"Only Booth and your inspector know that."

She held out her hand for the tape and Gabe popped the tape out of the player and handed it to her.

"They all know you're a cop, right?"

She sighed. "Yeah, I got that pretty much from the moment I arrived."

"Katy, let me help you."

"How?"

"I don't know," he said, desperately looking for something that would release her suspicious mind. "Give me something to do."

"Antonio's, the place where the girl worked. Did you know her?"

His eyes skipped off and settled on a corner. "That's not a crime. I'm all alone down here. I've been alone since I left the States. I'd like to go home, clear my name, have a life, but all I hear from you is, 'No, Gabe, that won't do.'"

She held up a hand. "Stop it." She sat drumming her fingers on the table top then said, "I'm here under duress, too. If I don't help either prove Spencer's the perp or uncover the real killer, Inspector Vignaroli will send you home in chains and you'll never be able to clear your name."

Tears welled up in his eyes and he reached out to grab both her hands in his. "You still love me, don't you, Whisper?"

She jerked her hands out of his, slid out from behind the table and with one hand on the door knob, looked back and said,"If you think…. Good God! You're still an idiot!"

He stood and reached for her, but the thunderous expression on her face stopped him. "Wait. Don't go yet. I'm sorry, I got it wrong again. Look, I've been living in a time warp down here, dreaming of you and home and everything I left behind, and then you appear out of the blue and all I can think of is how can I make it right between us. I don't want to mess things up again, so let me help, okay?" When she didn't bolt, he said softly, "Will you sit down again… please? I promise we'll only talk about the case."

She stood where she was, lips tight, her glare a tiny bit less than it was a minute before, except her hand was still on the door knob.

He watched for a sign that she might be weakening. "Come on, Katy, you name it, I'll do it."

"You want to help? Tell me about Antonio's and the girl."

He turned away to get cups out of the overhead cupboard, relief washing over him.

"I knew her, but not in the biblical sense. Way too young for me. Girls there are supposed to be eighteen, but they all have fake IDs."

"Like the sixteen-year-old I found in the water."

"It's no secret. They sell the prettiest ones on their way up to the border. They're broke, uneducated and desperate. How're they going to get all the way back to Honduras or Guatemala? Did you think the Mexican government gives them a bus ride home? That's the U S of A, sweet-cheeks, not Mexico."

He handed her a mug full of steaming hot water and a tea bag. "Sugar's in that covered dish. Look, the two of us can knock out that list in half the time. Then you can go home."

She picked up the spoon he handed her and punched her tea bag down into the hot water. "I need the local gossip on the magician's assistant, Astrid Del Mar. See if you can find out her real name, any connections to Spencer Bobbitt."

"Sure, I can do that. She lives on his boat, right?"

"No," she said, "that's the other one, Myne. Astrid said she lives aboard at Bandido's next to Baja Naval."

"Bandido's, huh? Yeah, I know it. Easy in and out. Do you know if she's working tonight?"

At her intake of breath, he laughed. "You aren't going to go all moral on me now, are you, Whisper?"

"Don't call me that, and if you get caught…."

"What—they send me back to the States in chains?" He turned to rummage through a drawer. Pulling out a folded black leather case, he tugged on the string and unfolded a set of locksmith tools.

"Burglary tools—is this the way you've managed to get by all these years?"

"If I told you they came with the trailer, would you believe me?" At the hard set of her mouth, he snorted. "Then don't ask if you don't want to know."

"If Raul gets a hint of what you're doing…"

His head jerked up. "It's Raul now, is it? You're the one who should be careful. If that big Mercedes says anything, he's connected."

"Oh, for heaven's sake Gabe."

"Crooked cops in Mexico are as common as flies. None of 'em make enough to live on, everyone knows that."

She tried to wave away the notion, but Gabe knew his comment struck home.

"Stick around for Christmas, why don't you? Then you'll see what I mean. Every ex-pat knows to carry a second wallet for when they get stopped. They call it a traffic violation, but that's just another word for *mordida*. Cops pick up fifty, a hundred a day and consider it their Christmas bonus. They sure aren't going to get it in a paycheck."

He'd asked around. Raul Vignaroli drove a very expensive Mercedes, wore handmade Italian suits, and didn't even apologize for it.

She held up the cassette. "I'll keep this, in case he is connected." Gabe put down the tools and followed her out the door.

"We'll talk tomorrow night. Goodnight, Gabe," she said, stepping onto the wobbly stepstool and then onto solid ground again.

"Wait," he said, touching her shoulder. He was holding out a flashlight. "Take it. That rocky downhill path is treacherous at night."

She nodded and hefted the long heavy black tube. "This is police issue, Gabe. Where'd you get it?"

"Will you get over yourself? Not everything down here is illegal. You can buy most anything at the local flea market. The batteries aren't great, so you might have to shake it once or twice, but it should get you home."

"Alright, I'm sorry. Be careful tonight, will you?" she said, and turned away to follow the weak beam of light along the bluff.

Taking a moment she stopped to admire the moon as the low, gun-metal gray clouds swept across it and then a cool sea breeze lifted her hair. The fullness of the moon reminded her of her "date" with Raul Vignaroli. Did she like him as a man? The answer was yes, she did. He had a gentleness that peeked out from behind the gruff policeman's exterior, and there was sadness, too. Maybe from the heavy load he seemed to bear as Chief Inspector for Ensenada, or maybe she simply wanted to imagine his marriage was unhappy. At least he didn't try to lay *that* old story on her.

Tomorrow she would show him the tape and see how he reacted. That would be the final test she needed to determine if Gabe's suspicions about Raul Vignaroli were true, that he was connected with the cartels. Though she was determined to withhold final judgment, there was a very strong part of her that fervently hoped that Gabe was wrong.

Patting the tape recording in her pocket, she adjusted her grip on the flashlight and found the rocky path leading down for the marina parking lot.

Without any handholds she cautiously took her time, shuffling her feet and feeling her way over rocks for the next level spot. The full moon suddenly took a dive behind the clouds and waypoints became dark smudges she could no longer identify. Going by memory and Gabe's big black flashlight, she continued down the path.

Then she heard a noise and a few small rocks skittered down to land at her heels. She swung the flashlight up, following the trail of dust, but couldn't see anyone. A night animal or someone's dog out for a pee on a bush? Either way, it was time to make tracks. Shrugging off her growing apprehension, she moved the beam back to the path and picked up her pace.

A rock rolled downhill, then another, until one sharply bit into the back of her leg.

She turned, glaring up the hill. "Who's there!" she barked, panning the weak beam across the top. Nothing. She clicked off the flashlight then ducked down and waited. The seconds ticked off, and then she heard it. Footsteps making tentative, stealthy movements as someone cautiously followed the path down after her.

Now glad for the extra cloud cover, she kept her profile low and scuttled along, moving faster.

Behind her, someone clumsily stumbled over rocks trying to catch up. She heard a curse as they stubbed a toe. As her eyes adjusted to the night without the flashlight she willed herself to move ever faster, knowing her life may depend on it.

She thought of the follower as a man, but there was no way to tell if the person was male or female, Mexican or American. However, there was no doubt that whoever it was they were after her to cause trouble.

Only a hundred yards more and she'd be down in the parking lot, but also totally exposed to an attack. She wasn't afraid of hand-to-hand combat, even in a knife fight. She excelled at the jujitsu and karate necessary to reduce an armed combatant to a puddle at her feet, but not if her follower had a gun.

Touching a large boulder to her left she saw that the path was about to bend around it. She would have to make her stand here and take her chances. Rocks were now tumbling with ever more frequency as her pursuer tried to close the gap.

Slipping around the bend she climbed up behind a large boulder and fisting the dead flashlight, hunkered down to wait.

The noise made by this guy as he stumbled down the path after her was enough to set her teeth on edge.

Then the night was suddenly quiet. A soft scuff of leather and a satisfied grunt.

She whirled around, rolling to one side as a dark shape flew at the space she'd just vacated. Her assailant cried out as he smashed into the rock and then he was at her again, clawing at her clothes as they both struggled for purchase on the uneven rocky surface.

Thick, wide shoulders said male and he had her by at least forty pounds.

Keeping this in mind, she put out a foot and yanked him across her hip and slammed him into the boulder behind her.

His breath exploded with the impact, and she heard him curse, *"Ay, mierda!"*

Mexican.

She stood over him and jiggling the flashlight, caught him in a spreading yellow light. "Who sent you? Who do you work for?"

The man was young, maybe twenty or so, unshaven, and looked more like a fisherman than a gangster. She kicked him on the side of his hip where it would hurt the most and asked again, "Who sent you?" and added a swear word to go with it.

He whimpered once, rolled away and before she could react, scrambled over the boulder like a dark beetle and disappeared up the path. She listened to his ragged breathing as he ran for all he was worth all the way up to the edge and over the top, his feet thudding through the RV park as he made tracks for somewhere else.

Now shaking from the lost adrenaline, she called out loud, "Got more than you bargained for, did you, kid?"

When she was sure he was gone, she gave the flashlight another jiggle and took the path down to the marina and then to her boat. She was never so glad to be home. And this time, she put in the hatch boards and used the combo lock on the inside.

Still shaken from the attack, she made herself a cup of tea and sat down on the settee to think.

It all came back to her in a mental merry-go-round: Dinner with Raul, Booth's body in the water, Astrid attacking Myne, the two girls fighting on the dock, Gabe slipping a tape into her hand. *You still love me, don't you, Whisper?* The memory of Gabe once again declaring his undying love only gave her the jitters. *Last time I put my trust in Gabe Alexander, he threw me out of my own car.* It was with some chagrin that she suspected Raul of the same when he demanded that she get out of his car. But there was an obvious reason for his actions. Surely Gabe was wrong about Raul Vignaroli. Astrid and Myne. She reached up and touched her cheekbone. Yes, she'd have a bruise tomorrow from trying to stop that fight. What was it with these two girls anyway?

The key had to be the tape with Booth's voice on it. Booth had underestimated his intended victim and died for it.

Katrina Taylor Hunter, she heard her daddy's voice say. *Gabe Alexander had the tape and a player. And look where he lives—nesting up there over the marina. There's your killer.*

Chapter Twelve

The next morning she awoke with a terrible headache and the feeling that her boat was in the middle of a storm. She rolled out of her bunk, winced at the lump on her shoulder from last night's scuffle with the young Mexican, undid the combination lock and climbed up the ladder. A line of sport fishing boats were on their way out of the marina—too many of them to be going out for the day. Bad news travels fast. A murder, an American police woman now involved was too much for these guys. And if Spencer Bobbitt was as connected as Raul said he was, there was no way the marina was going to get rid of him until he decided to leave or was arrested.

At the sound of her chiming cell phone, she dropped down into her cabin and answered.

Without preamble, David, her erstwhile fiancé, said, "Is it true? You're in Mexico?"

She groaned. "Yes." She waited, knowing David would be unable to allow empty air time.

"Katy, we really need to talk."

"About what?"

"About us, of course. When are you coming home?"

"In a couple of weeks—why do you ask? Did Karen Wilke dump you already?"

"Karen and I were never anything but friends. It's you I love, Katy, and if you'll come home, I'll prove it to you."

Katy drew a big breath, let it out. "Goodbye, David." Then she closed the cell and tossed it on her bed, watching it chirp and dance around on its own until she pulled a blanket over the noisy thing. Her sister had been right about David all along. He wasn't worth her time or tears.

Hearing bicycle wheels move over the dock, she looked out her porthole and saw it was the ill-tempered magician, Fred. Looking for a prop, she grabbed a bag of trash and followed him up the dock to where his forty-eight-foot yacht was end-tied. She noisily opened the garbage can lid and tossed in her small bag.

Fred turned to see who was making the racket.

"Morning," she said brightly.

His chin did a quick nod to acknowledge her existence; then he continued on to his boat.

She caught up with him. "I saw your magic act the other night at Spencer's. You put on a good show."

He looked her up and down, taking her curvy figure, and long, honey-streaked curls threatening to come loose from the ponytail. "If you're looking for a job as a magician's assistant, I might have an opening soon."

"That sounds like fun," she said, grinning. "What's the pay?"

"A lot less than you make in the SFPD, Miss Hunter," he said, the hooded eyes searching the dock for listeners. "It's already too hot out here. Come aboard and we'll have a cold drink and talk."

She followed him into a smaller version of Spencer's monstrosity, but it was still a football field compared to her Westsail.

"Jeff and Astrid are in town getting supplies, so I'm short of everything except Coke. Ice?" he asked, holding up a can and a glass.

"The can is fine, thanks."

He settled across from her in a club chair, crossed the long skinny legs, took a swig at a water bottle and said, "Admirable of you to alert the Mexican police about the dead girl in the water, but why on earth involve yourself in their investigation? Or did they get you in a trade of some sort?"

"Better me than the Mexican police, wouldn't you agree?"

He leaned back into his chair, the hawkish eyes carefully guarded. "I was here the night the girl was killed. I heard nothing, saw nothing and know absolutely nothing about what Spencer did or did not do with that girl."

Katy shot back, "Alone?"

Yes, alone." Then as if rethinking his answers, he added, "If you're thinking Astrid and I are… well, you can forget it. She's an employee, nothing else."

So he was touchy about his relationship with Astrid, was he?

"So, how does an entertainer like you get gigs? Do you go down to the docks where cruise ships come in and set up your magic box?"

His mouth twisted into a scowl. "Cruise ship work wouldn't cover a day's worth of fuel for this baby."

She mentally smiled. He was annoyed? Good. "Then why Ensenada? Problems with IRS, ex-wives, a warrant out for your arrest in the States?"

He uncrossed his long legs, readjusted his narrow butt in his chair and then re-crossed them on the other side. "I'm here on business, I'm all paid up on my taxes, and I make a handsome living at what I do."

Refusing to allow his sour mood to put her off, she poked at him again. "So how's that going—the magic stuff?"

"That's strictly a hobby," he snapped. "I'm here putting together a consortium of investors for a Vegas-style resort south of here."

"Oh?" She remembered the room where Myne dropped her clothes to entertain a crowd of cigar-smoking businessmen. "Then you're partners with Spencer Bobbitt?"

"No," he said, his voice spiteful. "I don't need Spencer Bobbitt's sort."

"You think he's guilty?"

"Isn't that why you're here?" He sat back and steepled his long fingers, now comfortable that he'd turned the tables on her. "Tie up loose ends so the police can solidify their case against him?"

She answered his question with one of her own. "Astrid got the short end of that catfight last night, and you said you might have a job opening, so is she leaving her job with you?"

He ignored her question, picked up his water bottle and emptied it. Finished, he put it down and said, "Those two girls are always in one sort of kerfuffle or another. Jeff will soon tire of them when he figures that neither of them is going to further his ambitions."

"Why would you say that?"

"Because I know a fraud when I see one, Miss Hunter. But no one is going to leave their present positions because of him. Now if you don't mind, I have appointments this afternoon and I'm in dire need of a shower." He unfolded his long body out of the chair and stood, fully expecting her to leave.

Deciding to oblige, she nodded and left the way she came in.

Walking back to her boat, Katy thought about the magician's responses to her questions. They were appropriate for a man who was anxious to wipe away an association with a murder suspect. Not that it seemed to be working out so well if he still had to perform his lame magic act at Spencer's party the other night. There was something else about him that bothered her; the man had a way of moving his head to one side that reminded her of a predatory bird, and she had the distinct feeling that he was always watching, evaluating, taking it all in to tick away into some private list for use at another time. Not entirely unlike Spencer Bobbitt, who seemed to have spies everywhere and used every connection to his advantage.

Of course. That must be it—Spencer had something on Fred. Why else would the man be here?

Katy was outside her boat, adjusting the lines and the four fenders, or "rubber-baby-bumpers," as Booth called them, when she saw Myne, stuffed into a pair of tight Capris and a captain's cap set at a jaunty angle on her head. The girl walked up swinging a big gold purse layered with metal and tassels. "'Mornin' Katy."

"Good morning, Myne. Nice day, huh?"

"Ain't it a wonderful day?" Her young face gleamed with happiness.

Katy couldn't help but smile. "You're in a good mood today."

"I am now."

Katy stated what she figured was the result of last night's fracas. "So, you left with Jeff last night. Does that mean you and he are an item now?"

"Sorry you got mixed up in the fight, but at least it settled Jeff's mind once and for all."

"We didn't get much time to talk at Spencer's party. Is there someplace we can sit down for a few minutes?"

The girl's rosy red lips rolled in and out as she looked over at Spencer's yacht and then said, "I don't think Spence wants me talkin' to you, but he don't own me. This here your boat?"

"Yes it is. We can talk down below if you like."

Unfortunately, Astrid and Jeff walked through the gate pushing dock carts loaded with their grocery shopping. At the sound of their cheerful voices, Myne turned sulky and at Katy's touch the girl shied away, mumbled something about talking to her later and stomped off for Spencer's yacht.

Jeff's eyes tracked Myne until she disappeared into Spencer's salon and Astrid squinted a pair of unnaturally bright green eyes at Katy, as if trying to think of a reason why she should speak at all. Then yanking on the heavy load in her dock cart, she got the wheels rolling again and over her shoulder aimed a warning at Katy. "Watch your back, lady."

Jeff, finally dragging his eyes away from Spencer's yacht, glared at Katy. "What'd you say to her?"

"Myne? She was all bubbly and happy until she saw you with Astrid. So I guess the question should be, did you make her promises you can't keep? Is that why she's now so unhappy?"

His jaw tightened. "Lady, you don't know anything. Why don't you go home where you belong?"

"I would, but as you well know I have a job to do here."

"So you're a cop, but who says you have to butt into everyone's business down here?"

"Do you have anything you want to tell me?"

She could see that the thought was making him sweat. "No, I don't. What about you? That inspector got something on you?"

Katy mentally reminded herself to find that dock snitch and soon. "We should talk somewhere more private."

Jeff shook his head, the smirk turning into a grin. "No thanks, I like it out here in the open, but I'll tell you one thing I bet you didn't know—Booth was doing much the same thing you're doing now, that is, until he got too drunk to see the end of the dock."

So that's why Booth's name wasn't on the list. "He was getting paid for his information to the police?"

"Hell, if it paid, they'd get a lot more informants on their tiny payroll. No, they paid him in heroin. Booth had stomach cancer and nothing works for pain like pure horse."

This was not looking good for Raul Vignaroli. Informants, yes, every police investigator had his or her informants, even drug users, but they didn't supply them with the drugs. "Spencer knew this?"

"Sure he did, he set it up. Spencer keeps a hook into everyone who works for him. It's what makes him successful, doesn't it? That way, he's always one step ahead in the game."

His words cut another notch against Raul's finer points as a policeman and as a man. "And, you? What does he have on you that you'd be willing to jeopardize a career as a professional captain to cover for him?"

Jeff Cook's mouth clamped shut, his chin tucked into a defensive posture.

She said, "The night of the girl's death, the police arrived to find the engines revved and you trying to clean up after a murder."

He blanched, his earlier bravado now shaken. "That was a mistake. I panicked when I saw all that blood and no body and I couldn't wake Spencer to ask him, so I called his lawyer in Mexico City and the guy told me to get the boat out of the marina to open sea."

"I've been told that's SOP for Americans involved in accidents, but you could still be charged as accessory to a murder."

He licked his lips and then ducked his head to stare at his feet. "I'm not proud of what I did, but Spencer's attorney has cleared it with the authorities here."

Confirmation of her suspicion that Spencer had already paid off the local police and at least one judge. But if there was no official investigation, why was Raul involved? For that matter, why was she?

"Who called the authorities?"

"I dunno. Maybe Booth, because he was working both sides. Still, I don't know why he'd do it. He owed everything to Spence. Booth brought the girl, I saw them come aboard. Later, I went to check to see if Spence wanted anything before I hit the rack. His door was open… and that's when I saw… all that… that blood. So, what's Inspector Vignaroli got on you, Katy—not heroin, I'll bet."

"Not even close," she said, turning away.

He grunted something that sounded like an expletive and pushed his dock cart for Spencer's yacht.

She went back to her boat to sit under the shade of her bimini and think about what she'd learned. Spencer built his successes by holding up a mirror to the weaknesses of others, justifying his own evil by magnifying the poor decisions of others, all of whom eventually became his victims.

Chapter Thirteen

In the marina shower, Katy pulled out her square plastic container of Ivory soap and with a natural bristle brush went to work on hands and fingernails. Turning her hands over she admired the whorls, arches, tents and valleys of her fingerprints.

Fingerprinting everyone who had reason to be on Spencer's boat the night of the murder must've kept this tiny police department sweating under the barking threats of the American's lawyers. How tempting it would be to simply let the rich and politically connected Spencer Bobbitt slide out of the marina for the open sea. After all, according to the part-time movie-extra tourist-guide sergeant, the dead girl was only a *puta* from Antonio's, where anything one wanted could be had for a price. If Raul Vignaroli was in Spencer's pocket, then why did he go to so much trouble to involve Katy in an investigation that could be so easily be swept under the rug?

Then there was the tape recording. She sorely hoped Gabe's suspicions about Raul Vignaroli were wrong. In the few short days since she met him, she had seen much to admire—and it wasn't just her completely unrealistic attraction to the man. Yet, she knew, as a police woman, to reserve judgment until she got all the facts. And whatever the facts were, this was still Mexico—police work, he'd told her was done differently here.

She shampooed her long, thick hair before returning it all to her second favorite scrunchy—Astrid had pilfered her best. Then, changing from shorts to a longer pair of lightweight pants, she switched the cassette tape to the pocket of the clean pants, stowed her shower kit in one of the rental lockers and went to wait for the taxi.

At the police station, a harried desk clerk immediately jumped up to escort her to Raul Vignaroli's office. She could hear the familiar rumble of his deep voice coming from the hallway and it sent her heart beat into embarrassing flutters. She mentally kicked herself, swallowed and waited.

"Hello," he said, his eyes crinkling in a warm welcome. "Are you here to see me, Miss Hunter?"

"Yes, I am," she answered, eyeing the sergeant next to him.

The chief turned, said a few words to the sergeant, and then motioned for Katy to follow him. Over his shoulder, he said, "Would you like a cold drink?"

At her nod, he leaned into an open door and spoke sharply at a deputy whose feet were up on the desk, hands folded over his chest. The guy's feet fell off, knocking over a wastebasket. His "*Ay, mierda!*" followed them down the hall.

The inspector chuckled. "He may appear to have been asleep, but I assure you he's awake now."

The amused crinkles around his eyes lasted until a smartly dressed woman came around a corner and charged at him with the velocity of a single-minded bullet. Ignoring his respectful greeting, she stuck a forefinger in his chest, gave him a few choice words in Spanish, then finished with, "Fuck you, Raul Vignaroli."

Katy stared after the woman. "Did that lady just…?"

"Regrettably and in English, too. La Señora Alvarez is part of a very old and very respected Baja family. I went to university with her eldest son. Unfortunately, I had to arrest her youngest son today. He was using one of his father's fishing boats to smuggle marijuana into the States."

He opened a door to a private office and invited her to enter. "I'm not sure if she's incensed because I chose to put her son in jail or because I impounded her husband's newest and most expensive fishing boat. But then I suppose that is why her son used it. It *is* his father's fastest boat."

"I presume they won't be getting the boat back anytime soon."

"No. It will be sold at auction. The money will be used to buy the supplies our police department needs. She'll be the one to buy it back, at a price she can live with, though I'm not so sure if the son will be returned to her anytime soon."

Here was another point in his favor. "Your country has a zero tolerance policy for drugs, so why turn a blind eye to Booth's drug use?"

Raul fussed with the opening tab of his can. Was he looking for an answer out of the ever-shifting sand of Mexican politics, or one that would simply suit his purposes?

"Booth," he said, a sad note entering his voice. "He was dying. Cancer of the stomach. You know I consider every sort of method in which to get my cases solved. Our way is very different than yours. If Americans don't like the way Mexicans behave, your government simply shoves them out of the country. It isn't so easy with us. I have a responsibility to weigh every decision when dealing with foreigners, especially American tourists, and shoving them out of the country is not always the best way to deal with a problem."

She nodded, her admiration at his ability to juggle the diplomacy of politics tainted by what she still didn't know and needed him to answer, honestly. "Then Booth *was* the man you had on the dock to watch me."

"We are understaffed, underpaid and overworked. I thought Booth a good choice for several reasons. But with his death, perhaps it is time for you to take your boat back to San Francisco and reunite with your fiancé."

The subject of her fiancé was not one she was going to address with Raul. "Are you telling me you no longer need my help?"

"I don't need the help if you don't trust me."

She huffed out a laugh. "I didn't think you ever stopped to consider how much you were asking, or for that matter, cared. What about Gabe?"

"You still care very much about him, do you not?"

"We have a history, if that's what you mean, but that's all there is to it."

He held up a forefinger. "Not all of it. I know that you were married to him for a brief period of time."

She visibly cringed. "We were kids. It was annulled, and if I hadn't bumped into him in the entry of your police station, I doubt I would've ever seen him again."

"And now you are engaged to another man, are you not?"

"I don't… what does that have to do with this investigation?" She licked at dry lips and plowed on. "I'm here because I found a tape, like the kind you use to record conversations, stuck in the dock next to Booth's slip. It might have something to do with why Booth is dead."

He leaned forward, his brows lowering over his glare. "Do you have the recording?"

"You *knew* he was blackmailing someone? Was it you, Inspector?"

His frown deepened, but wouldn't respond.

Then she caught him off-guard. "Someone tried to attack me last night."

He stood up, his chair crashing into the wall behind him as he rounded his desk to check her for injuries. "Were you hurt? What happened? Why didn't you call me?"

Her mouth dropped open. Then she tilted her face up to his, her unanswered question reflected in his eyes. "No. I wasn't hurt and there was no reason to call you. It was a kid, sent to do some damage, maybe warn me off. I gave him more than he bargained for and he ran."

He heaved a shaky sigh and let his hands drop to his sides. "I see now that you have a bruise on your right cheek," he said, tenderly. "He apparently got in one strike."

She reached up to touch the bruise she'd covered with makeup."I got that when I stepped between the catfight between Astrid and Myne. I'm okay."

He stepped back, breaking the intimacy of the moment, and went to his desk to rummage around in it for pad and pen.

"Have you listened to this tape? Do you have it with you?"

"No," she said, looking at her hands in her lap. "But I can get it."

"You didn't bring it with you, Miss Hunter?" he asked softly. "Is it because you still have doubts about me?"

"No, it's... just...."

He sat drumming his fingers on the desk, then making a decision, stood up, his jaw tight. "We're going for a ride," he said, taking the steps around his desk to grab her by the elbow.

With one hand still holding her elbow, he pushed through a back door and pulling car keys out of his pocket, beeped the key fob to unlock the doors, then opened the passenger side of his big Mercedes and motioned for her to get in.

A nasty thought crept forward to cut a chunk out of her confidence. If Gabe was right about the inspector, perhaps he was taking her for her last ride. First her, then Gabe. Oh, God, her imagination was running amok again. The question she should be asking was, would David come storming down here to look for her should she go missing?

The answer to that was probably the reason why, without a peep, she got in, buckled up and waited. Because with everything she'd seen of Raul Vignaroli, something told her that if she went missing, here was the kind of man David Bennett was not. This man would come looking for her and he'd find her, no matter what it took or who he had to kill.

Raul wheeled out of the parking lot, and taking a frontage road, crossed over a bridge, bumped through a back alley until he stopped in front of a large metal building.

"Miss Hunter, Katy. Look at the sign on this building. What does it say?"

She read the sign. "It says Vignaroli Canning Company." The building took all of a city block. "Yours?"

"It belongs to my family. We own a good portion of the fishing fleets and canning plants from here to the southern border. I am a shareholder in the company. It allows me to continue the lifestyle I was born to, but I am also part of a federal task force dedicated to fight the cartels. My family approves of this, they know that the work I do is important, if dangerous. I hope you understand now."

She blushed and looked at her hands. "You didn't have to do this, you know." Then she looked up at him again. "Why do you care what I think of you?"

"Is it such a terrible thing—to want your approval? Has no man ever done anything to show you that your opinion of him matters?"

"I'm... I'm not sure what it is you're saying."

His eyes took on a bemused expression. "Perhaps I'm not making myself clear. I am asking for you to trust me," he said, giving a quick nod towards her shoulder bag.

"Oh, yes. I see what you mean." She rooted around the inside of her bag and pulled out the small black tape recording. Holding it up she made a point of demonstrating that the tape wasn't going to fit into his CD slot.

He reached out and covered her smaller hand with his. "Will you *trust* me with it?"

Her hand opened and she offered up the little black cassette to him.

His smile of gratitude was tinged with only the slightest wave of regret as he pocketed the tape and turned his car around.

Katy insisted he not take her back to the hotel, but drop her off at a local grocery store, where she loaded up on basics for her boat. Then with her purchases, she took a taxi back to the hotel and pushed her loaded dock cart down the ramp towards her dock.

A long bank of fog now blanketed the horizon as it did every evening about this time. Overhead, stars pushed through the inky sky, and though the moon had yet to come up, the day was definitely gone.

She walked past boats with lights on, people talking over music, laughter as easy as the warm evening breeze on her face. Dragging her plastic bags into the cockpit behind her, she ducked under her boat bimini thinking how nice it would be to have someone to help. Not that her fastidious ex-fiancé would ever consider sailing to Mexico for a vacation. David's idea of roughing it meant having to do without room service. Of course, now her opinions were tinged by what she knew of Raul. What he said to her today—*has no man ever done anything to show you that your opinion of him mattered?*—and the way he'd said it wound ropes of longing around her heart.

Too tired to switch on the light, she laid the groceries on the galley floor, then reached into her icebox expecting to snag a long-neck Pacifico. Confused, she batted the empty space.

Behind her, someone burped softly. She stiffened and switched on the overhead light.

"Sorry," Gabe said. "Kept the lights off in case it wasn't you."

Her last two Pacificos were now empties on the table and ready for the recycling bin.

He stood up and offered to help with her groceries.

She stopped him. "Wait a minute—wasn't the boat locked?"

He grinned. "You need to give the tumbler a twirl if you want to keep reprobates like me out. You take that cassette to Inspector Vinegar?"

"I told you not to call him that. He has absolutely no idea who Booth might have been trying to blackmail and I believe him." Okay, not his exact words, but she wasn't going to allow Gabe another ounce of doubt about Raul to grow and fester where it shouldn't.

"Why? What'd he do for that?"

"He didn't promise me the moon if I *married* him."

"Ouch. Okay, I deserved that. I wish you'd give me a little slack here, Katy, I'm just trying to help."

"Where did you go last night?" she asked.

"What do you mean? I had a job to do, remember? Why? Have you change your mind about us?"

"No, Gabe. I left to go back down the path to the marina and someone tried to attack me."

"No! My God, Katy," he said grabbing her by the arms, giving her a once-over. "Are you hurt?"

She brushed his hands away. "I used that flashlight you gave me to beat him off or I would've ended up at the bottom of the cliff."

Gabe sank back down onto the settee. "I left right after you did. Went to check out Astrid Del Mar like I said I would. Did you tell the inspector I'm helping you?"

"You and I don't communicate anymore, remember?"

He seemed pleased with her answer. "Got what you wanted." He held up a small spiral notebook and flipped a page. "California driver's license number, address in L.A. and her real name is Astrid Woods, age twenty-six." He peeled off the lined page and handed it to her.

"That's great, Gabe," she said, praising him for the task but also guessing the ID was a fake, since that's the age she used to put her on own fake IDs. The girl looked younger, maybe closer to her teens. "I'll give this to my contact in California and see what he can come up with."

"I brought you something else," he said, reaching down to pick up a cardboard box. Opening the flaps, he pulled out a small orange-stripped kitten, its big ears chewed from fighting with its littermates. It also looked to have some kind of skin disease.

Katy shook her head at the kitten. "No. Sorry. My apartment building in San Francisco won't allow pets."

"Ah, come on. Every boat needs a cat on it. We got cockroaches down here the size of footballs and she's already cleaned my place of all the bugs."

Katy warily eyed the sleepy kitten. "Her feet are huge."

Seeing Katy was close to relenting, Gabe pushed. "This is a Baja fish cat. When she's a little bigger, she'll fish for her own dinner."

"She'll what?"

"It's some kind of a genetic mutation. See?" he said, spreading out the kitten's paws to show the deeply webbed skin between each toe. "They use their webbed feet to reach into the water and catch fish."

"Gabe, I just don't think it's a good time for me to have a pet."

"Tell you what," he said, putting the box on the table and edging for the ladder. "If you still don't want her by tomorrow, I'll pick her up and take her off your hands."

She looked at Gabe and then at the kitten in the box curled up on the rag and asleep.

"Well...." she said, looking at the kitten.

When she looked back, Gabe was already climbing her ladder. He waved to her over his shoulder. "See you tomorrow."

She pulled a beer out of the six-pack she'd brought home, tipped off the cap and up-ended the bottle till it was empty, then found a plastic tub suitable for a kitty box and hiked out the gate and scooped up enough dirt to use as littler.

Back in the boat she made a bed for the kitten out of a shallow pan and an old towel and let the kitten try out its new digs.

Tomorrow, she'd ask someone about a vet. The poor thing had some kind of skin problem. And it would need its shots and maybe neutering, if it wasn't too soon.

Gabe left her a present so he could keep a thread of communication open. Or he could have done it so that he'd know when she discovered he was the one who murdered Booth.

If she accepted Raul's explanation about his income and his work with the federal police against the cartel, then why did she tell him about being attacked but not that it was when she was coming back from Gabe's, or that Gabe was helping her with the investigation? Probably because she needed to hang onto the last vestiges of her distrust—something, anything that would keep her from making a fool out of herself and falling in love with a married man.

Just before she drifted off to sleep, she muttered, "Note to self: Do not even *think* about taking this kitten back to San Francisco."

Chapter Fourteen

Saturday morning and Katy awoke to the sound of Mexican mariachi music. Dressed, she went topside with her tea and watched the tents for a wedding reception go up on the hotel grounds. Soon caterers brought out tables, chairs and swags of flowers.

She'd brought her shower bag, with the plan of a shower and a call from the hotel phones to her partner at the SFPD. Then she would find a vet for the kitten.

She passed the wedding party, noting mothers in too-snug mauve dresses nervously measuring servings against the list of guests while dads slapped backs and schmoozed with business associates.

Weddings—they were the same everywhere. Tomorrow the fathers would groan under the weight of heavy heads and lighter wallets, and mothers would cry over the empty nest. At least the newlyweds looked happy as they ducked their heads shyly together, held hands and whispered to each other amid boisterous toasts to their fertility. From the look of the bride's waistline, Katy figured they already had a good start in that direction.

When her partner, Bruce answered, he grunted a quick hello and put her on hold. She got to listen to most of John Denver warbling about the Rockies before he came back on the line.

Eschewing pleasantries, he got right to it. "Let's see. First up, Jeff Cook. Quite the pretty boy, isn't he? All that muscle oughta be against the law. He doesn't have a rap sheet unless you count the one on the back of this eight by ten glossy I'm holding. I got to his agent who says Jeffy can still be engaged for strip parties complete with police uniform. On the other hand, he's got some unpaid parking tickets, and his last listed residence was with an aging actress who was *wonderfully* forthcoming about their short marriage—poor dear. Said she was 'old enough to know better' but she set him free after he forged her name to some checks. Any surprises yet?"

"Anything about his application to a maritime academy?"

"Are we still talking 'bout the pretty boy, or the forger?"

She got the point. No maritime academy in Jeff Cook's future, not with his track record. "What about the other one, Astrid Del Mar?"

"Not in the system, but the name does come up in reference to some really good tuna. You don't happen to have a driver's license number, do you?"

"You read my mind."

When she gave it to him, he asked, "You going to tell me what's going on? Or do I have to read it in the papers?"

"It oughta be the funny papers."

"What kind of characters are you running with down there?"

"Haha. Anything else? How about Wallace and Ida Howard?"

There was a bit of static on the line, but that didn't explain Bruce's silence.

"Still there?" she asked.

"You heard it too, huh? That great, long expanse of silence is coming to you courtesy of the FBI. You know what that means, don't you—someone is working a case on Wallace Howard. If I tiptoe real quiet, I might be able to get a Fibbie to tell me what's going on."

"The FBI? What…?"

"Dunno yet. Call me in a couple of days and hopefully I'll have the rest of the whole story for you."

She groaned. "Can't you just…"

"Can't rush genius, love. Call me on a land line in two—no, make that three days."

He hung up, leaving Katy with more questions than she had answers, except for one—add Jeff to the growing list of pathological liars. He was also a gigolo.

The hotel desk clerk not only gave her a recommendation for a vet, but insisted on chauffeuring her and the kitten in the hotel van. "It is no problem, Señorita Hunter, no one needs the hotel van this morning. I can have a man at your dock in ten minutes."

"Do you have any idea what it will cost for the veterinarian?"

"Oh, señorita, you will see, it is very inexpensive. Less than half of what you Americans pay in the States."

Sure enough, the vet was waiting for them, and cheerfully welcomed her to his clinic. Not only was he the only veterinarian in town, he also kept a spotless kennel for visiting Americans who needed boarding for their animals. And, lucky her, he just happened to keep all the supplies she would need; the grain-free cat food that would ensure the kitty's continued good health, the kitty litter, the covered and vented litter box that would prevent the cat sand from littering her nice interior wood floors, the pretty pink collar (because the kitten was a *she*) the name tag that goes on the collar, the must-have compact bed perfect for boats, the travel crate for safely transporting the kitten when off the boat, and of course, all the correct shots, a dose of flea meds, because that was the problem with her skin—fleas, not a disease—and the free advice to put garlic in her wet food every day to keep away any further infestation.

The kitten was too young to be neutered, but if the lovely señorita would bring her back in another month, the vet would be happy to neuter her for the low price of twenty American dollars. Before leaving, he tossed a squeaky toy into the kitten's crate. "A little gift for your new baby," he said, handing her up into the hotel van and waving as the van drove away.

By the time she got back to the marina, the hot, orange sun was working its way to China, and in its place a long line of thick gray fog hugged the horizon. Footsteps came and went as boaters wandered in from dinner, all of them accompanied by some form of conversation. Finally, she heard familiar steps—or thought she did. She waited. It was dark, and she didn't hear anyone call out her name. A guard? Or was it her attacker sent to finish the job?

She grabbed the small fire extinguisher latched next to the exit, quietly removed the hatch cover, and holding the fire extinguisher, leaned out to see who might be standing next to her boat.

It was Gabe. She signaled for him to come aboard and backed down her ladder and into the cabin. Closing all the portholes, and sliding the hatch cover in behind him, she lit a candle in a hurricane lantern and turned off the overhead lights.

He handed her a six-pack of Pacifico. "It's only fair. I drank the last of yours."

"Thanks," she said, wondering if she should be grateful, or wary of the offering. His last offering was now lapping up a bowl of milk.

"I wouldn't mind having one," he said, eyeing the beer. "That is, if you can spare it."

"Let me get you a cold one." She turned and reached into her cold box and handed him one of the cold Pacificos. "Now, what have you got?"

He leaned back his head, guzzled the bottle empty and belched. "Sorry. Hot out today. I was fixing the door latch on my trailer and must've got a touch of heat stroke. Felt dizzy for an hour or so." Then he looked around the cabin. "So, how's the kitten working out?"

"She's fine." Katy wasn't about to admit to buying all the stuff the vet convinced her she needed.

"I know they're illegal here, but I inherited a gun from the guy who rented me the trailer. You should take it. You got no way to protect yourself otherwise."

Should she accept the gun, give it to the chief inspector to check for ballistics? But if anyone was going to determine that Gabe was a suspect, it would be her, not Raul Vignaroli.

"No thanks," she said. "I have a fire extinguisher, a boat hook, and a baseball bat." She stood up. "Well, if that's it, we should call it a night."

Gabe sat where he was. "How long were you planning on being here?"

She glanced at the calendar on her bulkhead. She'd been eagerly marking off the days until she could go back to work. Now she was wondering if she would ever be going back to work. "A week, two, then I have to report to the commissioner."

"Don't you have some inheritance—from your father's estate?"

She sputtered, "That's kind of nosy, even for you, Gabe."

"Well, coincidences aside, and police departments being what they are, I was just thinking; what're the chances Detective Vignaroli hasn't already mentioned me to your boss? I mean, what if you do it all like you're supposed to, you go back to San Francisco only to get your walking papers anyway?"

Stunned, she stuttered, "I… I really hadn't given it a lot of thought, Gabe." There was no getting around it; one word from Raul Vignaroli and she could kiss her career goodbye. He hadn't told her chief yet—she was sure of it. Well, almost sure.

"Okay, then," Gabe enthused. "Why not live a little? Head south to Puerto Vallarta., take a real Mexican holiday."

The orange-striped kitten stalked her new toy, then leaped on it, making it squeak.

Katy looked from the kitten to Gabe and shook her head. "I'm not taking *you* anywhere."

"Ah, come on, Katy. You got me all wrong."

"If I do, I'll be sure to apologize before I leave. Now, if you don't mind, it's been a long day." She pointed to the ladder.

He stood and closed in on her. He stood within a few precious inches, the same as Raul had done a few nights back. But this was Gabe, not Raul, and she knew he was searching for a hint of the teenage love and devotion she'd had for him so many years ago.

"I've changed. Really I have. If only you'd let me show you."

Didn't David say much the same thing on the phone? If only she'd come home he'd show her how much he *really* loved her?

She turned her face away from the kiss he aimed at her lips and stepped back before she said something she'd regret.

Gabe, seeing she wasn't warming to him, shrugged it off and swung out of the boat.

She sank down on the settee, put her head down and gently pounded it on the table. One knock for believing in Gabe the first time, another for opening her mouth at the police station, and the last one to remind herself never, *never* trust Gabe Alexander again.

Awash in self-pity, she went topside to sit in the cockpit with a cup of hot tea. Melancholy hung on her like a thin coat of black paint. Pushing the recalcitrant tea bag to the bottom of her cup only frustrated her more. She put down the cup.

Why was she defending a childhood romance gone bad against the possibility that he'd be extradited back to the States? If it happened, he would testify, incriminating her, forever ruining her hard-won stripes in the police department—that's why. In the meantime, she was stuck here, scraping up evidence in a foreign country with no help to speak of, in an impossible case she couldn't imagine solving in the amount of time given her.

The kitten padded up the stairs and sat close to her, purring. "Thanking me for your nice bed and good food? At least you don't have any hidden agendas."

Over the sound of the kitten's gentle purring, she heard music wafting across the night air. It was coming from Spencer's yacht, but this time there were no lights and laughter.

Jeff said Spencer wasn't staying on his yacht, and since Booth's death, she'd seen no real reason to seek out anyone on the yacht.

Was Myne having a late night party?

She scooped up the sleepy kitten, took it below, slipped the hatch cover in, and quietly got off the boat to follow the music.

Except for the music coming from somewhere below, the yacht was dark and no one appeared to be home.

She tried the main cabin door. It was unlocked, and something about it made Katy uncomfortable. Taking the interior stairwell down a level, she followed the sound of Frank Sinatra music until she came to an open door.

Inside the spacious stateroom, a tall, thin man shuffled slowing as he clutched a nearly naked Myne to his chest. When they turned, she saw Wally Howard's long, sad chin resting on top of the girl's blonde head. His eyes were squeezed shut and a loopy grin was plastered to his face as he dreamily hummed along to "My Way."

For a moment Katy considered tiptoeing out the way she came, but when she saw a cord dangling from one of Myne's wrists, she stepped into the room. "What's going on here!"

Myne turned a damp face to Katy and boosted herself out of Wally's arms. Pointing at his shirtless, concave chest, she said, "See if you can talk some sense into this dumb shit. I meant it when I said I ain't goin' nowhere with you, Wally."

Wally flinched at the hurtful words, then tried to pull Myne back into his arms.

Katy stepped up and wrenched his arm around behind his back. "Get down. On your knees, now."

He slid to the floor, his head hanging down. Then he looked up at Katy. "I w—w-w—wasn't h—hurting her. Ask her. I s—saved her life."

Katy looked at Myne for confirmation of his story, but Myne was swaying on her feet. Catching the girl before she dropped, Katy gently set her down on her bed and turned back to Wally. "You stay put."

Then to Myne, she asked, "What's going on? Did he tie you up? Force himself on you?"

Myne, grabbed a discarded silk top off the bed and slipped it over her head. "I don't know what happened. I was asleep."

An empty bottle of Booth's favorite, Chivas Regal, and two glasses were on the bedside table. "But you finished a bottle with him?"

"Not him. I was asleep and next thing I know someone is tying my hands together. I fought back and pushed 'em off me, then heard yelling and a scuffling, an' the lights went on and there *he* was."

Katy turned to Wally. "Did you see who it was?"

He shook his head, the comb-over now hanging in his eyes. "Too d—d—dark. He Ran. T—t—tell her, Myne."

Myne tearfully rubbed her bruised wrists. "I'm grateful an' all, Wally, but it don't mean I want you to leave your *wife*!"

Katy looked from one to the other. "No ideas at all?"

They both did another head-shake, not looking her in the eyes.

They were hiding something. "It's a long way from your boat slip to here, Wally. You didn't see someone come aboard before you?"

Wally did another head-shake. Either he had something to hide or he wasn't willing to offer any explanation that involved more stuttering.

"Okay, Myne. In the struggle, you must've gotten an idea. Big, tall, short, fat, thin, young, old, alcohol on his breath, or food, or mints. How about bad breath? Did he say anything?"

She thought for a moment. "He was slippery."

"Sweaty?" Could the perp have been a repeat performance on some rough sex with Spencer's little plaything?

"You knew this guy."

"No! I swear." Myne turned on Wally. "I locked the salon door like I do every night. Jeff went out with his friends tonight, and I hate being alone on this big ol' boat… I locked it, I'm sure I did."

Myne jerked up off the bed, fists clenched at her sides. "*He's* got keys. You! You attacked me in the dark, tied me up and then made like you was savin' me so I'd be grateful, you pathetic ol' letch!"

Wally gulped and held up his hands in surrender. "I d—d—didn't didn't do it, Myne, you have to b—b—believe me."

There was no culpability on Wally's sad face, only the hunger for what would never be his. But if he wasn't guilty of attacking Myne there was still something else.

"You have the keys, Wally?"

He reluctantly drew them out of his pocket and handed them over to her.

She fingered the keys. "If you didn't attack Myne, were you responsible for killing the Mexican girl, and framing Spencer Bobbitt?"

He kept moving his head back and forth, shaking it as if the thought was too dangerous to consider.

Myne shot up off the bed. "That's it! Spencer always said Wally was his little mini-me, wanting what isn't his. Well you can't *have* me," she said, waggling a finger in his face. "I'm not up for grabs jus' a'cause Spencer ain't here."

Wally ignored Myne's outburst and got off his knees. He reached out to her but when she flinched away, he dropped his hand, his voice a low whisper, "Myne, you have to come with me. Spencer's not g—g—going to be able t—to take care of you."

She blinked, looking for confirmation from Katy. "I don't understand...."

"What Wally is trying to say," explained Katy, "is that Spencer may still be charged with murder."

Myne flopped down on the bed again, and fisted her hands in the silky quilt. "Well, that sucks."

"You see?" Wally enthused. "I'm your b—b—best bet, Myne. S—S—Spencer can't help you, but I c—c—can."

Myne looked up at him through tear-filled eyes. "I wouldn't go with you if you were the last ol' goat on the planet. Go on home, Wally," she said, waving him off. When he hesitated, she shouted, "What're you deaf as well as dumb? Go on, git!"

Wally hung his head in defeat and shuffled out of the room.

Katy wasn't sure if Wally was capable of murder, but he wasn't going anywhere, either.

Myne listlessly combed the curls away from her face. "How long were you there, watchin'?"

It was the way she said it that caught Katy's attention. Was it because Wally was watching her have some kinky sex with someone else and when it got too rough he stepped in?

"Who else was here?" Katy asked, picking up the empty Chevas bottle.

"Huh?"

Myne ignored the question and leaned into Katy, brushing her heavy breasts against Katy's arm. "I could be good to you."

Katy stiffened. Then remembered what she knew about desperate people and what they might do to get what they needed or wanted when their backs were against a wall. Myne probably still thought Katy was a lesbian because she was a police woman.

Katy moved Myne off her shoulder. "Sorry, but no. Now, will you tell me who was with you?"

Myne shrugged. "Nobody who can do me any good, that's for sure."

Katy was tired of Myne's willingness to cover for someone who, as Myne said, wasn't going to do her any good, when her own life was crumbling around her. Katy headed for the door. Pausing, she turned to look one last time at the tiny blonde sitting forlornly on the rumpled bed in the pink and frilly room that only a twelve-year-old would love.

"Good night then," Katy said, and quietly exited the stateroom.

The next morning, Katy decided her bad mood might be fixed with a good meal. She should go to town for lunch.

Better yet, invite Myne to go with her, have that talk they never finished last night.

She found Myne on the yacht, tucked in the shade and reading a book. She barely let Katy get out the invitation before she bounded up off the chaise lounge. "That's a great idea. I'm dyin' to go out. Let me put on some clothes and I'll be right back."

Wrapping a towel around her bikinied bottom she scampered for the stairs and disappeared. She was back in minutes, wearing a low-cut hot pink sundress, gold bangles on her wrists. She held out her wrist for Katy to inspect. "They're just like the ones your sister, Leila Standiford, wears, 'cept I can only afford the gold over silver version, but they look good, don't they?"

"They look great to me," Katy said, admiring the bangles.

"This is just the way she wears them, too," she said, stroking the bracelets. "I checked online. Two gold, then two enamel and gold, then two more gold. I'll bet hers cost a fortune, huh?"

Katy laughed. "I wouldn't know, but if you want, I'll ask the next time I see her."

Myne dimpled, now happy that she was rubbing elbows with a famous TV soap star's sister.

In the taxi, Katy directed the driver to stop at the fish market.

"Oh," said Myne. "I thought we were going someplace nice."

"You don't want to discount Ensenada's fish tacos. They're the best I've ever had and we can sit at a table to eat."

Myne shrugged, got out and reluctantly followed Katy.

Passing Indian women and children selling trinkets, the children, dwarfed in castoff clothing too large for them, held up Styrofoam cups and cheerfully begged. "*Dinero*?"

Myne started to dig into her purse for money.

"Wait," Katy said, taking two McDonald's coupons out of her own purse. "It kills me that these kids beg, but this way I know they'll get to eat."

She gave a handful of coupons to Myne, who bent down and put a couple in each of the kids' cups. The children stared into the cups, then fished out the coupons and handed them over to a woman with a nursing baby. The woman showed her disdain for the coupons by theatrically ripping them into shreds and tossing the now useless paper into the air like so much confetti. Lesson learned, the children scurried back to the streets to make up for their error.

Myne looked about to charge over and give the mother a piece of her mind. "So why ain't her kids in school?"

Katy took Myne by the arm and pulled her away. "The government pays for the classrooms and books, but uniforms, shoes and transportation have to be paid by the parents. The Indians just don't have the money."

Myne gave a disgusted snort. "I may have grown up dirt poor, but you wouldn't see my mother making me go out and beg on the streets."

"Where did you grow up?" Katy asked, dodging another unmarked pothole in the sidewalk.

"Here and there."

"Are your parents still alive?"

"My mom is, don't know about my daddy," she said, and then pointed at another pothole for Katy to avoid.

"Siblings?"

"One pissant trouble-maker—and that's all I'm saying about that."

Katy, distracted by her search for the right taco stall, let Myne's comment pass.

A hefty Mexican woman in a housedress and apron sealed the deal with a gold-capped smile, and loudly welcomed the two Americans into her open front café.

Myne squinted at the woman and then at Katy. "What's she yellin' at us for?"

"Actually, she's bragging to her neighbors that she's got American customers with American dollars and they don't. This is Ensenada's answer to McDonald's and let me tell you, it's just as fattening. Do you want fish or shrimp? Coke or orange soda?"

"Fish and I'd kill for an orange soda. Reminds me of home."

Katy held up four fingers to the cook standing ready over a boiling pot of hot grease and ordered. When they were ready, she showed Myne how to load up the taco from the relish dishes: cilantro, radish, onion, salsa and fresh heavy cream.

When Myne sipped the last of her orange soda she said, "Your Spanish sure is good. I can't speak nothin' but American and Spence says I don't do it no favors, either."

"How old are you?"

"My birth certificate says eighteen, but I oughta be thirty for all the living I've done. I been on my own since I was fifteen."

Add abused and abandoned and it could also be part of a ready-made repertoire meant to elicit the most sympathy. "How'd you meet Spencer?"

"Might as well hear it from me; I was dancing in a strip joint in LA 'cause all my dreams of gettin' into anything but porn had done been shot to hell."

"Leila saved her money and took acting lessons."

"She did, huh? Last boyfriend spent all my savin's for acting school fixin' up his motorcycle, and then he skeedadled. No forwarding address, either. Then Spencer came into the place and offered me a job."

"If things go bad for Spencer, will you go home? You could still go home, couldn't you?"

"Not an option. Mom's got a revolving door on boyfriends and I'm likely to shoot the next one."

"What's the problem with you and Astrid? Jeff?"

"Oh, that. We been spittin' at each other like two alley cats long before Jeff ever showed up. Nothin' you can do anything about it."

Myne wiped her hands on her paper napkin and took the trash to a can, signaling the conversation was over.

The ride back to the marina was quiet, both of them deep into their own thoughts.

Katy fingered the lock hanging open on her hatch-boards. Hadn't she snapped the combination lock when she left? Was Gabe crawling in and out at will again? There was no sound coming from below, but knowing Gabe....

Her hand went to her hip for the Glock she normally wore on her uniform belt, then remembered she wasn't in uniform now, she was in Mexico, where it was illegal for anyone but the police, and criminals, to carry side-arms. She selected a heavy winch handle and pushed back the hatch on her companionway, then stepped down the stairs into her cabin.

The place was wrecked. Her lovely new ultra-suede cushions slashed, their stuffing pulled out from the gaping tears in the fabric. The ultra-suede had the feel of real leather and was a luxurious expense she'd dithered over for months before she'd finally committed to it—now destroyed. All of it.

Heartsick, she felt the deed as clearly as if it were a knife between her ribs. She turned the lock over in her hand. The backside had been carefully pried open, leaving the innards exposed and vulnerable. Very expertly done, too. They'd taken apart the lock, then hung the empty shell back in place. To the casual observer, her boat would appear locked.

Though her possessions were tossed, the only thing missing was the list. It had been tucked between the backing of a picture of her and her dad. And gone with it any hope that she'd be keeping any secrets from the suspects in this marina. Obviously, the damage to the cushions was just for spite.

And where was the kitty? She called softly, opening cupboards, pulling up pillows, until at last she found the wide-eyed little fur-ball. Kitty had wedged herself into a corner behind the books on a shelf and hissed when Katy reached a hand in to her, then relaxed the moment she felt the soft stroking.

"Poor kitty. It's all right now." And lifting her out of the safety of the lair, Katy poured a cup of warm milk for the kitten, and a beer for herself.

Just to make sure the intruder hadn't decided to sabotage her engine, she checked her engine compartment. The door bolts were as she left them, the engine appeared fine and all hoses were connected in in their right places.

Katy knew thieves; most of them went about their B&E work with methodical care, picking up, putting down again exactly as found. This kind of damage told of someone with a stone in their craw. It was bitter act of revenge, and a warning. Go away, stay away, stop what you're doing.

She got out of the boat, and with her expression neutral, walked up to the hotel where she placed a call to Raul Vignaroli.

After he listened, he asked, "Do you think they damaged anything else?"

"Like what?" Drained of her tantrum, she weakly blew on a tissue. "My self-esteem? My cabin was tossed and the cushions were a statement and a warning."

"They were very beautiful cushions. Perhaps it's time for you to go sailing. Do you know Bandido's Marina?"

"Yes," she said, remembering Astrid's boat was berthed at Bandido's next to Baja Naval. Astrid had admired her family's photos on the bulkhead. The girl could have done this, but then so could have any number of people. This marina was populated almost entirely by thieves, liars, and at least one killer.

Chapter Fifteen

Slipping through the opening of the breakwater at the Ensenada harbor, she threaded through dilapidated boats, their anchor chains festooned in sea-grass and decks covered with the smelly guano left behind by seagulls and pelicans. Evidence of a permanent membership in Ensenada's Derelict Yacht Club.

Passing close to Baja Naval she felt a breath of longing for that first day before she so willingly went to the police station and the noose was tightened. But promises had been made, and slashed cushions aside, there was no turning back.

Aiming for the end dock, she cut her engine and glided up to where Raul Vignaroli waited dressed in a collared dress shirt over a pair of faded and paint spattered khakis, a pair of dock-siders and a captain's cap over his dark curls.

She threw him a line. "What's with the scrambled eggs on your cap?"

"Baseball player?" He let a small but playful smile tell her he was joking.

"No. You look like a policeman on your day off. Why the briefcase?"

"I have everything I need in here," he said, patting the hard-sided case. "I think it would be best if we leave the dock. Fewer people out on the water to overhear our conversation." He slid over into the cockpit, and with a roll of his hand, indicated they were leaving. "While you take us out of the harbor I will consider the damage done below."

Nodding, she put the tiller hard over, gunned her engine and they motored out of the harbor and onto the open bay.

He came up the stairs to sit next to her on the starboard side.

"You seem to have cast off your earlier unhappiness. Is it being on the water?"

She glanced at him, his arms crossed over his chest, his feet propped up against the cushions on the port side.

"That's a sailor's expression, you know," she said. "To 'cast off' refers to releasing the lines from boat and dock, but it has also come to mean letting go of life's cares. And, yes, I am more relaxed when I'm sailing. The sea relaxes me, it releases all my anxieties."

"Even when the weather is bad?"

"Unless I want to stay in a safe harbor, weather is an unavoidable part of sailing."

He nodded. "Ah, but Señorita Hunter, it's an experience you'll never forget if you have to make a living and it's blowing forty knots." A smile came and went and she noticed again the long dimples bracketing either side of his mouth. He was back to calling her señorita, but his manner seemed more teasing than anything. Then the wedding band on his left hand winked at her.

Well, she thought, *at least he isn't one of those jerks who takes off his wedding ring when he's out with another girl—oh, God, what am I saying? This isn't a date.*

They passed sunburned sport fishermen and Mexican fishing pangas returning from a long successful day. No one gave the little sailboat and its two occupants a second look.

Raul watched as her glance slid across each passing boat and its passengers without ever shifting her head. *Why do I find it so hard to believe that this small, compact, curly-haired and dimpled dulce would be a policewoman?* He knew the answer to that; because she was sweet and cute and every time he got close to her he wanted to reach out and.... He sighed a little too deeply, catching her attention.

"What is it?"

To cover his gaffe, he said, "Perhaps we could put up the sails?"

"She does handle the water better under sail and there's a nice afternoon breeze picking up," she said, nodding at the white caps skipping across the bay. "You don't get seasick, do you?" she asked, her tone hinting at a challenge.

"No," he said, matching her implied question. "Do you?"

She laughed. "Everyone gets seasick. Some sooner rather than later. If it's rough, I pack a lunch and stay topside."

She showed him how to hold the helm so that the bow stayed dead-on into the wind and went forward to raise the main. Securing the main halyard, she crab-walked back to the cockpit. Nodding her satisfaction at his ability with her boat, she tightened the mainsail and grinned. "Bear off to starboard, Cap'n, and let's get us some wind in our sails."

Raul bore off ten degrees and smiled when the mainsail greedily captured the wind. Katy unfurled the jib, and the small triangular sail soon filled and took its position next to the larger mainsail.

He did a little circle with a forefinger. "One minute, it's all wound up in a tight roll and the next, it becomes a sail."

"Never been on a sailboat before?"

He didn't want to explain that until this moment he had always preferred the hefty muscle of powerful twin engines to anything that poked along with only the wind. "No, I haven't and I like it better than I thought I would."

He watched as she tilted back her head to admire the salute of the colored tell-tales of her jib and main. Raul chose to admire the strong tan column of her throat as it met her shoulders in the sleeveless shirt. There was only a bit of air between his mouth her throat, those lips.

Still watching the sails, she explained, "Roller furling is the second best thing for a sailor as far as I'm concerned. I've never had to crawl forward in a blow to take down the jib and I don't ever want to have to."

"And I thought you a dare-devil, sailing alone."

She huffed out a laugh. "Whatever makes you think that? Bad weather pipes up I'm the first sissy to call for shortening the sail. No, no, I love sailing, hate the thought of drowning. I intend to be ninety, taking my leisure in a beachfront condo in Hawaii, and stressing over whether I should miss my tango lessons for a chance to crew aboard a racing yacht."

"And the first thing?"

"What?"

"You said that roller furling is the second best thing... so what's the first?"

She blushed again. She'd been caught unawares, and her blush sent the message that regardless of any quick response she came up with, he already knew the answer... *She likes me. In spite of everything I've done to her, she likes me.*

"GPS, of course," she blurted. "So, what's next?"

"Give me your hand."

"Wha...?"

"So that your prints will be accounted for," he said, holding up ink pad case.

Oh... yes... of course." She stuck out her hand to him and he carefully rolled her thumb and digits onto the pad and over to a waiting pad of paper. And then, for good measure pressed her palm onto the pad and finally all of it onto the white paper pad. Finished, he handed her a sealed alcohol wipe.

"Now, I shall go below and see if I can find more."

"Good luck with that, it'll mostly be my family," Katy called and then thought, *Oh, no. He'll find Gabe's prints down there too. Soon, very soon, I'm going to have to come clean about Gabe helping me.*

He balanced one foot on the top rung of the ladder and said, "I will need the name of your fiancé."

She hesitated. David? Her ex-fiancé might be messy with his relationships but he was a hardnosed attorney when it came to anything that smelled like a crime. "I'll have everyone's prints faxed to your office." She intended to leave David out of it for as long as possible. "It might get a little rough below. Are you sure you'll be okay?"

"I worked aboard my brother's fishing boats summers during college. I will be fine, thank you," he said, and disappeared into the cabin.

Katy resisted the temptation to worry over Raul Vignaroli's crime scene techniques. He was after all, American trained and employed by his federal government, so she stayed where she was and admired the clear cerulean sky as it arched overhead and sank into the deeper blue of the Pacific.

A ten-degree heel and not a wrinkle in her sails. Even the colorful tell-tales flew with military precision. It was almost perfect, that is if she didn't look down into the cabin where Raul was carefully going over her slashed cushions and walls with an eye for identifying a killer.

Raul ducked through the small hallway and into her small stateroom, thinking, *I can't imagine a more difficult scenario... though it could have been worse. It could have been Katrina lying dead on her cabin floor.*

He rubbed a hand across his jaw, surveying the damage: everything was as she had found it, the slashed cushions pushed over on each other, the pictures pulled out of their frames and tossed to the floor. He was grateful that she had resisted the temptation to tidy up.

Her drawers had been pulled out of their cabinets, the contents spilled onto the bed. Utilitarian white and colorful lace bras and panties scrambled into a messy pile as if discounted and discarded. He swallowed hard, closing off the image of someone tearing through Katy's personal life on a single-minded hunt for a simple list. The list he'd given her was not so very important, so why this kind of antipathy, this furious destruction? She was right, of course, the list was secondary to leaving her a message. She was a professional, but she was also vulnerable here on the boat in a Mexican marina where she had no friends. He winced at the immediate and visceral need to be the one to protect her. *Well, Raul, you know what you feel, but....* And that depressed him as much as anything. He could put a man on the dock to watch her boat, but he couldn't really protect her any more than he could make love to her. Shaking off the depressing thought, he went back to his task and in fifteen minutes he was finished, closing up his case and putting away his brushes.

At the top of the ladder he took a moment to admire the woman leaning out of the cockpit, her mouth stretched into a broad smile as she drank in the warm sun.

Reluctant as he was to break the spell, he cleared his throat. "May I trouble you for a soft drink?"

Katy ducked back into the cockpit, unscrewed the tiller lock and said, "You might as well make yourself at home, Raul. And there should be beer in the icebox," she called after him. *That is if Gabe hasn't drunk them all by now.*

He came topside, handed her one of the beers and stumbled over to the downwind side and sat.

Katy patted the seat next to her. "With the boat heeled, you'll be more comfortable on the upside. Brace your feet and you won't slip off."

He pivoted around and backed into a spot next to her.

His fragrance, that personal male aroma that either attracts or repels a woman, was definitely winding up her hormones again. *Don't give in to dangerous fantasies, Katy, the man is married, for cryin' out loud.*

To force herself away from uncomfortable thoughts, she said, "So, do you think you like sailboats?"

He lifted his large Roman nose and sniffed the air. "I love to be on the water. I even like to be on my brother's boat, unless the hold is filled with fish. But this is different, so quiet, so, ah—that's it, of course. You have turned off the engine and we are powered only by the wind."

Only the memory of having her boat cushions ripped apart and her personal life invaded kept her from completely enjoying the moment. It was time to admit defeat.

"It was easy enough to find the list tucked behind one of the photos I keep on my wall. So I guess the cushions were simply for fun."

"We arrested Spencer Bobbitt this morning."

"You have the evidence you need then?"

"Another anonymous tip and this time we found Spencer's gun jammed into an old tire in the arroyo below the RV park." His eyes were watchful as he said, "You know the place on the cliff above Marina Mar where the Americans live?"

"You mean where Gabe lives."

He didn't deny it, only nodded, watching her reaction.

"Do you suspect Gabe of being the tipster or the shooter?"

"I haven't decided."

"You're waiting for me to tell you? I don't know Gabe that well, not anymore, I don't. But you have someone watching him—to make sure he doesn't run?"

Raul nodded, apparently still wary.

"If you're thinking that I would protect Gabe Alexander at all costs, you're wrong, Raul. I won't. I don't want anything bad to happen to him, but if he's guilty, I won't protect him, either."

He nodded again, apparently relieved at her reply. "Then perhaps you have pricked a nerve somewhere. Other secrets someone does not want you to know."

"Why don't you help me out here? Tell me what *you* have on these particular people."

He said, "Other than her passport, Astrid Del Mar is a blank page, and Fred McGee is from L.A., and he works for your Internal Revenue Service."

She thought of Bruce's comment that the FBI was looking at Wally Howard. If the IRS was also investigating Wally Howard they would want to make sure they got any and all monies owed to them before the feds put him away for good. That would explain his sour disposition towards her interest in the case and his cover as a lousy magician.

Raul said, "If there are details that link Fred McGee and Spencer, I would be glad to know of it. Perhaps Jeff Cook might be willing to share with you."

His comment burst her earlier happy mood. "What, pillow talk? Not with me, Inspector. Besides, Astrid gets first dibs right after Myne is through with him."

Raul knew a mistake when he saw one, but what else could he do? Better this way than to allow his growing admiration for her to bloom into a flirtation that could go nowhere. "Dibs...? I see that you have learned important things already. Anything else?"

She hesitated, then said, "We both know Booth didn't walk off that dock; he was murdered for that tape I gave you the other day. Who he was blackmailing—Spencer? Wallace? Fred?"

He gazed pensively at the bug-sized cars hurtling along the *malecón*. "I don't believe it was Spencer."

"And my cushions? That could have been the work of a woman." She thought again of Astrid, and then of Ida Howard in tears, crying that it was "already too late." Why was it too late?

Raul interrupted, "You know, it may not have anything to do with Spencer. It could be that you have scratched at some secret by one of the witnesses."

Katy stiffened, her drifting thoughts knocked back into high alert by his words. Frightened suspects, she knew, can be as deadly as any killer. She licked dry lips and tasted the bitter truth. Her attempts to save her career ,or Gabe from prison, may now be the least of her worries.

By the time Katrina and Raul motored though the rock barrier, a cooling fog had blotted out the stars, dimming the city lights until everything—buildings, boats, people—was cast in a dull visceral rusty red. Katrina shuddered against the depressing sight and her own thoughts. She'd been lulled by the warmth of the blue sky and the Mexican waters until her lethargy had been slammed back into reality.

Unaware of Katrina's apprehensions, Raul jumped onto the dock, cleated the lines, then sat on the coaming of the cockpit. "If you will pass up your cushions, I will take them with me."

"Evidence?"

"No, no. Tomorrow, I will have a very reputable upholstery shop re-cover them for you. He will use only the finest materials and you will never know they were damaged."

"Great. How much do you think it will cost?"

"*Nada*," he said, curling his fingers in a manner to indicate she should start passing them up. He waited, expecting no objection.

"You don't have to do this, Raul."

"I want to—please." He smiled warmly, the light in his amber eyes directed at her with compassion and something else she didn't want to admit.

This was an unexpected surprise. His behavior, swimming between gruff disinterest and back to warm intimacy, left her constantly off balance.

His offer certainly appeared genuine, and if she didn't accept it, she would go without until she got home to San Francisco. Besides, he did owe her, so she went below and passed them up to him.

"I can help you carry them to your car," she said, looking at the pile.

"Not necessary," he said, and turned to whistle lightly. A young man pushed off from where he was leaning against the corner of Bandido's building and trotted over, picked up the cushions and disappeared into the dark.

Raul turned back to Katrina. "One more thing, I am putting another man on the dock at Marina Mar to watch your boat."

"You mean watch me."

He nodded. "That too. I will put another one at the entrance. So they don't stand out too much, they will both wear the hotel uniform. You have my number. If you need help, my man on the dock will come immediately."

She didn't bother to argue that a man watching her boat or her would do no good to someone intent on getting to her and without thinking, she asked, "But what if I want *you*?"

"I will always come—if you want me."

He gave her boat a pat, and then hefting his briefcase, vanished into the night, whistling a melodious tune.

Chapter Sixteen

Katrina steered her boat past the green and red entry lights to Marina Mar. Even with her foul-weather coat buttoned up against the cool night air, she shivered at the mounting dread spreading from her scalp down to her toes.

Cutting the motor, she drifted soundlessly into her slip, secured the lines and after feeding the kitten she then went topside with a cup of hot tea to watch the RV park's nightly bonfire. The fire crackled and spiraled high into the rust-colored fog until the flames punched holes into the night.

When the fire died down and the sounds of laughter quieted she took Gabe's flashlight and her boat knife, and scrambled up the rocky path next to the marina and pounded on his door.

"Go away," the truculent voice called back.

"Gabe, open up, it's me."

The door jerked open and Gabe poked his head out the door. When he saw who it was, he growled, "What're you doing here?"

"I came to see you," she said, thinking it might not have been a good idea after all. His eyes were bleary from drink and she thought, rather belatedly, he might not be alone. But when she started to back away, he reached out and pulled her inside.

Unsure of what she should do now, she watched him flop down at his dinette and put his head on the table. Turning to leave, she said, "I'll talk to you tomorrow."

"No, wait," he said listlessly.

"Sleep it off, Gabe. Today has been bad enough without having to deal with a drunk."

His eyes were bloodshot, his tanned face pasty under the dim overhead light. "I'm not drunk. We held a wake for the guy who owned my trailer and it turned into an all-day affair." He stroked the smooth surface of the dinette, then, looking around the interior as if seeing it for the first time, said, "Guess it's mine now. I'd say it's about the same size as a federal prison cell, wouldn't you?"

Not drunk, just feeling sorry for himself.

"Saw your boat go out today," he said. "Thought you decided to go home."

"I went for a sail." So she thought to unburden herself to someone who understood her, who would empathize with her position, stuck as she was investigating a crime in a foreign country. Silly now to imagine she might be able to think that person would be Gabe.

He rubbed at the bloodshot eyes. "Well, then… hungry?" The sagging cheeks lifted in a lopsided smile. She hated this, seeing him dull-witted and boozy.

"Then would you like a drink? No beer but I got whiskey… ah, not whiskey. I remember, rum and coke, right? That's still your drink of choice, isn't it?"

The gesture, serving her up her favorite cocktail, made her feel ashamed of herself. Unlike her, Gabe had nowhere to go.

"Okay. Light on the rum please." Besides, after today she could use one.

He nodded, got up, threw open cupboard doors and handed her an ice and Coke topped with a splash of rum, a slice of lemon on the edge, and laid the glass on a cocktail napkin in front of her.

She smiled. "That was very smartly done."

"Tended bar in Panama for a while."

No doubt he'd held twenty temporary jobs while he was on the run.

She pushed at the ice in the drink with a finger. "My boat was broken into today, Gabe. The cushions slashed and Raul Vignaroli's list of witnesses taken."

He reached out and took her hands in his, genuine worry on his face. "You weren't there? Thank God. I told you to give the tumbler on that lock a good couple of spins. You should stay here tonight. "

She pulled her hands out of his. "I locked it before I left. Someone took it apart and then set it in place to look as if it were untouched. I would've thought it a job by a pro except for the job they did on my cushions."

Gabe snorted. "And you think those slashed cushions were no more than a momentary lapse of good manners by some burglar? You're not safe on that boat anymore, and the Mexicans are no match for the likes of someone with Spencer Bobbitt's influence. You should stay here with me."

"Thanks, Gabe, but that's not going to happen. The police arrested him this morning," she said, carefully watching his reaction. Hadn't he told her he didn't know Spencer or Booth? "They got an anonymous tip about the weapon that shot the girl and it's no surprise that it belongs to Spencer Bobbitt. Want to guess where they found it?"

He rubbed the back of his neck and stared at a shadowy corner of his trailer.

He knew? To keep her disappointment in check, she knocked back the last of her drink. "Someone dumped it into that arroyo that meanders under the footpath up to your trailer park. Any thoughts on how it got there?"

He swirled the ice in his drink before answering. "You don't think I had anything to do with killing that girl, do you?"

"No, but I have to ask, were you in on Booth's blackmail plan?"

"No!"

"Then did you find it, or did you take it from him before you pushed him into the water to drown?"

Gabe's eyes widened. "I swear to you, I didn't have anything to do with Booth going into the water." Then he blinked. A tell she knew well from her training as an investigator in the SFPD. He *was* keeping something from her and the knowledge of it made her ill.

"You're lying! The girl? Did you drop that gun in the arroyo? Were you there, in on it with Spencer Bobbitt? Tell me, what did you *do*!"

"Kat, you know me better'n anyone. I may be a lot of things, but I'm no killer."

She waited.

He reached up to wipe away the beads of sweat layered his forehead. "You really have changed, haven't you?"

"I'll take that as a compliment. Start talking."

"Whatever you do, don't turn your back on Spencer Bobbitt."

"I don't see any cloven hooves on the man."

"Yeah, well you won't until you feel the pitchfork up your ass."

"You speaking from personal experience?"

He sighed deeply, as if his broad shoulders were unhappily carrying around the weight of too many secrets. Then he got up and took the drink glasses over to the sink and sloshed soap in them, then sluiced water around each and set them in a wire rack to dry. He turned back to her and leaning against the counter, said, "Ever hear the story about the blind mule? No? Well, Buddy wouldn't pull his own weight unless the farmer pretended he had another mule in harness. He'd call out, 'Giddy-up Buddy, giddy-up Dandy.'"

Already exhausted from her long day, his delaying tactics were beginning to grind on her last nerve. "Is there a moral to this story?"

"Yes, there is. Chief Vinegar is letting you do his dirty work and you're just as alone in the job as old Buddy the mule. You shouldn't be here, doing any of this shit, not on my account. I told you I can take care of myself, fade into the hills, hitch a ride south on a boat or a truck. There's no reason why you should put yourself in harm's way."

She didn't bother to remind him that she was just as stuck here as he was. "I appreciate that, Gabe."

He sat down again, rubbing at his scalp as if a genie might appear and make it all better. "I was outside, having a smoke. Heard this sound, like a mewling kitten. After it didn't stop, I followed the sound and found her. I was afraid to pick her up, she was bleeding pretty bad. If I'd only known ...."

"Known what—that I'd be the one who would find her floating on a patch of sea-grass out in the Pacific? Are you saying that you dumped her in the water to drown?" Shocked, Katy was also furious.

He put up a shaky hand. "No, that's not the way—I was going for help when I bumped into Booth. He said he'd make the call if I'd stay with her. I did and he came back with a Mexican kid—"

"It was a Mexican kid attacked me after I left your place a few nights ago."

He licked at his lips and continued, "Booth brought the kid and a blanket. I thought they were going to take her to the hospital. Come on, Katrina, don't look at me like that. Mexico has free medical care but you've got to have a way to get there and I don't have a car.I couldn't call an ambulance, either 'cause I didn't have the cash to pay for it, but Booth did, or at least, he *said* he'd take care of it."

"Did you see Booth the next day? Ask *him* what happened to the girl?"

His face lost all expression.

Of course he didn't. It might involve the police and where his passport might be—things that could get him thrown into jail. And there was the obvious exchange of favors to consider. He had kept it secret, thereby banking a favor should Spencer be the killer and that might come in handy. At least he understood that Spencer's pitchforks and cloven hooves were no match for what he owed Katrina Taylor Hunter.

"Then instead of taking her to the hospital, Booth threw her into the sea to drown."

Gabe sighed deeply and gazed at the fly specks on his ceiling. "It may have happened that way, I wasn't there, I swear."

Katrina suddenly felt sick and claustrophobic. She stood up. "You'd better be telling the truth, Gabe, or I swear, this time I'll let you rot in a Mexican jail."

He gulped, mashing his callused hands together in a knot. "Katy, I've been eaten up with the guilt of it—but what else could I do?" He looked up at her. "What a fine reunion this has turned out to be, huh?"

Reunion? She had the insane desire to throw back her head and howl with laughter. Their so-called reunion started out in the police station and just like last time, had all the earmarks of a train wreck.

Back on her boat, she started a new list and this time she chose a hiding place where no man would consider looking… a Tampax box.

Someone had carried the bleeding girl to a car, but instead of taking her to the hospital where she might've been saved, they chose to take her to the RV park instead. Was that because they hoped to incriminate Gabe or was it to dump the responsibility for the body on him?

Could the timid Wally have what it takes to murder a teenager in order to incriminate Spencer and secure the patronage of his mistress? No, surely not Wally. He'd been the first to jump in the marina water to help secure Booth's body into the sling.

Too weary to brush her teeth, she did remember to put in the hatch boards that would keep the kitten from wandering off the boat, but since her only working fan was in the main cabin, she left open all the portholes in the off-chance a breeze would cool the interior. Then she put away the list and crawled into her bunk. Tomorrow, she would find a way to tell Raul about Gabe finding the girl and Booth coming to move her.

A persistent knocking jerked Katy up and out of her bed. The sun was up and when she looked at her watch; it was already nine a.m.

"Who is it?" she called, pulling on her shorts and a sweatshirt.

Astrid was standing outside, anxiously scanning the dock.

"Good morning, Astrid," she said, looking around the quiet dock. "I'm just up, but come aboard and I'll make some coffee."

Astrid scrambled down the companionway so fast that Katy hardly had time to get out of the girl's way. At the sight of the settee and its missing cushions she visibly shuddered. "Oh. It's true, then. Someone slashed your cushions. I didn't do this," she said, pointing at the flat wood peeking up between mismatched cushions. "That's… that's just not me, you know?"

"Why would anyone think *you* did it?"

The girl's green eyes widened. "Jeff thinks… Look, I'm crazy jealous when he talks to other girls, I can't help that. I love the big dope, an' now he's all mad at me and stuff. I just thought…"

"What?" These two girls were going to be in for a major surprise when they learned Jeff was a pro at conning women.

"If you told him I didn't do it, he'd believe you."

"He'll believe me, but not you. Is that because you have a history of lying?"

"That's not true! It's just that I can get in and out of really small places like you wouldn't believe. I'm Fred's best assistant ever, just you ask him if you don't believe *me*."

"Is this a part-time job, or is there school or something else for you when you go home?"

"I… I haven't decided about college yet."

"You look like you work out."

"That's how I met Jeff," she gushed. "At a gym in Ventura. We're leaving for Puerto Vallarta soon as… soon as he gets some things settled. It's just about the most romantic place in the world to get hitched, you know?"

Of course, this left out Myne's plans for Jeff, but who was she to argue? "When're you leaving?"

Astrid looked down at her lap, her buoyant mood slipping. "That may have to be put off for a bit. He still has some… well, one little problem to fix."

"You mean like telling Myne he's going to leave with you instead of her?"

Astrid's chin quivered a bit in the delivery but she stubbornly plowed ahead. "Exactly. That conniving little bitch is finally going to get what she deserves."

"And what would that be?"

Astrid's lips tightened and she had the look of someone who now wished she hadn't been so forthcoming.

"Okay," Katy said. "How many times have you two fought over some guy that probably doesn't love either of you?"

"Of course he loves me!"

"Why? Because he says so?"

Astrid's natural hazel eyes stared back at Katy, and for the first time, Katy noticed what she hadn't before. There was a familiarity about the girl, as if she'd seen her somewhere before. And then she had it.

"So, is Jeff the real problem between you two?"

"I told you, I missed out on my one and only big chance at *American Idol*, and it's all her *fault*!"

"And, you're honor bound to take Jeff back, no matter what."

"Well, he was mine to start with."

"People don't belong to us, Astrid, you know that better than anyone. Your sister is selfish, but I doubt she really understands why you're so angry with her."

"Sister! What makes you think…?"

"There is a resemblance, you know. You two have the same shaped face and you both have that little crooked pinky that some siblings have. I notice things like that. It's my job, and besides, I have a sister and we've been fighting and making up for as long as I can remember, so your behavior towards Myne makes sense."

Astrid looked down at her chest. "We *were* born on that dumb catamaran, but it was my mom who jumped ship in P.V." Astrid raised her head to meet Katy's eyes. Was it to gauge Katy's ability to swallow her story? "My dad kept us with him until they worked out the divorce and then they split us up. I went to L.A. with him 'cause I'm the oldest and Myne went with our mom to Texas."

"Uh-huh. I guess that explains the East Texas accent."

"Yeah, yeah, and tomorrow she'll have an Aussie accent. She thinks she's an actress. I hadn't seen her in nine years and she decides to come out to L.A. and live with us. She made the round of Hollywood agents and totally *bombed* her screen test. If she'd stuck with the singing act we put together, she might've had a shot at Hollywood, but she left after we had a fight about it and I haven't seen her until we landed here. So here we are again, living on the water, only the boats are whole lot bigger."

"This is childish you know. You don't really want Jeff. You're just mad at her for the loss of your audition, aren't you?"

"I didn't come preloaded with the double-D's but I'm a better singer than she'll ever be. She was just eye-candy, anyway. She got mom's figure, I got daddy's brains."

"You don't have to look like Dolly Parton to get an agent, Astrid."

"She still screwed up my big chance at *American Idol*."

"If it makes you feel any better, she's going to be out in the cold now that Spencer's been arrested."

She hooted, "Lost her meal ticket, has she? Sweet."

"Sisters don't always do it right," Katy said, thinking back to when she shot her sister's stalker. Maybe if she had tackled him instead of wrestling him for his gun she wouldn't be down in Mexico. But then she'd probably still be planning a wedding with a fiancé she no longer wanted, either. Which made her think of Raul Vignaroli again. Why was it every time she thought about David, Raul's image popped up? It was becoming a habit she would need to shake.

"Tell you what—I'll talk to Jeff," Katy said, giving Astrid her most sincere smile. It wasn't a lie; she had every intention of questioning Jeff again. "If you'll tell me what you know about Fred."

"Fred?" Astrid was suddenly cagey. "I mean sure, what can I tell you?"

"For starters, how did you get the job with him?"

Astrid's easy posture went rigid and her hands quieted. "Newspaper ad."

"Been with him long?"

"Two years. But I told you Jeff and I are leaving."

"Uh-huh." The best way to crack Astrid was to push at her defenses. "You can tell me, do you suspect that Fred had something to do with the girl's murder?"

Astrid jumped as if she'd been pinched. "Fred? Good God, no! I mean, he's more likely to kill Spencer. No. Forget I said that. Besides, I hear they finally arrested Spencer, right?"

Katy was now suspicious. "But you know something about it, don't you?"

Astrid, eyes wide, shook her head. "Not me. I wasn't even here that night. I was on my boat, asleep, alone."

"How about the night Booth was found in the water? You were there."

"I was there to see Fred. We were going over his next show. You should ask Wally and his wife about Booth. They're the ones who plied him with rum to get the dirty on Spencer, and that's all I'm going to say about that." Astrid mumbled a quick excuse and was gone in a flash.

Rum *and* narcotics? That would have been a lethal cocktail. Raul supplied a dying man with heroin, and yet Booth gambled on blackmail as a way of getting some ready cash. Odd. Surely not for himself. Was he helping someone else? Perhaps Myne, as a way out from under Spencer's thumb?

She was getting ready to take the trash out of her boat when she heard someone else calling her name. "Katy, Katy! I'm so glad I found you," she cried, throwing herself into Katy's unsuspecting arms. "Where you been? They arrested Spencer yesterday!"

Katy put an arm around the sobbing girl and pushed her into the boat. "Yes, I know, but

The little blonde collapsed onto the settee with its odd assortment of temporary pillows. Noting her lack of interest in the missing cushions, Katy deleted Myne as the list thief and cushion slasher. She poured a cup of coffee for Myne and handed it to her.

"Will they let you see him?"

Myne knuckled her reddened eyes. "This wasn't supposed to happen. He told me he paid off a judge and the police. Now I gotta go talk to his lawyer, see if there's anybody left that can get him bail."

"The police found his gun." She started to say more but decided against it, not if Myne was still willing to cover for Spencer. "Well, the law is different here, Myne. Their laws are based on the Napoleonic doctrines—guilty until proven innocent. There's no bail for a murder charge."

Myne sniffled then sat up straight. "Oh my God! They'll impound his boat, too."

"You should go stay with someone. Maybe one of Spencer's friends?"

Myne's next words stunned Katy. "He said anything should happen to him, I should come to you."

Katy stuttered. "M—m—me?" Then she did a mental head smack. That first night on Spencer's boat, the smoke signals between Spencer and Booth. If it all came apart, Spencer, already under suspicion, saw Katy as the perfect foil; but did he do it so that Myne would be safe or was he setting up his mistress/employee as a spy in the opposing camp?

"Dry your eyes and tell me what you know about that night. And don't tell me you didn't know he had a prostitute at the boat," she said, thinking of Myne's entertainment of Spencer's prospective clients.

"I never said I didn't know. I just thought that passel of lawyers he thinks so highly of woulda been able to keep him out of jail."

"Myne, someone has been giving the police anonymous tips. First, when the girl was murdered and now someone told them where to find the gun. Would that be you?"

"The man still signs my checks. Why would I wanna bust up that deal?"

"How about Jeff?"

"I don't know. Maybe. Jeff said he was moving off the boat 'cause Spencer owed him wages, but I never took Jeff for a snitch, least ways, I didn't think he was."

"If Jeff is off Spencer's yacht, where'd he move to?"

"He moved onto Fred's boat, which I'm sure suits Astrid just fine and dandy."

So that was why Jeff might or might not work out. The war between Astrid and Myne was heating up again.

Myne picked at the crumbled tissue in her hand. "Are they sure it's Spencer's gun?"

"'Fraid so. Where were you when the police first came for Spencer?"

"My room's down the hall. I don't sleep good most nights, so I took a pill. I didn't hear nothin' till Booth woke me up and said I had to talk to the police. I told them I didn't know if he had a girl aboard or not, 'cause had girls from Antonio's delivered several times a week, and I wouldn't have had anything to say about it if he had six of 'em every night."

It would have been ludicrous for Katy to try to imagine herself in Myne's platforms. Katy looked down at her aged deck shoes and grimaced at the neglected shape of her own tanned legs.

Seeing Katy's frown, Myne slouched over her hands and murmured, "I guess you being with the police an' all, you seen a lot worse than me, huh?"

Katy held up a palm. "I'm not judging you, Myne."

"I owe Spencer a lot."

"I understand. He got you out of that strip club. But now you and Jeff are together, you can leave, start a new life, right?"

"Maybe, maybe not. I'm still sore at Jeff for leaving me all alone on that big ol' boat."

"Do you know if he had a favorite?"

"Jeff don't go for the girls at Antonio's… oh, you mean Spencer. He didn't have no favorites, only that they had to be young. Spence likes 'em young." There was a momentary wistfulness that passed across her face. "I was just a kid, fooling myself to think he would marry me if I was preggers. That little scare got him a vasectomy and me an abortion." She shrugged. "It was either take care of the problem or he was going to kick me out. After that, it was all business between us."

"He's married, you know."

She dismissed the idea with a floppy wave of her hand. "They have an arrangement. She stays out of his hair and she gets to keep her high falutin' lifestyle."

This was the typical married man's version as told to a gullible girl, but what was the real story?

Myne swiped at the tears threatening to spill. "He gets convicted, I'm out of a job *and* a home."

"If the police were going to seize Spencer's yacht, they would've done it already. I think it's safe for you to go back."

Myne tilted her head, considering. "You think so? Gee. That might be okay, then. I'll be by myself, but I can do that. There's plenty of food in the fridge… and nobody to bother me. I can do that." She dimpled once then frowned. "I gotta go see the lawyer. Will you go with me?"

"Of course," Katy said, thinking of the fan she still needed to replace. "I have some chores to do in town anyway. Why don't you go get your purse and a hat," she said, nodding at the girl's sun-pinked skin. "I need to take a shower. I'll come by in say, half an hour?"

Myne was once again all smiles.

At the marina showers, Katy took out her favorite hyacinth soap went to work on the grime under her toenails. Then taking a razor, she carefully lathered her legs and rid them of the last of the stubble and, deciding she had the time, washed and conditioned her hair, blew it dry and pulled it all into a thick shiny ponytail. Donning a clean, sleeveless khaki shirt over a pair of walking shorts, she turned around to admire herself in the mirror. She was going to the police station.

Never knew who she might run into there.

Chapter Seventeen

Slinging her kit bag into the cockpit for later, and making sure the kitten had food and water and that her lock was secure on the hatch boards, Katy walked to Spencer's yacht, took the steps up to the sun deck and tried the sliding glass doors to the living room. The only thing she saw was her own reflection in the mirror behind the bar. It was locked, and probably a good idea, since Myne was living alone now.

Over the hum of the AC she felt a faint, throbbing base beat against the glass doors. Taking the stairs down to the lower level she followed the sound. She tried the exterior doors that would lead to hallways but the handles wouldn't turn. Stopping at the porthole where the music appeared to be coming from, she went up on tiptoe and looked inside.

This was Myne's all pink room with its pillow shams edged in lace and plumped together over a matching satin comforter. But where was Myne? Then she saw movement on the floor next to the bed. Two short legs ending in bare feet with the gumdrop toes sporting the cyanic blue polish Myne favored. Katy banged on the porthole. Nothing could be heard over the loud music. All the doors were locked. Depressed at losing Jeff to Astrid and Spencer to a murder rap, had she decided to end it all with an overdose of her sleeping pills?

Just as Katy was about to go for help, she noticed a large pair of bare feet sliding down the girl's legs to sensuously cuddle the pink toes. The girl's feet returned the caress.

Sighing, Katy settled back onto her feet and left.

She gave it another half hour and went back. This time the slider was unlocked, the lights on and Myne waved her in. "I'll be with you in a jiffy, soon's I get this dorado filleted and in the fridge."

Myne adjusted the apron she wore, hefted the heavy carving knife and went at the fish with a vengeance.

"I came by earlier. Door was locked."

"Probably in the shower," she said, grimly whacking the fish.

Considering the knife and what was left of the fish, Katy asked, "Is that fresh dorado?"

Myne shrugged and turned away. "A *friend* brought it by," she said with a sigh, moving the fish onto some paper and then carrying the limp remains over to a lidded trash can and dumping it all into the can.

Wiping her hands on her apron, she smiled weakly at Katy. "I don't know why I thought I had to fillet that damn thing, I can't cook."

Removing her apron, she came around the counter in a man-shirt over a pair of black tights, the Leila Standiford look-alike gold bangles at her wrists, and diamond ear studs big enough to feed a small country.

When Myne noticed Katy's interest in the earrings, she self-consciously lifted a finger and adjusted the heavy stones. "I never wear 'em."

Her bad mood brightened as she admired her reflection in the mirror behind the bar. "But maybe it'll cheer him up some, since he bought 'em."

Or maybe it was to remind Spencer that ten grand was hanging on his ex-mistress' ears and out of his reach.

"You think I'll get mugged?"

Katy smiled. "I think you'll do just fine."

Myne lowered her eyelashes and a sly smile curled at her lips. She shrugged a huge gold lamé purse onto her shoulder and a pair of dark sunglasses on top of her forehead. "Let's do this then."

"Hat?" suggested Katy.

Myne coyly moved a lock behind her shell pink ears to show off the diamond sparklers. "No thanks. I wouldn't want to ruin the effect."

This should be interesting.

In the taxi, Katy watched Myne's growing nervousness as she kept touching the stones as if to remind herself they were there. Then with a small sigh, she let her hand trail down her neck to drop quietly into her lap.

Yes, Myne had a plan and Katy would give a lot to be a fly on the wall when the girl went to visit Spencer. She'd also like to know if it was Jeff with her on the floor of her bedroom today. Knowing what she did about him, she had to wonder if he was the one who pushed Myne to wear the diamonds and why.

Spencer's lawyer was a vigorous man in his early forties, expensively attired in a handmade silk suit and tie. He greeted them with the hearty banter of a man about to make some serious money. Avoiding the dangerous ground of what to call Myne, he didn't bother to address her as anything that might get him into trouble. Instead he lightly kissed the back of her hand. "I am so very glad to meet someone who is clearly on Mr. Spencer's side," he said.

His composure, however, did wobble a bit when Myne bent over her purse and gave him a breathtaking view of some very abundant décolletage.

To break the awkward moment, Katy commented on the polo awards on a nearby shelf.

"Yes," he said, clearly relieved at her distraction. "We are very proud of our club here in Ensenada." He shot a glance at Myne, who was now rummaging fitfully through her bag, and continued, "Polo is a very popular Mexican sport. You should come to one... sometime," he added, smiling weakly.

Myne waved her checkbook at him. "Got it. Now, ah'm prepared to write you a check for his bail."

The lawyer, in an obvious attempt to set the time on this fool's errand, unstrapped his Rolex watch and laid it on the desk.

"I'm sorry, but that won't be possible. There is no bail for a murder charge here in Mexico."

If Myne's narrowed eyes were twin barrels, she would've shot him full of holes. "Ain't there some judge you can bribe?"

He thoughtfully tapped a forefinger to his lips, perhaps considering who was left to bribe at this late date. "Tempting as that might be, I'm sorry, señorita, but the opportunity for good will has already passed. They found the gun, you know."

"Oh no! He can't stay in jail, it'll kill him."

The lawyer tipped a canny eyebrow at the obvious playacting. "Of course, if you have any evidence that would prove him innocent...?"

Myne flicked the tip of her pink tongue at the corner of her mouth. "I... I don't know anything Are they sure it's his gun? They got prints and stuff?"

The lawyer moved the tissue box closer to her side of the desk."I'm sorry, but at this time, it appears that he will be charged.

"However," he said, nodding at her checkbook, "if you would be so kind as to write out the check for my retainer, I will see what I can do."

He then pushed a piece of paper with a number on it across the desk, clearly expecting her to fill it into her checkbook. Myne leaned forward to peer at it, again giving him an eyeful of her very abundant chest.

The lawyer stood up, shot his initialed cuffs, and strapping on his expensive watch, indicated an end to the meeting. "If there is anything more that I can do for you," he said, coming around the desk to grasp her small hand between both of his, "please feel free to call my office at any time."

Myne, her lips tight around her teeth, yanked her hand away, hiked her bag up onto her shoulder, and without a backward glance, marched out of his office.

At the secretary's desk, she ripped out the check, and handed it to her. "Tell him to fill in any ol' number he wants. And tell him he'd better be worth it or he'll answer to Spencer Bobbitt's friends!"

Out on the street, Myne clutched at Katy's arm. "That asshole lawyer good as said Spencer's goose is cooked."

"It's the gun, Myne, they have his prints on it."

"But he could still be innocent, couldn't he?"

"Sure," Katy said, impressed that Myne saw the lawyer for the bottom feeder that he was. "If something or someone comes forward with evidence to prove he didn't do it."

Myne shook her head. Then she giggled. The giggle turned into laughter until she was almost doubled over with it, holding onto her stomach with one hand and Katy with the other. "If… if I'd done it like Spencer told me… take him his checkbook first, so he could sign it for the lawyer's retainer… I never do it right… and this is so funny! I told that son of a bitch to write in his own number, but if he writes it for more than two hundred dollars it'll *bounce."*

"That would be funny… only…"

"What?" Myne's effervescent mood dissipated like bubbles on the air.

"Well. If it bounces, what's your back-up plan… if this lawyer quits?"

"Oh, shit. I guess we better go see Spence and get his John Hancock on one of his checks' for that crook he's got for a lawyer."

Katy shot her a look. "Pot calling the kettle black?"

"Oh." She giggled again. "You're right about that."

"Then let's just hope that the lawyer has less soot on him than Spencer Bobbitt."

Chapter Eighteen

Katy watched the jailer lead Myne over to an elevator and punch the UP button for her. Myne dimpled sweetly for the officer then turned to give Katy a tremulous smile and a thumbs-up.

She managed to return the gesture without screaming, *"I'm not your girlfriend! I'm Raul Vignaroli's personal spy!"*

Determined to find the chief and end this charade, she backed up and tripped over his feet.

He reached out a hand to steady her, and the heat of the connection snapped and crackled but he didn't let go until she looked down at his hand on her arm and her eyebrows moved up a notch.

"So," she said, "we should talk."

He thumbed over his shoulder. "Not here, please," and with a proprietary hand at her back ushered her down the hallway to his office.

Katy momentarily stiffened at the intimacy of his broad hand heating up her body but waited to break the contact until they moved through the door.

Inside, they each took their appropriate seats—Raul behind his desk, still littered with piles of folders, and Katy on the hard plastic chair in front of it. On the wall was the same kind of big school house clock that only a short week ago inched painfully through the hours of her life.

He laced his fingers together and said, "He didn't deny that it was his weapon and his fingerprints are on it."

"Anyone else's?"

"No."

She sat forward in her chair. "Time, water, weather will deteriorate any viable prints."

His dark eyes held hers for a moment longer and then he smiled. "Did you know that fingerprinting analysis was discovered by an Argentinian by the name of Juan Vucetich in 1891?"

"Fascinating, but you still don't think he did it, do you?"

"What I think doesn't stand up to the evidence, the gun, his prints."

"I hear that the FBI is putting together a case against Wallace Howard."

He leaned back in his chair. "Yes, but it is Spencer Bobbitt who is of interest to my government, and subsequently how I became involved with this investigation. Your government wants to be sure of his innocence before they have him extradited back to the States."

"Back to the states? What for?"

"They weren't interested, until his accountant Wallace Howard offered them information about a shipment of stolen case-goods to be transported across the border, which of course were packed with guns and drugs because that's what the Sinaloa Cartel does when they transport anything in trucks. Naturally, the FBI alerted our federal task force and the shipment was seized."

Then she remembered Wally begging Myne to let him take care of her because Spencer would soon no longer be her benefactor. Wally must be the anonymous caller. "Turning in his boss to the FBI would also get him immunity from prosecution, right? From what I've seen and heard about Spencer—I will be surprised if—"

"Yes? What is it you're thinking?"

"Wally tells Spencer he's retiring. He has his game all in place. He tells the fed about the shipment, implicates Spencer. Spencer finds out about it and turns the tables on Wally."

"How?"

"Because Wally got the equivalent of a horse's head in his bed."

Raul was quiet for a minute. "The movie. You are speaking of The Godfather, are you not?"

"Uh-huh. Spencer got Wally and his wife down here to Ensenada with promises of a nice new sailboat as his retirement gift. The sailboat turned out to be a wreck. Spencer's little joke and a message that Wally's plan was going to backfire on him."

"And you think Wally killed the girl as revenge?"

"Yes, I do. And I also think Booth knew the whole story, and as Spencer's consigliere, tried to blackmail Wally out of testifying."

"There's only one problem. Wally Howard has stomach ulcers and was in our local hospital that night."

Katy blinked. "But he could've hired someone to do it like he hired that Mexican kid to push me off the cliff."

Raul spent a few seconds absently-mindedly shuffling papers around on his desk, then stood up. "I see you brought Myne to see Spencer. I can arrange for you to talk to him, if you like."

"I think I'll pass, at least for now," she said, disappointed that Raul didn't jump to the idea of Wally as the killer. If anything he seemed distracted.

"Myne thought Jeff Cook was in love with her," Katy added, "but the guy's a gigolo…"

"*Mujiero*," he added thoughtfully.

"Yes, a womanizer. He's got a reputation for fleecing middle-aged women. He's also romancing Astrid Del Mar, the magician's assistant. You caught their gymnastics the night Booth was found in the water. And, if it means anything, Astrid is a pathological liar and a kleptomaniac… she stole my favorite scrunchy."

"Scrunchy?" His quick smile caught her by surprise.

"Yes, like this one." She indicated the colorful, fuzzy band holding her ponytail.

He tapped at the pile of paperwork on the desk, looked as if seeing it for the first time, and then asked, "Will you please have dinner with me tonight?"

She searched his face for some hint of an answer to her questions, but Raul's eyes remained on her waiting for her answer. She looked at his hands resting on the desk and once again thought how much she liked his broad palms, the blunt fingers with their clean, pared nails.

"Alright. Where?"

"I will pick you up at the entrance to your marina tonight."

"Italian again?"

"Something different, if you will allow."

She hesitated, still annoyed that he wasn't taking her theories about Wally as the killer seriously enough, then shook it off. Tonight. Dinner. A break from all of this. She'd enjoyed the last one, hadn't she?

"What time?"

"I will be there at six-thirty, unless that is too early?"

"No, that's fine, I'll be there."

He didn't walk her out the door and back to where he found her in the waiting room. Instead, he simply nodded at the pile of work on his desk and she was dismissed.

Katy left the way she'd come in, her footsteps echoing down the hall as she wondered at his sudden shift away from the investigation. When she got to the waiting room she saw Myne surrounded by Mexican cops and decided she needed to rescue her before she caused a minor riot amongst all the testosterone in the police station.

She gingerly helped the wilted Myne into a cab and thought the girl had the look of a whipped puppy

"He wasn't amused by the diamond earrings?"

"I don't want to talk about it," Myne said, her voice squeaky with recent tears.

She might've felt sorry for the girl, but then she remembered the helpless sixteen-year-old who'd been shot and tossed into the water to die.

"Are you going to be okay?" Katy asked.

"I… I don't know." She held up a folded check. "He signed a check to pay for the lawyer, but then I don't know what I'm going to do for money next week. He says he's broke."

"I suppose you could sell those diamond earrings?"

She brightened for a minute while she fingered the earrings, then gave Katy a rueful grin. "I would but they're not mine, they belong to Mrs. Bobbitt. He just lets expensive stuff like this sit around in drawers while I gotta look through his ol' pants pockets for food money."

"Was it Jeff's idea for you to try the diamonds?"

She shuddered and looked away. "I was a fool to listen to Jeff. Spence told me if I tried anything like that he'd have me fitted for cement shoes. He could do it, too. He has people who can do it for him. He can do anything he wants, even from jail."

This only strengthened her conviction that Spencer hired the Mexican kid to try to kill her. "So, what do you think your chances are with Jeff, now that you don't have any money?"

"I thought I knew. Right up to when he brought me that fish, banged me one last time and then tol' me he wasn't coming back unless—unless I can come up with some dough for us to live on."

That explained the hatchet job done on the Dorado.

"Myne, you don't need Jeff Cook. He's not what he purports himself to be. He doesn't have a captain's license and he's not enrolled in a maritime academy, either. He's a part-time actor with a reputation for fleecing older women out of their money."

Myne sat quietly for a moment, and then straightened, her eyes twinkling. "Does Astrid know?"

"Uh, no, I haven't told her yet."

She reached out and grabbed Katy's hands in both of hers, the bangles tinkling against her wrists. "I'll do anything, *anything* in the world—if only—please, please don't tell her about Jeff."

She didn't dislike either of these girls, but she also didn't like the idea of a promise she might have to break.

"I'll tell you what. For now, if it doesn't cause any harm to Astrid, I'll agree to keeping mum on the subject of Jeff's inadequacies."

"Oh, you know about that too, huh? Well, I suppose sooner or later that would come out. And to think I tol' him size don't matter."

Time to take her home, get a shower and meet Raul for dinner and see if she could get him to explain why her theory about Wally wasn't working.

At the appointed hour, Raul turned into the hotel driveway and up to where Katrina waited under the shade of the portico. He got out, opened the passenger side and when she hesitated, he said, "I think we can dispense with the chauffeur act from now on."

He smiled as she swept aside her skirt, got into the car and buckled up.

Behind the wheel, he pulled into traffic and adjusted the AC to her preference from last time.

She nodded her thanks. "So where are we going?"

"It's not far from here," he said taking a turnoff from the highway onto a mountainous road winding upward past gated properties. The car climbed up over hills until it glided along a high adobe wall and stopped at a gate with a bronze plaque on the wall that proclaimed this was *Los Sueños*. A touch of a button on his visor and the double bronzed gates slid open and the car moved quietly down a graveled path, then up and around a thick grove of olive trees.

The view opened up to the ocean below. She got a peek of a flat copper roofline jutting out from a cliff as the car swept down into a garage.

With wonder in her voice, she asked, "Whose home is this?"

"Mine. Come, I will show you the view," he said, getting out of the car and going around to her side, offered her a hand.

Katrina hesitated. "And your wife…?"

He bent down to her eye level. "Will you trust that I'm not leading you into the den of iniquity?"

"That sounds like a dare, Raul—and you know what I'm talking about."

"Yes, yes," he said, sighing. "And I promise you an answer that you will approve. Come, we will go around to the main entrance so that you will have the full effect of the view."

He opened the front door and they stepped inside. The foyer was dark when they walked in, then hidden automatic recessed lighting warmed the room. Katy looked down to see that she was standing on a solid piece of black marble. It was still light enough for her to see beyond the entrance. And what she saw astounded her—the house appeared to be airborne with nothing to stand between her and the wide open sky.

"An optical illusion," he said taking her arm. "It's a bit disconcerting when you see it the first time, but if you step closer you'll see that it is only because the living room is sunken."

Feeling disoriented, she kept close to Raul and shuffled her feet along the solid cool marble until she came to the edge.

Where she thought nothing existed but a great expanse of sky, now there were floor to ceiling windows and a wide living room with a sunken seating area.

At the sound of his keys tumbling into an art glass bowl on a metal pedestal she was startled to hear a woman's voice calling, "*Cena, querido*!" And then there was the laughter of children.

Shocked back into reality, she started to speak and the voice called again. This time she cocked her head. There was something about that voice; the timbre was the same in each call, but still… the lilting, modulated tones of a woman's voice, almost as if….

Katy turned to him, a surprised smile on her lips. "Is that…?"

"Come," he said, taking her hand, "I will introduce you."

Chapter Nineteen

Katy followed Raul down a long hallway and into a modern open kitchen, complete with contemporary appliances, a butcher block island and a breakfast nook, which was occupied by a large wire cage. In it was, what might or might not be, a bird. It had the beak and the rounded head of a parrot, but except for a few pin feathers on its head and wing tips, it was entirely bald.

The bird whistled a greeting at Raul, then seeing a stranger, immediately turned a large yellow eye in her direction and stretched out a long wrinkled neck to inspect this newcomer. Somehow the result appeared to be less than satisfying and he opened his beak wide as if to say something, then seemed to change his mind, and fluffing phantom feathers, turned his back and hunched his head down onto naked shoulders.

"Wow," Katy breathed. "I've just been dissed by a bald parrot. What happened to his feathers?"

Raul handed her a glass of red wine and said, "He doesn't like people talking about him so we'll discuss this in the living room."

Katy huffed out a quick laugh and saw that he was serious.

"I think you will like the wine," he said. "It's from my family's vineyard."

She lifted the stemmed glass and sniffed the heady bouquet. "Nice. Italian?"

"My father brought vine cuttings from Italy and planted them here in the hills behind Ensenada. We already produce enough to export to the States."

"This in addition to the cannery, your brother's fishing boats and your uncle's restaurant?"

"I'm a very silent partner. My sisters run the winery and the vineyards," he said. Turning to the oven, he donned oven mitts large enough to be used in a glass blowing factory and extracted a hot dish.

Katy breathed in the delicious-smelling casserole. "Lasagna's my favorite, and though the parrot has got the voice down pat, I presume he doesn't cook."

He chuckled quietly and cutting even portions, served them onto plates. Then with a bowl of salad in one hand and his plate in the other, said, "The living room is back through that hallway and to your right, if you will carry your plate and my wine glass?"

She nodded and silently moved out of the kitchen and down the hall to the huge sunken living room. A towering fireplace reached thirty feet above them and in front of it was a beige leather sectional and a shiny black marble coffee table complete with a cache of stubby lit candles and silverware for two wrapped in napkins on a couple of thick placemats.

She set down her plate on the coffee table and giving the wine a swirl said, "Did you come home early to prepare all this then?"

He put down his plate on the placemat and said, "My sister brings me dinners once a week and I asked her to bring enough for two tonight. Please. Sit and let's eat before this lovely meal is cold or I will never hear the end of it."

"It sounds as if you have a wonderfully close family."

"Mmm-mm," he said between mouthfuls. "That's why my uncle was so thrilled to see us at his place last week. I don't see him or my aunt enough and they're good people."

Katy was beginning to get the picture. "Mother? Father?"

"My father died three years ago, but my mother is living, and she has six grandchildren and a private girl's school to run, so she is content."

"There are enough wealthy families here in Ensenada to support a private school?"

He closed his mouth around another bite and silently shook his head, asking for a moment while he swallowed. With a quick swipe of his napkin, he explained. "It is private so that she can do as she pleases. My mother is determined to educate poor girls through high school and, when she finds the exceptional student, into college. She has this huge old limousine that she bought, or stole, from some deposed South American dictator—it has bullet holes on the driver's side, which she refuses to have repaired, and she has a driver, Marco. Every morning at five a.m. he waits at several assigned places and then drives them to the school where they get a hot meal and a decent education."

"Indians too?" she asked, remembering the Indian children begging with their mother near the fish market in town.

"When my mother can browbeat the parents into allowing them away from the fields. When you were at Baja Naval, did you meet Roxanna? She's the bookkeeper in the office."

Katy remembered the marina office receptionist. A self-confident young woman with flashing almond-shaped dark eyes and a humorous mouth. Roxanna was the one who called Raul for her. and getting no satisfaction, gave the phone a slam-dunk back onto its cradle. Yes, she did have the look of the local Indians.

"The revolution here was about the old land grants that had been gifted in the millions of acres and held for centuries by absentee owners who seldom lived here. The revolution threw out the charters and divided the land up into smaller family plots and gave a voice to the Mestizo—the people who are Indian and Spanish. The condition, that the property had to be improved in fifty years or it would revert to the government and be sold, meant corruption, theft and in some cases murder, where land, especially attractive seaside property, was acquired so that developers could make a profit."

"I have a friend who is Mexican-American," Katy said. "She bought a condo in Puerto Vallarta, only to have it repeatedly on her. Something about the land being stolen from the poor? She got a Mexican judge to reverse the order, but it's still dragging through the court."

"Yes, the developers pay off the lawyers and the poor are left with some rocky acreage up in the hills as recompense. Change comes hard to Mexico."

Katy, replete from the good wine and delicious lasagna, quietly asked, "Why does the parrot have no feathers, Raul?"

"Parrots develop a life-long devotion to a mate of their species or an owner. And if their mate, or in this case, owner, dies—they grieve and drop their feathers. My sisters say I am mad to keep him. But I thought if I kept him with me that someday he would recover and they will grow again."

She turned the wine glass around, wondering if Raul had recovered yet. "It must be terribly painful to come home and hear your wife's voice calling to you. Does he do that '*Dinner, sweetheart*' every night?"

He sighed and stood up. Stacking the dishes onto a nearby wheeled butler's trolley, he said, "Come and sit on the couch with me."

Katy settled next to Raul on the big comfortable cushions of the sofa. He sat a little farther away than she would have liked, but he stretched an arm across the back of the sofa and lightly stroked her shoulder then let his hand fall away as he began his story.

"My dead wife's voice, the laughter of my children—my daily penance, my monthly scourging and my annual sacrifice, such as it is, for their deaths."

Katy waited for him to continue as the seconds turned into minutes.

"I was a lawyer then. I got my law degree in the U.S. as my father wanted me to, married to a good girl from a good family and we had two young sons. I was representing Ford Motors in *La Ciudad*, as we call Mexico City. Ensenada was considered a haven away from places like Mexico City, which was, and still is, the world capital for kidnappings. So, what did I have to worry about? You've seen the gate and wall outside? It was built after they were murdered, so I don't know why I bothered—I was too late. The house was a design of my father's and he had it built as a wedding gift to us. I loved this house once, but I don't see it anymore... do you understand what I mean?"

"I think I do."

"There had been some problems with what I thought of as the local bad boys smuggling marijuana into the U.S. but my wife was uneasy. She noticed that several homes here on the mountain had been bought by strangers and there were parties and cars coming and going all hours of the night. We had servants, but I hired a guard to watch my family and check incoming visitors.

"One evening, my wife and sons were on the patio next to the house, where the boys liked to play. My sons, I'm told, heard popping sounds, and thinking it fireworks, went to see. The bullets hit my older son first. When my wife screamed and ran for him, more bullets hit her, then my youngest. The servants, to their own peril, dragged them behind the house to safety, but it was too late. I flew home on a friend's private jet…."

"Raul… I…."

"The shooters, the killers, were never found. As well as my family, the police found the occupants of the house next door murdered. I had that house, and all the other houses on this mountain burned to the ground.

"When I finally accepted that the killers were never going to be brought to justice, I became a federal agent for the Mexican government. At first I worked only in Mexico City, but our federal government, even with a more progressive president, had no hope of stanching the bleeding that has become part of this country with the cartels. So, I came home to be close to my family again, and now I work for El Presidente and report on the cartels' activities from Ensenada."

"That's all very dangerous work."

"I did say penance, didn't I? And I have the parrot, his name is Sal Mineo, we call him Mineo. I see my family more often now, and they are very patient with me. I have to tell you something that will amuse you. When I asked my sister to fix dinner for two she was ecstatic. Of course, tomorrow I will have to repay her with information. She will want to meet you. They all will."

Katy thought back to their first dinner out and his comment that he'd have to report in to his family the next day. As wonderful as the house was, it was obvious to her that it had become a mausoleum for the man and parrot.

She looked down at his hands, at the gold wedding band on his left hand. "You date, but not here in Ensenada."

He touched the ring and said, "It doesn't do much to thwart the ambitions of the local matrons with eligible daughters, but until now I have not had a reason to remove it." He searched her face for understanding. "I have friends and another home in Puerto Vallarta, Katrina, but no one woman that I truly care for."

Taking all this in, Katy was at first amazed that she didn't see it from the beginning. But then, she'd been too busy handling Gabe's problems, and the investigation, and Raul… that was why… and every time she thought she saw something in his eyes that matched hers… she'd been right the first time, she just didn't want to think she was falling for a married man. But the attraction between them *was* real.

She shook her head and laughed, startling him. "Aren't we a pair? You, a grieving widower, and me, limping down to Mexico where I can hide from the fact that my fiancé dumped me and my job with the San Francisco police department may just be in the toilet."

"He dumped you? You are no longer engaged to be married? I read the San Francisco newspaper notice of your engagement. You were to be married in a month."

"I was actually relieved. But Raul, where do you think this could go, this attraction for each other? Certainly nowhere else but this room, and your wife and children live here still, and will, as long as you have that parrot. And if that isn't enough, you're hoping to catch the men who killed your family. What do you want from me, Raul?"

He looked from her eyes to her mouth and back again, memorizing her face for when she was gone again. "Is it not enough that I fight with myself to keep from coming to you at all hours because I can't bear to stay away? I'll tell you what I want," he said, moving closer to her. "I want to be with you, for as long as you want to be with me. For a day or a lifetime. What do we have to lose, Katrina Hunter?"

She opened her mouth to answer then closed it, and unable to speak she reached out and put a hand on his cheek. He covered her hand with his own, turned it palm up and ran a forefinger lightly along the crease next to her palm. "This is your lifeline, *cara mia*, it is yours to do with as you please. No one but you can choose. So, choose, Katrina."

And that was when she heard a raspy voice calling, "*Oigame! Tengo sueños.*"

"We're keeping him awake?"

Raul sighed and looked at his watch. "Mineo's bedtime. And if we don't shut up soon, he'll—"

"Tengo sueños!"

"—keep it up until we do shut up." Raul stood, drawing her into an embrace. "Perhaps I have been too blunt and you need to consider? I have said what I want, but I don't know if I can stand the rejection—not tonight."

She raised her face to his. "The answer is yes, but surely not here?"

Raul smiled, his eyes crinkling at the corners as he brought his mouth down onto hers for a long deep kiss and then pulled back."We keep an apartment for guests and clients at the winery. No one will be there tonight but us."

She looked at him and nodded. If tonight was all they had, she'd gladly take it.

They said little on the short ride over the mountains to where a wide valley opened up under the clear moonlit night. He drove with one hand, the other folded over hers as if reluctant to miss out on one single moment of their time together.

Following a dirt road between vineyards, she saw a cluster of outbuildings in the distance. Raul drove up to an iron gate ornately decorated with vines and grapes and an overhead arch with words stamped out in metal. "It's too dark to see now, but it says Angelita Winery," Raul said, releasing her hand long enough to punch in the numbers that made the gate swing open and drive through.

He punched the gas, and without waiting to see the gate close behind them, pulled into a cobblestone yard next to a huge barn.

He got out, came around to her side and offered her his hand. When she slid out of the car, her nostrils immediately flared to the scent of hay, horses, old oak barrels, grapes and the simple singular note of new wine.

Raul unlocked a door and asked her to wait. Soon the seams of the barn leaked a warm light from within and she heard a sound as the big barn doors slid open on motorized tracks. The place was enormous, with barrels and wooden crates and tractors and forklifts.

He led her down the center and then upstairs to another level, turning off the lower lights as he pulled her into a darkened room. He hit a switch by the door and recessed lighting showed a fully furnished and very masculine apartment. The walls were of a natural seasoned and grayed wood, the furniture dark brown leather couch, loveseat and a club chair and tables. Against one wall was an entertainment center and on the opposite side of the room was a compact kitchen with granite countertops and stainless stove, dishwasher and fridge.

"This is lovely."

"Thank you. It's better than anything Ensenada has to offer when clients fly in, and besides, it keeps negotiations here at the winery."

He stepped around a bar and brought out two wine glasses and a couple of bottles. "Last year's Barbera is very good, or would you rather have the chardonnay?"

"The Barbera, please, but first, your bathroom?"

He nodded towards a door to her right. "The switch is on your left." Then he smiled silently and dug the opener into the cork.

Katy opened the door, hit the switch and gasped. She had opened the door not on a bathroom, but a large bedroom with more recessed lighting and French doors that opened onto a second-story veranda. There were no window coverings to mar all the moonlight flooding into the room. She walked over to them and opened one, breathing in the night smells of the winery, then turned back into the room and walked over to the king-sized bed where she pulled back the spread.

She used the master bath and returned to the living room, where Raul was waiting for her with a glass.

He touched the rim of his glass to hers, sending a tinkle of a two-note song into her heart. "To new beginnings."

She took a sip, nodded her approval, then put it down on the bar, and taking his hand said, "The moonlight won't wait all night, Raul."

He kissed her lightly on the lips then drew back, his expression searching as he scanned her face for doubt.

She raised her chin and leveled her eyes to match his expression, then broke into a grin. "I have no doubts about tonight, Raul. Now, please take me to bed."

He smiled warmly and arm in arm they walked through the door and into the bedroom.

Chapter Twenty

The short ride back to the marina was quiet until he drove under the portico at the hotel.

"I admit I saw your police connections as a bonus and I am grateful that you have discovered another suspect in Wallace Howard." He got out, went around to her side and opened her door, offering a hand out. Still holding her hands in his, he said, "But now I would like for you to move your boat back to Baja Naval, have your boat prepared for shipping."

"But…" She was confused by his willingness to let her go.

"I want you away from here, not away from me," he said, gesturing towards the darkened marina where yachts quietly lined the docks. "Leaving this marina will send them all a message. The case is closed and you are no longer a threat."

"Then you do think one of the people here killed the girl, and not Spencer?" She tried to pull her hands away, but he held on.

He pulled her into his arms and kissing her forehead, said, "The case is now too close to the Mexican cartel, and they have spidery tentacles into every facet of our government and I won't have you subjected to even the tiniest bit of their interest. Besides, you and I need a real vacation. I do not keep talking parrots in my home in Puerto Vallarta. Will you consider it?"

"What about Gabe?"

"Gabe can have a bus or plane ticket to anywhere he wants," he said, kissing her cheek and then capturing her mouth for one last hungry kiss.

She was abruptly dropped back into the moment when Raul said, "Perhaps you will have an answer for me when you arrive in Baja Naval."

"Yes," she said, planting one last quick kiss on his mouth. She started to turn away, but Raul caught her hand, lifted it to his lips and said, "*Nunca que las sombras olvidaron mis mentes.*" She smiled at the promise and turned away to head back to her darkened boat.

The literal translation to his comment was *Never will the shade cover my memories*, but it really meant that no matter what her decision, he would never forget her.

Walking along the marina fence in the warm moonlight, she let her hand drift over a recently trimmed privet hedge until she came upon a single red geranium sticking up like a revolutionary flag above the tightly sculpted greenery. The Mexicans saw what others missed; the importance of beauty and color and life to the otherwise bland green hedge. It reminded her about what was best in the Mexican people, their generosity to the less fortunate, their courage and heartfelt love of country. This was what Raul was talking about, why he felt so ashamed that the cartels had enveloped the land in a dismal shroud of pain and suffering and no one, least of all him, seemed to be able to do anything about it.

At her gate, she noticed a bundle of rags, probably old clothes left for the dock boys, and put out a foot to toe it aside, but recoiled when it moaned and said her name.

She squatted down next to him. "Gabe? What the hell...." There was a whiff of alcohol and the vomit that comes before passing out in the street. "Good grief! Can't you show some restraint?"

"Some—somebody sandbagged me."

"Here?"

"Depends. Where am I?"

"You're at the gate of my marina. It's three a.m."

"Guess the bar closed without me... ugh. Help me up, will ya?"

She pulled him to his feet and with his arm anchored across her shoulder, she turned for her boat. "Try not to make any noise till we get back on board."

They lurched in the direction of her boat slip, Gabe groaning with each step.

"Can you try not to do that?"

"They kicked me in the ribs. I think one's broken."

Shocked, she started to question him, then hoisted his arm up higher and in a few more steps they reached her boat.

She gave him a push up into the cockpit, but as he rolled over the side, she heard a feminine squeal.

Gabe cursed and growled something and then she heard him say, "What the hell—Leila?"

Katy scrambled in after him, hit the cockpit light and confirmed her worst nightmare.

There was just enough light for her to see her sister, her long straight blond hair bunched up on one side of her head , hands on her hips, staring open-mouthed and obviously surprised at the sight of Gabe Alexander with Katy.

"I can't believe this! You and Gabe?" Her voice was scratchy, her eyes heavy from sleep.

Gabe held onto his head and watched the two sisters out of bleary eyes. "Katy, you got any whiskey?"

"Shut up, Gabe. Leila, please, let's take this downstairs and I promise, I'll tell you everything."

Inside her boat, she reached into her fridge and tossed Gabe a package of frozen peas. "This is my last bag of frozen peas, and no to the whiskey. I need you clear-headed."

He gingerly held the package of peas to the back of his head. "Gonna be a lump the size of Kansas."

Leila glanced from one to the other. "I thought I'd come down and give you a nice surprise. Poor thing, all alone in Mexico, so down on yourself at losing David to Karen Wilke. But I see I was off base—again."

Katy lit the stove and started the kettle. "Leila, honey, this isn't a good time."

"Oh yeah? Looks like fun and games to me." She squinted at her sister and said, "You still got the hots for Gabe Alexander, after all, huh?"

Gabe squinted up at the sisters. "Who's David?"

"Shut up, Gabe. Leila, just... just sit on it for a few minutes, will you?" She handed out mugs of hot water and tea bags and three ibuprofen to Gabe. "Gabe, take the pills with the tea and tell me what happened."

"I went to Antonio's." He blew at the steam on his mug and smiled shyly at Katy's sister. "Nice to see you again, Leila. You're looking beautiful as ever."

Katy tapped him on his head. "Not the time, Gabe."

"Ow. Okay, okay. I went there 'cause one of the trailer guys said a girl from Antonio's was looking for me." Gabe, unable to forgo a chance to embellish his adventures, turned his attention to Leila. "All of them are illegals, Leila. They come from all over the southern continent, even a Russian girl last week, though she's already gone. Someone comes in the night, picks them up and they disappear into some house of horrors in New York City. You can bet she won't be coming back this way again."

Leila gasped, both repulsed and entranced by his story."White slavers? Oh, my God, go on...."

Katy growled, "Get to it, will you, Gabe?"

"Don't nag," he said. He tossed back the three tablets with a swallow of the tea and continued. "If they try to form friendships the bosses break it up. See, two or more could work up the nerve where one may not be brave enough."

"To escape?" Leila squeaked. "That's horrible! Can't anyone break it up?"

"Bosses don't have to worry about that." Gabe straightened and then grimaced at the ribs. "The cops here all get a cut of the take."

Leila scowled. "That's despicable. Ensenada's only a few hours from the border."

He looked at her through bleary eyes. "They have stash houses full of girls just across the border in Tijuana. Bet your Vignaroli knows all about it."

Leila turned on her sister. "*Your* Vignaroli? Who's... ?"

"Later. I promise."

Katy wasn't about to tell Leila about her romantic evening with Raul, at least not until they were alone. "What happened after you got to Antonio's?"

"Bartender said my beer was on the house so I sat down and drank it. I wasn't drunk, I just couldn't seem to move."

Katy groaned. "Roofies."

"Oh shit," he said, rubbing the back of his neck. "You mean they had their way with me and I never knew it?"

"Very funny. Anything else?"

"It was all hazy after the drink. Damn. Why'd they have to hit me?" he asked, gingerly testing the lump on this head.

Katy moved the frozen peas up a notch. "They were probably worried you'd come around and put up a fight."

Leila was anxiously eyeing Gabe's pain-filled eyes. "What about his ribs, shouldn't he see a doctor, get them taped or something?"

Katy inwardly groaned. She really had to explain Gabe to Leila, but not until they were alone. "They don't do that anymore. It inhibits the breathing and can bring on pneumonia. The ribs will heal as they are. I've had a few broken ones myself, and though it's no picnic, I can concur that the new method is for the best." She reached into the overhead cabinet and pulled out several extra pillows, a sheet and a blanket.

"You'll breathe easier and sleep better if you use all the pillows. The settee is yours for the night, Gabe."

"How's the kitten doing?"

"She's fine," she said, motioning her sister up the steps. "Now go to sleep, Gabe. We'll sort this out in the morning."

Gabe flopped over onto his side, grimaced, sighed and closed his eyes.

Topside, Katy settled in to tell her sister everything, but Leila, always the first to jump into any argument, beat her to it.

"What kind of a place is this? I came down here thinking we were going to sun ourselves on the veranda of the hotel, and you're here with Gabe Alexander? No, no, don't tell me. I'll get to him later. What's going on with the white slavery? And, who's Vignaroli? The way Gabe said the name makes me think it's a cop. Am I right? What's up with that?"

Katy took another sip of her tea, hoping to find a place to start. "Please, let me start at the beginning. Then if you still have questions, I'll answer them."

Twenty minutes later, all but two of Leila's questions were answered.

"The producers at *All My Tomorrows* would kill for this story. You and Gabe. How he talked you into running with him then pushed you out of your own car and made off for Canada? Better than anything we've got for plot, that's for sure. They die in a horrible fire, tragic car accident, no body to recover, then come back two years later with a new face. Course it's a different actor, but the fans don't care. So, what's with you and this inspector Vignaroli? And if Spencer Bobbitt… that's a great last name, I don't suppose his wife's name is Lorena, is it?"

Katy refused to add any more fodder to her sister's growing admiration of the circus she was living right now. "Never mind that. As for Raul, I haven't had the time to think it through yet."

"Huh. That why I got my signals mixed. You had that satiated look of a woman who'd just been successfully bedded, but you were with Gabe. You're sleeping with Raul—great name by the way—aren't you?"

"With Raul? Tonight was our first. I don't know where it's going, or if it's going. It isn't a good time for you to be here, either."

"Are you trucking the boat home, or are you going to sail her on her little bottom?"

"I'm moving the boat tomorrow to the downtown working marina and from there I'll make arrangements to have her trucked home. Raul is sure that whoever is behind the murders will consider me out of the game."

"But are you? Off the case, I mean?"

She sighed. "Yes, I think so. He's not going to hold Gabe, so there's no real reason for me to stay. Now, if you don't mind bunking with me, I really need to get some sleep."

"Sure. This is way cooler than anything I imagined for a vacation."

Katy woke to strings of light playing across the walls and floor and a cool breeze coming through the portholes. She wiggled her toes, stretched and momentarily digressed into a childhood game of 'where am I?' but instead of a ten-year-old's daydream of India and elephants, her nose smelled diesel, and there was the strange buzz-sawing coming from somewhere. Rolling over, she came face to face with her sleeping sister, the kitten curled up on the end of her bunk, the striped tail covering most of her face, except where one eye was carefully watching her. Katy sat up, put out a hand and stroked the orange fur, and after a few soft strokes it purred a strange, if somewhat musical, accompaniment to Gabe's snoring.

She quietly edged down to the bottom of the bunk, got dressed, and carrying her sandals, tiptoed past Gabe, his arm dangling off the settee. She picked up the wet package of soggy peas he'd used on his injured head and dumped it in the trash bin under the sink and put on the coffee. None of which seemed to bother Gabe or Leila.

She took her coffee and went up the stairs to nestle into the cushions of her cockpit. If she were in San Francisco, she'd be following autumn leaves cartwheeling down Sacramento Street to her favorite coffee shop. In her fantasy, she still had her job and it was the weekend and her engagement to David was now only a shadowy memory, but she had someone special in her life, someone who meant the world to her, someone darkly handsome whose rumbling voice woke her in the mornings with—

"You're up early." Gabe, his hair looking like the barbed wire contraption had nested on his head and his eyes red and swollen and crusty from sleep and the drugs he'd tossed back with his beer last night. He held up his cup. "I'd join you if I knew where to find the coffee pot."

"Small pot, blinking red light on the machine. Or just follow your nose, Gabe." And as an afterthought, said, "Stay below. I'd rather keep you a secret for a few more hours. At least until I talk to Raul."

He shrugged and disappeared. Having lost her connection to a happier early morning fantasy, she followed him below. He was slumped down on the settee, yawning into his mug of coffee. Shirtless, he still had on his khaki shorts from the night before.

"How're the ribs?"

"Not so bad," he said, gingerly pressing his bruised side.

"Remember anything else?"

"Not yet. With Spencer arrested for the girl's murder, you going home?"

"Yes. I'm moving the boat to Baja Naval today and Raul will give you a plane or bus ticket to anywhere you want."

He was ignoring the kitten cleaning herself as she sat next to him on the settee.

"The very reason I don't have pets," she said. "You could douse yourself with kerosene and juggle flaming torches and that cat would go on licking her butt."

"Oh, I don't know," he said. "Bet if I added a kitty toy to the juggling I'd get her attention. Listen, I've been thinking…."

The cell phone in her pants pocket vibrated. She pulled it out and saw she had a text message.

She paled and then said, "When Leila wakes, tell her to stay on the boat and I'll check in with her later."

"You want me to help you move the boat to Baja Naval?"

"Leila will do it, but stay put until I get back, okay?"

"Your sister sails, too?"

"Of course she does. Don't you remember? *Pilgrim* was Dad's boat. Leila and I both grew up sailing with him."

"Then it's not yours?"

"It's mine and Leila's, want to check the documentation, ask Leila. Now please, don't go topside and *don't* talk to anyone on the dock. Can you do that?"

"Where're you going?"

"I've been summoned to an interview by the great Spencer Bobbitt," she said, grabbing her sunglasses and handbag.

As she walked by *Consolation Prize*, Ida Howard popped out of her boat, waved a dish rag at her and scrambled down the rickety wooden steps.

Breathlessly, she said, "I understand they've arrested Spencer for the murder of that young woman."

"That's what I hear. I'm leaving soon, but Myne could use a friend about now."

"Would putting a stake through her heart help?" The older woman huffed out a laugh. "Oh, come off it, Katy, surely you know she's a blood-sucking little vampire, but I suppose if Spencer's going to prison she'll climb into some other man's wallet and that will be the last we see of *her*."

"Do you think he did it, then? Murdered the girl?"

"Of course he did. That the police were stymied by the absence of his gun has been resolved, hasn't it?"

Katy's antenna went up. "A gun? I didn't think the police said anything about a gun."

Ida tossed her gray bobbed hair and sniffed. "Gossip, I suppose, but you'd know, wouldn't you—working with the police chief on the investigation?"

Katy decided to forgo the game playing. "Yes. An anonymous caller told them were to find it."

Ida swiveled around to stare at the rocky path cutting a line in the sandstone up and over the ditch. "Well, then... done and as it should be."

Katy examined the other woman's response with interest. She hadn't told Ida where the gun was found. "And what do you know about the murder, Ida?"

"I know that with Spencer in jail, Wallace and I might have a chance."

"Want to explain?"

"Let's not pretend you don't know about Spencer transporting stolen case-goods to Mexico. At first they offered a deal to Spencer, but now that he's in jail for murder, the FBI will choose Wallace instead."

"That's great, but it's also a terrific motive for murder, Ida."

Ida sucked in a breath. "Yes, we wanted the FBI deal. If anyone deserves a break it's Wallace, not that devil. He's dragged us along with his nasty business deals until it was too late to get out, but Wallace would never resort to murder!"

"Then what about Booth? It appears you were the one who plied him with rum the night he either walked off the dock—or was pushed."

"Why would we do that? Granted, Booth was Spencer's evil little minion, always procuring girls for the man, but kill him... no. And as for plying him with drink, the man could put away a fifth a day and not stagger, no help was needed in that department."

"But add that to the heroin he was consuming and it could have been a lethal combination."

"And Wallace has a lethal heart condition, but that doesn't stop *him* from drinking. Look around you—there's nothing else to do down here. Oh, wait, I forgot, they can eyeball Spencer's mistress, not that it will do them any good. She's not for the likes of anyone without cash. So, pardon me if I show no sympathy to Spencer's whore, but neither of us killed that girl or Booth. You want to look into Fred, he's the one with motive."

"How's that?"

"Fred was angry enough to frame him for the murder."

"What's Fred's beef with Spencer?"

"He's certain Spencer is holding his daughter prisoner. Idiot man. The silly girl doesn't want anything to do with a respectable father, and why should she, when all she has to do is lay on her back to get a paycheck."

That explained a lot of things: The empty bottle of Scotch and Myne saying her earlier night time visitor wasn't able to do her any good. Fred must've bribed Jeff with better wages to show Myne that Jeff's interest was only where the money was, not her. Poor Myne. Then there was Wally begging Myne to come with him. Poor Ida.

"Then Fred's not associated with Spencer, that is, other than trying to get his daughter away from him?"

Ida shrugged. "I've never seen him before we got here. If my husband had kept to what he knows, instead of attempting to get one over on Spencer Bobbitt, we wouldn't be in the mess we are today. And no, I don't know anything else about Fred McGee, I've got my hands full with keeping my husband out of trouble."

Katy turned to walk away.

Ida called after her, "Then you'll tell that Mexican police chief that we're not to be pestered anymore, won't you? We'll be escorted back to the States soon."

Another person asking for reassurance that was not hers to give. Katy shook her head. "I really have no influence here, Ida. The Mexican police do so as they see fit with or without my advice."

Ida was clutching at straws. She had to know that her husband wanted Myne instead of her. Was Ida the one who tried to tie up a sleeping Myne? Ida was a hefty woman and hadn't she dead-lifted that anchor? She could easily pick up Myne and toss her over her shoulder, then into the sea. Booth was small for a man, and except for his belly, he probably weighed only a few pounds more than Myne. But was Ida capable of shooting a young girl in cold blood to save a husband who didn't want her?

Moving down the dock, Katy could feel the woman's eyes boring a hole in her back.

Chapter Twenty-one

The usual assortment of wives, mothers and relatives at the police station had been replaced with hard-eyed young men in military riot gear, helmets and automatic rifles across their laps. Phones rang, instructions were shouted across the room and police scurried in and out of offices.

Katy waited by the door until she found a familiar face. Sergeant Moreno, his head down, shambled past without looking. Sweat stained the underarms of his shirt and the tight crease of his uniform pants had long since been destroyed. The sergeant blinked at her greeting, then gave her a weary smile.

"Ah, Señorita Hunter! I did not see you."

The feeling was mutual. She would never have recognized this rumpled, tired version from the Hollywood wanna-be of a week ago.

In Spanish she asked, "Is the chief in?"

"Oh, no, señorita. The *jefe* is away. Please, you must leave, we are *muy* busy." The sergeant must be very distressed to allow his near perfect American English to slide.

"When will he be back?"

He shrugged, already signaling to someone over her shoulder. "If you will excuse me, I must get back to my men."

She followed his glance to what appeared to be a SWAT team filing through the entrance. "What's going on?"

The sergeant chewed on the end of his black mustache while he considered. "There was an incident in El Sauzal."

"El Sauzal?" They'd passed a sign for the small community where Raul's home perched on a hilltop. "What happened?"

The sergeant pursed his lips and scratched wearily at his thick dark hair. "You are an American policewoman so you know that I cannot tell you much, but—the *jefe's*… someone set a bomb at his house. It is completely gone now."

Katy felt as if the bottom of the floor had fallen out from under her feet. She grabbed onto the sergeant's arm. In the shock of the moment, her emotions spread across her face. "Is he… is the chief okay? Please, can you tell me?"

"I cannot say, señorita. Please, you must leave now," he said, pulling her hand off his sleeve.

He couldn't be dead! He was with *her* last night at the winery. A wonderful moonlit night filled with the kind of lovemaking she'd always dreamed about and he didn't bring her back to the marina until almost three a.m. where she found Gabe, beaten and dropped at her gate.

But Gabe's beating wouldn't compare to Raul being murdered in his bed. No, this couldn't be happening, not now.

Then she thought of Spencer Bobbitt and her heart sank. That devil! This was his doing, she just knew it. She pulled out her business card, the one with her police ID on it, and handed it to the sergeant. "Please call me the minute you can tell me more?"

The sergeant pulled his eyes away from the army boys, took the card and slipped it into a breast pocket, then snagged a passing officer, but before he left, he patted the shirt pocket over his heart to show that he wouldn't forget, and then handed her off to the jailer.

Katy allowed herself a slight smile at the sergeant's kindness, even in the midst of a crisis like this one. Oh God, please let him be alive, and she followed behind the officer up the elevator to the prisoner's visiting room

At the end of the hallway, a guard stood and let her into a small side room with no windows. She sat down in one of two beat-up and filthy plastic chairs and stared at the bilious green and pockmarked walls.

She spent the time waiting to calm and clear her agitated mind. It would do no good to appear weak or weepy in front of Spencer Bobbitt.

Ten minutes later the door opened and Spencer sauntered through the door, his graying blond hair slicked back on his thin face.

"I got your message," she said, trying to keep the edge out of her voice. "You wanted to talk?"

"I do, but have you seen Myne this morning? She's supposed to bring me food every day, not just when she feels like it. I pay for a private cell or I'd have three other lice-infested wetbacks for roommates," he said, taking a chair across from her.

"I'm sure the *wetbacks* would prefer you have your own cell, too."

"I give her one simple job to do... she's probably sunning herself on the deck and painting her damn toenails."

"I'd think you'd be more worried about getting off a murder charge than about the whereabouts of your mistress."

He turned his head to stare at her; the effect was like having a large lizard turn its disinterested eyes on a potential meal. "That's being handled."

"You mean the deal you thought you had with the feds?"

He slouched down in his chair, arms folded, now relaxed and sure of himself.

"You have quite the arsenal of toadies at your disposal, Spencer, but the feds have picked someone else to testify, so you get to stay in a nice Mexican jail until they decide they have the resources to prosecute you."

Spencer hung an arm over his chair and said, "I'm innocent."

She wasn't about to give him an inch, not when she was sure he was behind the plot to murder Raul. "You had the chief inspector's home blown up last night, didn't you?"

"It's sad, but I ran out of options when I needed them most. Which brings me to you. I think I can make you an offer you won't be able to refuse."

There it was again. That eerie similarity to *The Godfather*.

"You're kidding. Do you really think I'd do anything to help you, knowing you murdered Raul Vignaroli? If nothing else, I'll plant some evidence just to make sure you stay in a Mexican prison for the rest of your life."

"It's nice to know that for once my sources were right, you were in love with that annoying policeman. Well, my dear, I have no intention of waiting for the Mexicans to send me to one of their horrid little prisons. I want you to do the one thing no one else has been able to do—get me released from his hell hole."

"Not in a million years."

"Oh come now. It'll be easy. I already have the paperwork for a transfer by an American Marshal to the States. Unfortunately, Raul got wind of it and had him picked up at the Rosarito checkpoint, so you're going to be my safe passage out of this jail."

"Congratulations, Spencer. You've just managed to piss off the last person in Mexico who could possibly help you get out of jail."

He tipped an eyebrow at her. "Touché. And, if I may say so, you have some *cojones* on you for such a little thing. Myne should take lessons." He reached into his pocket and extracted an envelope and handed it to her. "Here is the paperwork. You will notice that your passport is also in there. Go back to your boat, get your police ID and come back here in one hour. I'll be waiting. Don't worry about the Mexican police, they're too busy chasing their tails."

She crossed her arms over her chest and glared at him. "You're out of your mind."

"Oh, did I forget something? Yes, sorry, completely forget to tell you—your sister is now in the hands of my associates. She will be waiting for us at the airport. Unless, of course, you refuse to do as I ask, and then I will have her body bulldozed into a Mexican dump."

"Leila's in L.A."

"No, no. Seems your dear sister was worried about you, flew down to give you moral support. Beautiful girl, your sister. Maybe I'll give her as a thank-you gift to my new Mexican friend, the head of the Sinaloa Cartel. I'm sure he would appreciate a real live American television actress."

Katy closed her eyes. How the hell did this happen? Gabe, Leila. She'd left them both on the boat. Then what happened to Gabe?

"Ah, I see you're considering my offer. Your Gabe was so helpful, led us right to her, good man that he is. Ask anyone, I never forget a favor… or a slight."

She should have anticipated something like this, but it hurt to think Gabe would betray her to Spencer. "I don't believe you."

He reached into his pocket and pulled out a cell phone, punched in a couple of numbers and waited. He spoke into the phone. "Put her on, please?" When he handed the phone to Katy, she gingerly held it by two fingers and away from her head.

"Katrina? Is that you?"

It was Leila.

"Where are you?" she asked quickly and just as quickly the phone was yanked out of her hand and closed.

She pushed back the chair and leaning over him, pointed to the cell phone. "I'll take that."

Spencer smirked, stood up and banged on the door.

She was surprised to see the door swing open so fast. The guard must've been standing outside waiting for instructions.

Spencer nodded at Katy. "She needs to leave, now."

She reached out and made a grab for his cell phone, but Spencer easily held the phone above her outstretched arm.

"Nah, nah, nah—we'll have none of that. I have a steady supply of these little gizmos and this one will be long gone by the time anyone gets around to asking about it. Which, by the way, may be much later than any late night date you might have planned. The Mexican federals are swarming around the bomb site like so many angry bees, looking for clues, and of course, your boyfriend's body."

Raul might still be alive, but the fact that he boasted about the bombing of Raul's home made her anger rise up and she was tempted to smash in his ugly nose.

Spencer simpered and giggled, as if this was all a fun and funny practical joke. "I always wanted to say this," he said, then lowered his voice into a theatrical snarl. "Do as I say and your sister lives. It's so menacing, don't you think? Come now, I don't have all day, so chop-chop."

He exited the room and his guard manhandled her out the door, down the stairs and soon she was standing in the hot sunlight blinking at the foreign landscape. Nothing was the same anymore; not the street vendors with the smell of tacos bubbling in a nearby pot, not the careless motorists speeding by. Her sister had been kidnapped and Raul was probably dead.

The devil incarnate he might be, but he wasn't going to twist Katy Hunter around his finger. She'd get her sister back and then Spencer would rue the day he ever tangled with her.

She wiped at the unshed tears, took out her cell phone and tried Raul's phone again. The line buzzed with a busy signal. She desperately wanted to hear his voice again, to reassure her that he was still alive, still willing to wrap his arms around her and tell her that there was still hope for them. The last honest policeman in Ensenada, and he wasn't going to be able to help her. She snapped the phone shut. Time to go find her sister.

Chapter Twenty-two

All the way back to the marina, Katy continued to try Raul's cell. She hopped out of the taxi, paid the driver and power-walked the distance from the hotel to her marina gate, hoping against hope that Spencer Bobbitt had been lying, or that Gabe had somehow foiled Spencer's henchmen and at this very moment they were sitting in her boat, laughing about high-school antics.

Raul's cell phone finally connected to voicemail. Breathless, she slowed her pace and with the minimum of details told him what she was doing and where he could expect to find her within the next hour. It might be nothing more than wishful thinking, but it still gave her a sense of hope. If Raul Vignaroli was still alive, he would come for her, she knew it.

She clicked the cell phone closed and willed him to call her back, then hurried through the gate and ran for the boat. It was empty, the hatch board out, the lock hanging off the hasp. Leila's big white sun hat was on the settee, her tea mug still warm on the counter as if she'd just laid it down to answer a knock on the hull. Where was Gabe? Off someplace counting the blood money he got for selling her sister to Spencer? Myne. Could she be in on this with Spencer? Although nothing so far indicated Myne would go along with a kidnapping plot, she might have caved under the pressure from Spencer, especially if the threat came with a promise of some much needed cash.

She ran to Spencer's yacht, pounded on the locked salon door then took the stairs down to the lower level, counting portholes until she came to Myne's room. The room was dark and empty.

Back on top again, she looked across the marina parking lot and saw Gabe casually sauntering through the parking lot as he made his way to her gate. She ran down the dock and opened the gate.

"Uh, hi," he said, showing her a pack of cigarettes. "I know you told me not to leave, but Leila was out, too and…what's wrong?"

"Where's Leila, you bastard!"

"Whoa," he said, putting up his hands to wave at her anger. "What're you talking about?"

"You sold my sister to Spencer so I'd get him out of jail," she said, grabbing his left thumb and forcing his arm behind his back and up to his scapula.

"Owww! Quit that! Good God, Katy. What the hell are you talking about? Where's Raul?"

"Like you didn't know. Spencer had Raul's home blown up to create a diversion for his escape."

She was listening to him grunt and swear and make excuses for himself and… "What did you say?"

"I *said*, she asked for cigarettes and I went back to my trailer to get some. Katy, please, you know me, I wouldn't hurt a hair on Leila's head."

She let go of his thumb and turned him around to face her. The only thing on his face was worry, not guilt.

"Come on," she said, "I'll apologize later, after *you* help me find my sister."

Inside the boat, she gathered her police ID and the Glock she had taped under a floor board. She shrugged off Gabe's stuttered amazement that she dared to stash a weapon on her boat. "If it comes to killing the bastard to get my sister back, I'll deal with the charges later."

"Fire extinguishers and baseball bats be damned, huh? You sure have grown up, Katy. So what's next?"

"The police station was crawling with federal police looking for evidence at Raul's home. I don't have time to wait for help. It's you and me, Gabe."

"I'm in, you know I am. Tell me what you want me to do."

Katy was thinking she was going to need someone at the airport for backup. "Have you got access to a car? Someone you can borrow one from?"

"Not today. All the guys are at jobs."

"Fred's got a car, we'll ask him."

"But isn't he still on the inspector's list of suspects?"

She thought back to her partner's comments that Fred was an IRS agent. Then finding out that he was Myne and Astrid's dad made up her mind. "It's time I found out who I can trust and right now I need the help."

Gabe followed her to Fred's boat.

Astrid, her cheeks red and her face blotchy from crying, motioned them inside and closed the slider. "We were just having a father-daughter talk about Jeff Cook."

Fred stood up when he saw Katy. "What's wrong?"

Choosing her words carefully, she addressed Astrid. "Remember how I told you that sisters don't always do it right? Well, my sister picked yesterday to come down for a visit. Only problem is, Spencer kidnapped her right off my boat while I was on my way to see him in jail. I've been instructed to help him escape or he's going to have her killed."

Astrid gasped.

Fred raked Gabe with his hooded glare. "And where were you when all this happened?"

Gabe shot back, "I was out, picking up cigarettes for Katy's sister."

Katy turned to Gabe. "Even with Gabe off the boat, there are all sorts of people on the dock this time of day. I still don't understand how they could do it. Wait—uniforms, they had to be wearing marina or police uniforms. They could've told her they'd take her to me. Leila wouldn't go more than a few feet without becoming suspicious, asking unwanted questions. She'd want to call me. If they objected… Oh my God." Katy walked out onto the deck of Fred's yacht and they all followed.

She pointed out her boat, measuring off the distance someone would have to go with an unconscious woman over their shoulder, through the gate, to a waiting car.

"She's right here on this dock. Astrid, do you know where Myne is?"

"I'm here, Katy." Katy turned around to see Myne, her long hair wet from a recent shower.

Astrid went to her sister and protectively put her arm around her shoulder. "She wouldn't have anything to do with kidnapping your sister, Katy, she's been here all day."

Myne let out a squeal. "Your sister—Leila? Leila Standiford is here? Where? What's she wearin'? I can't wait to meet her. Oh, Astrid, you won't believe this! Katy's sister's a movie star!"

Astrid looked fondly at her younger sister. "Hon, I think we need to find her first. Seems Spencer had her kidnapped."

"He wouldn't!" Looking from her sister to her dad to Katy and seeing the grim looks on their faces, she said, "That bastard! Does he have any idea who she is?"

Katy said, "My sister would not go willingly with kidnappers. Not after all she's been through."

"She'd kick up a fuss, huh? I knew it. She's as tough as her character on TV."

Katy wasn't about to ruin Myne's hero worship, not when she needed Myne to help her find her sister. "I'm thinking she's still on this dock. Maybe even on Spencer's yacht."

Myne turned her head to look at the long expanse of Spencer's boat and said, "I locked it up before I left, but Jeff still has one."

Katy nodded. "And he would wear his captain's uniform to convince Leila he was the real deal."

Fred said, "Just a minute. I'll be right back."

When he left, the two girls started chattering.

"Daddy was right about him…"

"And to think we both…"

"I'm sorry I didn't listen to you…"

"I'm sorry too…"

Katy held up a hand. "Ladies! Can we leave it for later? My sister's life is hanging on a thread. I have to find her before Spencer has her moved to the airport."

Myne dug into her pocket and came out with her key. With her arms around her sister, she said, "We'll help you find your sister, Katy, it's the least we can do."

"Now girls," said Fred, holding a machete. "If anyone gets to punish that good-for-nothing Jeff, it's going to be me. Then it's Spencer's turn."

"Daddy," Astrid said, "you don't have to go that far. Katy's a policewoman and she knows what to do."

Fred looked down at her from his considerably long nose. "Well, do you? Know what you're doing, Miss Hunter?"

Katy lifted a finger and they all stopped talking. "Myne's got a key. We think my sister is on Spencer's boat."

Gabe touched her arm. "This could go either way, couldn't it?"

"He's counting on the pandemonium at the police station to cover a getaway." She looked at her watch. "We've got thirty minutes, tops. She may have been gagged or drugged and unable to respond. We'll break up and go through every room."

They went in different directions, the girls with their dad and his machete, Katy with Gabe and her Glock. Katy quietly opened doors, went through closets and turned on lights. With time running out, and her search of guest and crew cabins showing nothing, she and Gabe went to the lowest level and to the heavily insulated engine room.

"This would be the perfect place to hide Leila," Katy said, switching on a light. "No one could hear her scream for help."

There was a metal grate walkway down the middle of the room with engines, lockers and work benches on both sides. Katy had Gabe wait by the door at the opposite end of the room as she looked into lockers and under tables. She stepped off the metal grate and wove through the machinery, looking around and under conduits and pipes, softly calling her sister's name.

About twenty feet away, next to some machinery, was a dark shape. She hurried the four yards until she was standing over what she thought might be a body under a pile of rugs. Instead, it was a lumpy pile of oily carpet.

Picking up a corner, she pulled it up—exactly as advertised—two oily old carpets bunched together, but no Leila.

She signaled to Gabe that the carpet didn't have Leila in it.

Then she heard a break in the hum of the air conditioner and a hiccup in the pressurized compartment as the entry door opened.

She waved a warning at Gabe and was relieved to see him quietly slip out the other exit, closing it behind him. She rolled herself under the dirty carpet, holding up a corner so she could peek out.

Two men walked past her narrowed line of sight but all she could see were legs; one with long pants and huaraches and the muscular legs and sailing white shorts of Spencer's boat captain—Jeff, the rat, was her sister's kidnapper and he'd brought someone with him to pick up Spencer's get out of jail prize

A hinge creaked open and the voices faded as they clanged down metal steps. Steps down? She'd completely forgotten about the bilge!

Throwing off the smelly rugs, she scrambled up and removing her shoes, tiptoed over to look down the hole into the bilge. There would be more pumps below, watertight bulkheads against a breach to the hull and a good place hide Leila.

Katy removed her gun from her jacket and quietly took the metal stairs down to what she hoped wasn't her sister's grave.

A Mexican was down on his knees working at the knots of a rope holding the limp body of her sister to a post and Jeff stood by impatiently directing the other man's efforts.

She pointed her Glock at them and shouted, "Stop right there! Put up your hands!"

The two men whirled around. Jeff tensed when he saw the gun then relaxed. "I found this Mexican on the boat and when I questioned him, he admitted to holding this girl for ransom. I convinced him to let her go."

Katy, never letting her gun waver, glanced at the wide-eyed Mexican cowering at the sight of her gun.

Out of the corner of her eye she saw Jeff reach behind him, grab a length of rusty chain and throw it at her legs. She tried to jump out of the way, but a few links caught her ankle, knocking her to the floor. When Jeff made a dive for her gun a large foot kicked it away and out of his reach

She looked up. Gabe. He offered Katy a hand up while Fred stepped around them and planted the tip of his machete at Jeff's forehead. "Give me a reason and I'll gladly slice you in two, you scumbag."

Katy went to her sister and kneeled down. She called over her shoulder to the others. "She's okay!"

Leila was groggy, but awake. She put up a hand to the back of her head and winced. "Where's the bastard that clocked me?"

"He's going to jail; we'll see to that. Now, let's get you out of here, sweetie."

Fred and Gabe tied Jeff's and the Mexican's hands behind their backs and led them off the boat. From the dock, Fred called hotel security and within minutes they were surrounded by guards who took the two men away.

Katy looked from Gabe to Leila and said, "I'm going to the police station. I need to see if anyone can tell me about Raul. Here, Gabe," she said, handing him her Glock. "Tempting as it is, I can't take this into jail with me, and in any case, I'm going to enjoy telling Spencer his plan backfired."

Fred tossed her the keys to his car. "Take my van. It's the gray one by our dock. And give him a swift kick for me?"

She bounced the keys in her hand. "Is Myne the only reason you're interested in Spencer?"

"Officially? I work as an investigator for the IRS. This yacht is just one of the props I used to get closer to Spencer Bobbitt. My sector chief knows our family drama, so he sent me instead of someone else, with the agreement that I'd see if I could find Spencer's hidden assets. Is it true that he planted a bomb at the chief inspector's home?"

"Yes," she said, her voice catching in her throat. "Though nothing's official yet as to whether or not he was in the house at the time."

"I'm sorry to hear that. I understand he was one of the good ones."

"Yes, he is—or was."

"Well, good luck with Spencer, then."

The police station had emptied of most of the officers. Sergeant Moreno was nowhere in sight, and a pimply faced youth sat at the reception desk, obviously uncomfortable at having to answer questions since he didn't know the whereabouts of either the sergeant or anyone else in authority. He was, however, suitably impressed with her American police ID and happily escorted her upstairs to the visitor's room, where he haughtily ordered the jailer to present the prisoner to the American police woman post-haste.

Still worked up from the last hour of drama, she paced the tiny room until at last the door opened and Spencer walked in, his face devoid of expression.

"Perfect. You're here and just in time."

Katy lifted her chin."You're completely out of bargaining chips, Spencer. I found my sister on your boat and Jeff and the Mexican are now in custody."

"I figured as much. Never let a boy do a man's job, I always say." He drew out a gun and pointed it at her. "Which leaves me with you. You're still going to be my ticket out of this God-forsaken country, and if you're a very good girl, maybe I'll ransom you to your wealthy family instead of giving you flying lessons from three thousand feet."

He pounded on the door and when it opened, he was handed a linen jacket which he laid over his gun hand, and pulling another envelope out of his pocket, he handed it to her. "Copies of the paperwork you will need."

Then he motioned the jailer to clip on a pair of metal cuffs, his left wrist to her right hand. With his right hand tucked under the jacket, they took the elevator downstairs.

"You can't possibly think you're going to get away with this."

"Of course I will. The plane is waiting and all you have to do is follow directions."

When they were downstairs, he stood close to her, the gun dimpling her side while she handed the paperwork to the young officer. When the young man gave her a quick look, Spencer lifted their cuffed wrists to show that he was indeed in her custody.

Outside, a taxi pulled up. The driver, seeing the two gringos, waited only long enough to hear the man say airport before popping the clutch and lurching into afternoon traffic. Katy wasn't surprised that he never gave his passengers another look. He was intent on driving two Americans to the airport in a timely and safe fashion, and then getting paid with a nice tip for a job well done.

If only Raul was alive and got her message before she was dropped out at three thousand feet above the Sonoran Desert. Pushing away the sorrow and pain of her loss, she reminded herself that she wasting time. It was up to her to find a way out of this predicament before it was too late.

At the airport, Spencer instructed the driver to take a side road around the small terminal to where a guard waited at a closed gate. At Spencer's nod, the guard opened the gate and let them through. With the gun still at her ribs, Spencer told the driver to aim for a line of private jets lined up at the far end of the tarmac. He shoved a fistful of dollars at the driver and motioned for Katy to open her door.

Katy sighed and did as she was told as there was no sense in taking a stand here where the driver might be shot in the melee.She got out first, Spencer scrambling after her and kicking the door closed. The taxi driver never looked back as he sped off in a cloud of dust. She looked around. Nothing but a line of private jets and this one, the steps down, the pilot at ready, the engines revved up for takeoff.

Now was the time to make her stand. "Unlock the cuffs, Spencer. I'm not getting on that plane with you."

"Oh, I think you will. A simple phone call can connect me with someone to finish the job on your sister."

"You already tried that once and it didn't work. She's now safely surrounded by friends and out of your reach."

Spencer showed her his big teeth. "I still have influence." Then he reached into his pocket and pulling out a key, unlocked the cuffs. "You have a choice; go with me and know that your sister is safe, or take the chance that you can warn her in time."

Glaring at each other, neither of them noticed the black Mercedes speeding up the tarmac.

Raul Vignaroli got out and with his hands up so Spencer could see that he was unarmed, he walked toward them. "Let her go, Spencer!"

Spencer held her in front to act as a shield, and backed up for the steps of the plane/ "Oh, but I have. See?" He held up the handcuff now only attached to his wrist. "She wants to come with me, don't you Katy?"

Katy called a warning to Raul, "He has a gun!"

Raul nodded, keeping his empty hands where Spencer could see them as he continued advancing. "You can leave, but you must let her go."

Spencer backed awkwardly up the steps, dragging Katy along while Raul stood helplessly at the bottom of the steps. At the last minute, Spencer pushed Katy down the steps and ducked inside.

As Raul rushed to break her fall, the jet revved its engines and the steps retracted.

Raul crushed her to his chest, dragging his mouth across her wet cheeks, her eyes and finally her mouth.

She pulled back, her voice shaking with the adrenaline of the last few hours. "Took you long enough." Then she reached up and touched his face. "I thought... I thought you were dead."

They turned to watch the jet ready itself at the end of the runway. "Can't you keep him from taking off?"

"No, I can't stop him without a squadron here to close off the runway and I didn't want to take the chance that you would be on it."

"Then he's just going to get away with everything he's done? Murder, extortion, kidnapping?"

"I don't think Spencer Bobbitt is going to get very far."

They stood together watching the wheels fold as the jet rushed up to meet the thin hot air of Ensenada. There was a part of her that was glad to see the last of Spencer Bobbitt.

As the jet soared up and over the barren hills of Ensenada they heard a popping sound and then the air was rocked by the blast of a tremendous explosion. The jet was now a fireball, metal pieces falling back to the earth.

Katy clutched Raul's arm. "What...?"

In the distance she heard sirens.

"I suspected as much," he said, turning her toward his car. "The Mexican cartels do not like loose ends and Spencer Bobbitt was now more of a liability than an asset."

"Raul, please don't take this the wrong way," she said when she was in the passenger side. "I'm happy to see you and all, but where have you been?"

"I'm sorry, but I had to set up a command post to sort out who had engineered the attack on my home. It was determined that this was not an act of terrorism but a simple attempt on my life by one of Señor Bobbitt's henchmen. And since I survived, the Sinaloan Cartel, being the pragmatic sort that they are, determined that Señor Bobbitt should be eliminated."

In his car, and away from spectators, he drew her into her arms and held her tightly.

She pulled back. "Your home… is it completely gone?"

"Yes," he said, kissing her forehead.

"I'm so sorry. What about the parrot?"

He drew back. "You know, until this moment, I'd completely forgotten about him. Poor thing. I don't suppose—no, once the explosives took the foundation, the entire structure went over the cliff. It's a miracle no one below was hurt as it went down that mountain. The house, the parrot. Do you know something? I believe... yes, I am relieved. I am finally free. That's a good thing. Yes, I believe it will be a very good thing. Would you want to—"

"Yes," she said, holding onto his hand as he drove. "Let's go somewhere. Puerto Vallarta, anywhere."

"What about your sister... and Gabe?"

"My sister... oh dear. Of course. Let me check on them first, okay?"

When they got back to her dock, Leila shouted a greeting from the transom of Fred's boat and ran to meet them.

"Where've you *been*, sis? You've missed all the fun! Gabe makes the best margaritas, and I can't think of a better painkiller for all we've been through." Leila ogled Raul, winked at her sister and put out a bangled hand for him to shake. "I presume this is Chief Inspector Vignaroli? Gabe has told me so much about *you*."

Raul, to his credit, smiled warmly at Leila and taking her hand, lightly kissed her knuckles.

Leila, obviously into her second or third margarita, giggled and rolled her eyes at Katy.

Katy looked at her sister and laughed. "How many of those painkillers have you had?"

"Oh, Katy, don't fuss at me now when I'm finally having fun. Come on," she said, tugging her sister along to Fred's boat.

Gabe and the girls were up on the aft deck.

The girls stood and rushed over to hug Katy, both wanting to thank her and tell her how much they loved, loved, *loved* her sister.

"She's going to introduce me to her acting coach," Myne gushed.

"And I'm going to go back to school. Leila says UCLA is a great school for screenwriters."

Leila shoved a couple of margaritas into their hands and insisted they join them.

Gabe said, "So was Spencer surprised to see you?"

"Well," said Katy, "not exactly." Then she told them all of it. At the end of the story, Leila's face was sober and the girls had stopped giggling.

Katy said, "So Myne, you are really and truly free of Spencer Bobbitt."

Myne nodded. "What about Booth and the girl? Do you think we'll ever find out if Spencer was really guilty of their murders?"

Katy put down her drink. "Has anyone seen Ida Howard today?"

Fred answered. "I took the liberty of announcing to Wally and Ida that they were to be ready for a US Marshal to accompany them back to the States tomorrow."

Katy, knowing that Ida wasn't Wally's first choice of companion, wondered how that was going to play out. Then she thought of something. "Gabe. Remember the night you found the tape?"

"Yeah, and sorry I ever thought to give it to you, since you thought I was responsible for Booth's death."

"Okay, got it, Gabe. But remember you said you came down to the marina because you heard a woman's voice shouting?"

"Yeah, that's right, I was coming down to see if you needed help."

Leila leaned into Gabe. "That was so gallant of you, Gabe. Wasn't that gallant of him to do that, Katy? Isn't he a sweetheart of a guy?"

In another time and place, Leila's antics with Gabe would have come with a lecture. Instead, Katy quietly motioned Raul over to the rail. "Would you do me a favor and check on Wally and Ida?"

He slanted a glance at her then nodded. "Yes, I see what you're thinking. I'll be right back."

When he was gone, she said, "Leila, if you think you'll be okay tonight without me, Raul and I would like to have dinner alone. Then tomorrow we'll move the boat to Baja Naval and get it ready for transport back to the States."

"Sure," said Leila, hearing the note of sadness in her sister. "That's a great idea. Gabe says he knows where he can get fresh oysters. We'll fix dinner on your boat and catch up on old times."

Gabe was signaling behind Leila's back, hoping she wouldn't mention the possibility that Leila's dinner might involve climbing over fences to get those oysters.

Leila pushed Katy for the steps. "Go on, have a night out." She leaned closer and whispered, "Let tomorrow take care of itself. Stay the night. Go for it, you may never get the chance again."

Katy kissed her sister and said, "Watch yourself, sis. Gabe's a dear but he's… well, he's still Gabe."

Katy went to her boat, threw a change of clothes, toothbrush, and her favorite perfume into an oversized purse, swung off the boat and walked the length of the dock to find Raul standing next to Wally and Ida's boat. He was talking to a guard. The guard did an about-face and hustled for the gate.

Raul, his mouth set in a grim line, kept her from going any closer to the boat.

"What is it?" she asked, fearing the worst.

"They are both dead. It looks like she killed him, then herself," he said, handing her the handwritten confession.

"Ida admitted shooting the girl, not because she wanted to frame Spencer, but because it was mistaken identity. She had lifted Wally's keys to Spencer's boat and picked up Spencer's gun meaning to shoot the man who had ruined her life. When the bed covers moved, she fired. Seeing it was a girl and not Spencer, she dropped the gun and ran, not thinking anything other than getting away. She ran into Jeff and Booth and they told her they'd 'fix' it for her. Of course, Jeff has admitted to moving the girl to the RV park and throwing the gun into the arroyo, but he says he didn't know that Booth wasn't going to take her to a hospital."

Katy said, "That's why she told me it was too late. Wally found out what she'd done and told her he would not take her with him into witness protection. He wanted to take Myne, instead, the poor slob."

"He was going to turn her over to the Mexican police, so she killed him and then herself."

"Then Spencer was innocent of killing the girl? He was drugged and slept through all that?"

"The girl might've drugged him with the intention of robbing him before she left. I've spoken to the President, and he's made it his mission to clean up the human trafficking in Ensenada. We're going to close Antonio's."

Katy shook her head sadly. "Then Ida killed Booth to keep him from talking. That's the voice Gabe heard arguing with him the night she pushed him into the water. What are you going to do about their bodies?"

"I have made arrangements. The bodies will be taken off under the disguise of carpentry repairs for the boat."

When she started to object, he said, "This marina, and certainly the hotel, has had enough bad publicity. We try for damage control when we can. You and I are done here."

"You're right, of course. Booth was dying, why would he go to the trouble to blackmail anyone?"

He put a hand on her elbow and gently steered her for the gate and his car in the parking lot. "Booth had a local woman as his wife. In the states you call it common-law. He wanted her to have some money." He stopped and looked at her. "I know you think me heartless that I allowed Booth to have heroin for his illness. But I paid him in cash, too. And I will see that she gets the money from the sale of his trawler."

"That would be very kind."

"Now, no more about these people. I know a place where we can have a simple but hearty dinner and watch the moonlight with a glass of wine."

She put her head on his shoulder and said, "I thought you'd never ask."

Chapter Twenty-three

Raul lay with his arm around Katy, her head on his chest and her bare leg over his while she drew circles in his chest hair. Dawn was limning the eastern slopes in anticipation of another sunny day.

"You're awfully quiet," she said.

He moved his arm out from under her head, pushed up onto the headboard and then drew her into his arms again. "Yesterday, I was offered a position as liaison between our government and your American drug czar."

She pulled away to look him in the eyes. "Are you going to take it?"

"I would have to move to either San Francisco or DC and I was hoping you might help me make a decision."

"You would be away from your family."

"My family will always be here for me. But, most importantly, the house is gone, the parrot is dead, the past is now truly buried. I can start my life again. So do you have an opinion?"

"When do you have to make a decision?"

"This week," he said, lifting his head to look at the streaks of morning light in the east. "Today, actually. I have nothing to take with me, except the few clothes I keep here. Regardless of what city I choose I will be busy traveling between the two and sometimes I will fly to Mexico City to talk with our president. So, Katrina Taylor Hunter, will you help me out here? DC, or San Francisco?"

"It's hard to find an apartment in either of those cities."

He chuckled. "I wasn't fishing for an invitation to live with you. You Americans. You get it all backwards."

"It's freezing cold in DC. You'd hate it."

"And San Francisco is warmer?"

"Oh, much, much warmer."

"I will call the Mexican Consulate then. They will provide me temporary quarters until I can find something that suits me."

"San Francisco is small, easy to get around. I'll take you sailing."

"We will date. I will court you. Meet your mother as you will meet mine. Do you like baseball, the opera?"

"Is the pope Catholic?"

"I will get season tickets for us, then."

"Good luck with that," she said, nibbling on his chin.

He chuckled at the tickling. "It shouldn't be impossible."

"Oh yeah? What else you going to do for me?"

"I will love you. And in time, if you see that my love and devotion for you is what you want to live with, then we will marry."

"Oh boy. That's... that's a lot for a girl to think about."

"I am not a frivolous man, Katrina. You've brought fun and humor into my life and when I think of my future, I see us together, for many years to come."

"Then, Raul Vignaroli, you definitely should come live in San Francisco. My mother is going to love you as much as I do."

Raul smiled, kissed her, threw back the sheets and, naked, pulled her onto her feet. "Shower with me and we'll go back to the marina."

"Breakfast in town?" he asked as they approached the fork in the road.

"I should get back to my sister. After everything she's been through, I owe her a nice breakfast at the hotel. Then she'll help me move the boat to Baja Naval."

Outside her gate, he said, "I'll walk with you, say goodbye to your sister and then go to see Gabe."

Gabe. She hadn't given him a moment's thought since last night. As they walked through the gate, Katy thought how different the marina looked now with many of the sport fishermen gone. Soon Fred would leave with his girls, Wally's wreck would be taken out into the bay and sunk, as it could only bring bad luck to anyone who thought to buy it.

And her boat… Wait. Where was her boat?

Katy counted slips, the empty one next to where her thirty-two-foot Westsail was supposed to be berthed.

Slip thirty-two D. Printed in black on the dock box, wasn't it?

Empty. She gaped at Raul, unable to come up with a good reason why her boat wouldn't be there.

As she and Raul tried to speculate on the whereabouts of her boat, a guard trotted up, saluted and handed Raul a note, and an envelope to her. "The man said to give you this letter as soon as you came back this morning, señorita."

Raul scanned the writing on the single page then looked up at Katy. "The parrot, my parrot was saved. Someone found him alive, completely unharmed, sitting by the road outside the gate to my property." His eyes searched hers. A link to his past was back to haunt him. Would he be able to let go and start anew as he'd promised? "My sergeant brought him here to your boat because he thought…. But where is…?"

Katy looked up at him and waved her two-page handwritten letter in front of his face, laughing. "Your parrot has been shanghaied."

"Shanghaied?"

"It's only fitting, you know. Pirates and parrots go together." She scanned the second page and snorted. "Listen. She writes, '*She* only speaks Spanish but it's such a pathetic little thing we thought we'd take her with us, teach her some English. The kitten seems to like her so when our adventure gets us to Puerto Vallarta, I'll take the bird home with me. This girl needs some new feathers and I'm the one to give them to her.'" Katy shook her head. "My sister thinks your bird is a *she*. Oh. That's why... Raul, I told Leila about your parrot, the house, your family. This is Leila's gift to us."

He smiled, the long dimples giving his face a simple joy. "Then she has my blessing."

"I can't believe I didn't see it coming."

"That she would take your boat and my bird?"

"Not that. This has Gabe written all over it and Leila just happened to be ripe for the picking."

"You're not making any sense."

"The sailboat, as my sister Leila likes to remind me, was left to both of us, and Leila is on vacation and Gabe has talked her into taking him with her. I only hope he doesn't convince her to take him back to the states with her."

"Would he do that?"

"Oh, yes, my darling, he would definitely try," she said, reaching out to grab his hand and lead him away. "Let's go have that breakfast you promised me and I'll tell you the whole story."

The End

HURRICANE HOLE, the sequel to *A Dangerous Harbor* on Amazon Kindle, coming September, 2013

Excerpt:

Burdened with the majority of the groceries, Gabe struggled to keep up with his boat captain, the one whose bad mood trailed behind her like black smoke from a busted tail pipe. "Leila, slow down, will you?"

Leila stopped mid-stride, anger rippling across her beautiful features like the scheming vixen she played on *All My Tomorrows*. "I did all the grocery shopping so you could buy some decent clothes, and you come back with a shirt that smells like diesel?"

He lifted the collar and sniffed. "I guess the guy had this batch stowed in the bilge. Did I tell you he's Hawaiian? Sailed all the way from Hawaii in his catamaran."

"And all he had left was the one shirt that screamed *tourist*?"

Gabe squirmed uncomfortably. He looked good in this shirt; he knew he did. The color bought out the aqua in his eyes. He bought it to impress Leila, but attention was the last thing he needed, and they both knew it.

Twenty years ago, he'd scooted across the border into Mexico on a hopeful cloud. Unfortunately, the fluffy stuff was now showing signs of evaporating under his feet. This was Leila's final stop before leaving for the States—which meant he would be left to shift for himself in another backwater Mexican town—unless he could talk her into taking him with her.

"And, while I'm at it," she said, pointing at his long feet hanging over the run-down flip-flops. "I see you forgot the shoes."

"I can always get shoes tomorrow."

With a derisive flutter of her lips, she stomped off toward the ramp where cruiser dinghies were tethered like restless ponies. At the steep incline, she leaned back, and let the card slide down the uneven boards to land safely in front of her dinghy. She smiled, and the famous Leila Standiford dimple momentarily appeared. But her quick smile at the minor triumph soon disappeared.

"This humidity is unbearable," she said, wiping the sweat from her brow. "Isn't it supposed to cool down by the end of October?"

Gabe looked at the bright blue sky reflected on the water. Even with the clouds stacking up on the horizon, it didn't look like they would get a break in the heat anytime soon.

"A nice rum and Coke on ice will make you feel better."

Maybe a drink would fix his captain's bad mood as well. Reaching up to scratch under his 49ers ball cap, Gabe wondered exactly where his plan had gone wrong. She was losing patience, and this morning's threat—that she would leave him on the dock if he didn't find a place to stay, and soon—only added to his worries. *They'd been here for four days, and she thought he was procrastinating? Hell, he wasn't procrastinating—he was hanging on for all he was worth.*

Leila interrupted his train of thought. "Gabe! You coming?"

Gabe let his cart full of groceries lead the way down the wobbly wood dock, loaded his bags of food after hers, then when Leila was comfortably settled, he startled the little three horsepower into life, and they motored toward the fleet of cruising sailboats bobbing at anchor.

Thrifty cruisers appreciated the free anchorage, shelter from southerlies, and a place to resupply before moving on. Most did move on, but disillusionment with the dream of cruising caused more than one sailor to take root in the silted-up bay. He'd soon become one of those casualties—if he didn't come up with another plan, a better plan, and soon.

For more about RP Dahlke

www.rpdahlke.com

FACEBOOK PAGE: www.facebook.com/RPDahlke

GoodReads: RP Dahlke

Twitter: @RPDahlke

Praise for RP Dahlke's Dead Red Series:

A DEAD RED CADILLAC:

"Ex model and motorhead, Lalla Bains, pilots us through a murder investigation with more twists and turns than the coast highway and with an ending more satisfying than the purr of a perfectly tuned '58 Cadillac." ~Lesley Diehl, author of *A Deadly Draught*, Mainly Murder Press; *Dumpster Dying,* Oak Tree Press www.lesleydiehl.com http://anotherdraught.blogspot.com/

"Fresh and fun! With its engaging, down-on-her-luck sleuth, homicidal Caddy and a decades-old mystery, R.P. Dahlke's promising debut, *A DEAD RED CADILLAC*, will keep you turning those pages and guessing wrong right up to its surprising conclusion." ~Kris Neri, Lefty Award-nominated author of *Revenge For Old Times' Sake*

"Fast paced and fun with an outwardly tough but inwardly vulnerable lady-pilot, drug smuggling and plenty of eccentric characters." ~Rhys Bowen, award-winning author of the Molly Murphy and Royal Spyness mysteries. *Bless the Bride*, March 2011

A DEAD RED HEART:

"Author R P Dahlke has combined suspenseful murder and even humor in the creation of *A DEAD RED HEART*. I found myself changing my opinion about each character at least once as I turned the pages. And I have to admit, I didn't come up with the real murderer until the end. This author really kept me guessing and changing my mind." Martha Cheves, Reviewer, Stir, Laugh, Repeat

A DEAD RED OLEANDER:

5.0 out of 5 stars **What a fun read.**, August 10, 2013
By **dialeigh**—See all my reviews "This is one book that has it all! Who done it, chases, explosions attempted kidnapping, attempted rape, hitmen, the mob, plane chases and best of all wrapped in humor. I would recommend this to anyone who likes a good story line and more than a few laughs along the way. It's a family I'd like to read more about. You can't loose with this one, I assure you you'll enjoy it from page one til the end."

More of Lalla Bains can be found at Kindle:
http://tinyurl.com/6hdg3bf

Made in the USA
San Bernardino, CA
17 January 2018